To every thin
and a time to every purpose under the heaven.
Ecclesiastes 3:1

Every one knows that Christmas is the time of miracles, joy, and love. There's the story of Bethlehem with the blazing star and wise men bearing gifts for a baby king. There are lavish celebrations and presents, and the delicious satisfaction of pulling off ribbons and wrappings to find exactly what your heart desired.

It's never too late to recapture the wonder of the holiday, to wish again for your deepest dreams to come true. The backdrop of lights twinkling in the darkness and boundless good will make Christmas the perfect time for love, as the heroines in these four romantic novellas will see.

Come along as storytellers Yvonne Lehman, Loree Lough, Tracie Peterson, and Debra White Smith weave magical holiday tales of gifts that are "just right" and loves that are "meant to be." From a sparkling ring to a long-awaited trip, from a heartwarming surprise to the thrill of lifetime commitment, these gifts, and the loves that give them, will draw your heart and imagination into a splendid *Season of Love.*

Season of Love

Yvonne Lehman

Loree Lough

Tracie Peterson

Debra White Smith

BARBOUR
PUBLISHING, INC.
Uhrichsville, Ohio

ISBN 1-57748-350-2

Published by Barbour Publishing, Inc., P.O. Box 719, Uhrichsville, Ohio 44683
http://www.barbourbooks.com

Printed in the United States of America.

Season of Love

The Gold Star

Yvonne Lehman

Dedication

To Sylvia

Chapter 1

The first time Connie Turner saw her, she was sitting in the dirt, making mud pies. Her tattered dress and face were streaked with mud. Turning toward the clothesline, Connie pretended not to see the child and bent to pick up another piece of wash. She tried to keep her mind on the mild September day, and thought it a good decision to wash out a few pieces and hang them on the line rather than try and find a laundromat. Then she saw the child stand, look, and take a step in her direction.

Hurriedly, Connie put the wet towel back into the basket, picked it up, and almost ran into the duplex apartment. She locked the door behind her and peeked out the window. The girl stood still, staring dejectedly at Connie's apartment. Then she wiped her muddy hands on her dress, turned and walked across the dirt road, and went into the apartment directly across from Connie's.

Connie sat down at the kitchen table, her hands trembling and her heart pounding. The sight of a mere child could revive the memory of the awful day in March which was as clear as if it happened this day. The day when she had a husband of two years and a three-month-old baby girl.

John had been a proud father and didn't mind changing a wet diaper. He had offered to take Julie to the store to pick up a few supplies while Connie had attended her first missionary meeting since Julie's birth. After the meeting, a friend had taken her home. Connie was disappointed that their car wasn't in the carport. John hadn't yet returned and her friend wouldn't get to see the baby.

A little later, she heard a vehicle in the driveway and went to the door. She was startled to see not the family car, but a police car. Two policemen came to the door and asked if they might come in.

The accident had involved only one vehicle, they reported. Perhaps John had to swerve suddenly. A witness said the driver seemed to reach over to the right, then the car went out of control. It rolled down a steep embankment, overturned completely, and came to rest on its side. John had died from a broken neck. Julie didn't have a scratch on her, but had died of suffocation from the airbag.

For months, Connie was in a state of shock, frequently taking drugs prescribed by the doctor to calm her nerves and control her blood pressure. For a long time, she refused to believe what happened. She stayed isolated at her parents' home, wouldn't see friends, or read cards of condolence. It wasn't sympathy she wanted—she wanted her beautiful family back again.

Connie did not return to her kindergarten job that fall. It seemed impossible that she could ever return to the school where she and John had met when he was a third grade teacher. Nor did she return to the church although all the members had been loving and sympathetic. She was not a Young-Married person anymore—she was single. She no longer belonged in the class for married couples, but how did a married mother return to being single again? Impossible!

She did not spend Christmas with her family that year. The previous Christmas had brought her a baby. This one, only sorrow. She returned to her home after making it clear she wanted no visitors—not even family.

After the first of the year, Connie enrolled in a computer class. Little by little, she began getting rid of John's clothes and belongings. Her mother took Julie's clothes for her sister's newborn whom Connie could not bear to see. Connie hadn't thought she could feel any more desolate or empty, but as each possession was taken, she felt that another piece of her life was gone. Every time a single man called to ask her out or even to go to church, she felt they were desecrating her memory of her husband.

For a long time, all she could think about was John and Julie. Then she began to force herself not to think of them, but to concentrate on TV or the computer. To fill her time and mind, she took a job with a firm who sent out secretaries on temporary work assignments as needed by various businesses, such as a six-month job with a YMCA fund-raising campaign.

That second Christmas, after the accident, she tried to interact with her family but found that being around happily married couples and children was too painful, and ended up making everyone around her miserable.

Finally, after endless, meaningless months passed, Connie told her parents she had to leave and didn't know where she was going. She wanted to go to a city large enough where people didn't have time to become involved in the personal lives of those around them. She made the two-hour drive from Columbia to Greenfield, South Carolina, checked into a motel, and in three days had found a small apartment and was looking for a job.

Connie's thoughts were interrupted by a faint knocking at the back door. She felt the tears on her cheeks and brushed them away with the back of her hand.

The knocking came again. She unlocked the door and opened it. There stood the little girl who had caused the flood of memories.

Through the screen door, Connie saw that the little girl's face was almost clean. Her blue eyes were large, clear, and filled with the joy of living. A stray wisp of sun-bleached beige hair was caught back by a bobby pin into the rest of her uncombed hair. Connie wanted to scream at her to leave. She didn't want to wonder what Julie would have been like, had she lived.

"My name is Sylvia, what's yours?" she inquired.

Surprised at the beautiful, musical name on such an unkempt little girl, she replied without thinking, "My name is Connie Turner."

"I like it," Sylvia said approvingly. When she smiled, a dimple appeared in each cheek.

"Your mother will be looking for you," Connie curtly stated.

Sylvia paid no attention. "I saw you hanging out

your clothes. Your hair is pretty. I wish my hair was pretty like yours. You have pretty clothes, too."

Connie's throat closed. She had neither spoken to nor touched a child in over two years. She did not want the pain of remembering. Julie's hair would have been beautiful...clean and soft, with a pretty bow in it. Connie put a hand up to her own plain brown, short hair—pretty or not, it was the farthest thing from her mind. And her clothes? She looked down at her jeans and plain white T-shirt. She could not even say a polite "Thank you," to this child.

If Sylvia had any inkling of Connie's feelings, it didn't show. She tilted her head to the side slightly and asked in a sweet, imploring tone of voice, "Will you take me to church tomorrow?"

"No, I don't think so," Connie said quickly. "I don't go to church." She had gone to church most of her life and had been taught about God. But of one thing she was now convinced: God, if He existed, was not a personal God. She had no desire to worship a God who would take her husband and child away so cruelly and unexpectedly. She could not love a God like that, and she was certain He did not love her.

"Oh, please. It's only a block away." Sylvia pointed up the street, but Connie didn't look. She passed the church every time she went downtown and knew, if she looked, she could see the steeple from her back door. "My mommy would take me, but our baby is sick and Mommy won't let me go across the street by myself." Her pleading turned to a note of desperation. "If I don't go, I won't get a gold star."

Connie had to get away from her. It kept going through her mind, *What if she were my little girl making such a request?* She stepped back, her hand on the door, and answered just so Sylvia would leave. "If I can go, I'll come by for you in the morning, but I might not be able to."

"Okay," Sylvia said, as if Connie had agreed to go. She smiled, turned to go, and lifted her little hand in a wave of good-bye.

Connie closed the door and leaned against it, wishing she could put an end to all her nothingness, loneliness, and bitterness. Somehow the child had managed to loosen the tight grip she held on her aching heart.

Chapter 2

"I don't have an aversion to church-going, it just doesn't hold any meaning for me anymore," she told her reflection as she washed her face. *But that doesn't mean you should play a part in destroying a little girl's faith in people or in God. Surely, you could take a little child to church,* her conscience scolded.

To quiet her nagging thoughts, the next morning Connie dressed for church, walked across the backyard, up the steps of the little brick apartment, and knocked on the weather-beaten doorway.

Sylvia came to the door. "I can't go," she said, trying to hold back her tears. Through the screen, Connie could see a young woman sitting across the room holding an infant. She didn't come to the door or invite Connie in, but as Sylvia opened the door wider, the woman introduced herself as Reba Wahlen.

"The baby isn't feeling well," she said. "Perhaps we can all go to church together sometime. It's the one up the hill, a block away. Thank you for taking an interest in Sylvia."

"It's all right," Connie said.

"You look pretty," Sylvia said, her big blue eyes looking up at Connie. Her smile dimpled her cheeks.

Connie said good-bye and went down the steps, turned and walked along the dirt road between the rows of brick apartments. She was across the street and halfway up the other block when she realized she should have gone back to her apartment. *Well, since I'm this far and dressed for church, I might as well go on—and just maybe my conscience will let me sleep tonight.*

At the church, she was greeted warmly by a woman going up the front walk the same time as Connie. The woman directed her to the Singles' Class and introduced her to Betty Smith, the teacher, a middle-aged woman with graying, short blond hair. Betty's warm smile, friendly eyes, and kind words welcomed Connie and she had the others introduce themselves.

Connie knew she probably wouldn't remember any of the names, but she felt less self-conscious, seeing that most of the members looked as if they were in their late twenties and mid-thirties. Announcements were made by the apparent leader of the group, a rugged-looking man with an unusual reddish-gold cast to his dark brown wavy hair. Connie filled out a visitor's card, putting on it her address, telephone number, and where there were blanks for single, divorced, or widowed, she checked "single" rather than have to go into any explanations.

She handed the information card to Betty, who glanced at it. "You don't work?" she asked.

"I'm looking," Connie replied. "I just moved here."

"What kind of job are you looking for?" Betty asked.

Connie hesitated, feeling uncomfortable. "Maybe. . . secretarial. I might just work from home with the computer."

"The church is looking for a part-time secretary," commented the leader who had made the announcements.

Connie nodded, but she wasn't interested in working at a church and was glad the subject changed.

Several made prayer requests to deal with their difficult situations. *They don't know what difficult is*, Connie thought. After Sunday school, she left the quarterly on the seat, and walked to her apartment, her heels clicking on the pavement. There was no need to attend a worship service. It wasn't that she resented the faith of other people—she envied it, and wished she could have it too.

Turning the key in the lock, her heart was heavier than before. Perhaps unconsciously she had hoped for a spark of faith to be renewed. Somehow it wasn't quite so easy to forget all she had been taught and believed since she was just a small child—about Sylvia's age.

She kicked off her shoes and massaged her feet. *Next time I'll drive.* She changed her clothes and fixed herself a sandwich. Connie sat gazing out her kitchen window while she ate her lunch. She didn't see Sylvia. *What kind of life did the little girl have, cooped up in a small apartment, with only a strip of dirt road to play in?* Her mind drifted to her childhood—she had a big backyard to play in, and an open field behind that. There were many neighborhood children to play with her, her two older sisters, and brother. The memory of laughter and shouts from playing children drummed at her heart. Whomever had said those were the best years of her life had been right. Every child should have a happy childhood—something good to remember.

The phone rang, startling Connie from her memories.

"Hello?"

"Hi, Honey, how are you today?"

"Hi, Mom. Good—I went to church this morning," she quickly told her. She knew her mother would be pleased that she had gone to church. Connie didn't bother to explain she'd gone without meaning to because a little girl had invited her.

"Oh, that's wonderful. I was telling your sister. . ." Her mother droned on about how worried she was about Connie and went on to relay all the details about her family's lives. "You know we'd love to hear from you anytime, Connie."

Connie knew how hard it was for her mother. She just didn't know how to help or what to say to her daughter. "Please give everyone my love, Mom. I just can't be involved with them yet. Please try to be patient with me."

"It's progress, Honey, that you're getting back into church. You know we're here for you and love you." Connie could hear the tightness in her mother's voice as she said good-bye.

Throughout the afternoon, Connie carefully and deliberately took stock of her existence, and planned a course of action. She had promised herself she could never buy anything for herself with John's and Julie's insurance money. But maybe she should put it to some use and find a way to make little children's lives happier. *The church seemed to be important to Sylvia—perhaps they had a program that could help her!*

When the phone rang again later on, Connie expected it to be her mother again.

"Connie, this is Betty Smith, the coordinator for the Singles' Class. We like to welcome our new folks personally and I would love to bring my daughter by to meet you. She's divorced and has a special feeling for singles. Would you mind if we came to visit you this evening? I'd like to tell you about all the groups we have in the congregation and the special kinds of help they give to young and old alike."

"I have other plans," Connie told her.

"I understand," Betty replied kindly. "I am just so pleased that you attended the Singles' Class today. I do hope you'll come again. I'll ask the church secretary to send you a packet with information about the programs we have, if you like. We're especially excited about our new program for single parents with young children."

"That would be fine, thanks," Connie replied. She appreciated the call, but that wasn't what elevated her spirits slightly. It was the thought of doing something for Sylvia and her mother—in honor of John and Julie—without having to get personally involved.

Nothing had sparked such an interest in her since the accident. Come to think of it, she hadn't seen a man over there. Perhaps Reba had lost her husband, too. Sylvia was the only person, in over two years, who had stirred up a spark of concern in Connie's heart for anyone. If she could just learn a little about what Sylvia and her mother needed. . .

The next morning, when she thought Reba would have had time to do early morning chores and maybe put the baby down for a mid-morning nap, Connie walked across the backyards, up the steps, and knocked on the doorway just as she had the morning before.

There was no answer.

Perhaps Reba Wahlen was busy with the baby.

Connie waited, then knocked again, louder. No answer. She opened the screen door and peered through the glass in the wooden door. She could see the straight-backed chair against the opposite wall where Reba Wahlen had sat with the baby. She could see the kitchen countertop, which did not look as if a small girl and a baby lived there. Nothing was out of place. Not one glass, or a bottle, or a spoon lying around.

She saw no toys. An eerie feeling washed over Connie. It was as if she were looking at an empty house. Bewildered, she walked around to the front. There were no drapes. She opened the front screen and knocked loudly on the door. She called Reba's and Sylvia's names.

"You looking for somebody, honey?" a voice behind her said.

Connie turned. A short, middle-aged woman stood on the front porch of the next apartment. "I'm looking for Reba Wahlen," she said. "She lives here."

"Maybe you got it mixed up," the woman said. "All these apartments are alike."

"No, I was here yesterday morning. It's across from mine. I live right over there." She pointed toward her door.

The woman walked over to the banister, closer to Connie. "I've lived here five years." She shook her head. "I don't know anybody by that name you said. But I do know this—nobody has lived in that apartment for three weeks."

Chapter 3

As Connie walked toward her own apartment, she glanced at the weather-beaten doorway with the muddy fingerprints, the dried and stepped-on mud pies on the bottom step, the mud hole in the dirt road where Sylvia had sat, the stick she played with lying beside it. *No, I did not imagine those things; nor did I imagine Reba and Sylvia. It was not a hallucination. They were real. I talked with them.* Reba had even said she went to the church up the hill. She even said they might go there together sometimes.

Connie wondered why she hadn't seen them leave. *Why hadn't the neighbor lady noticed them living there?* There were too many unanswered questions.

Connie tried, but couldn't forget the Wahlens. She sat down to read the job ads, but every time she put the Wahlens out of her mind, they returned. She kept wondering about the mystery of the whole thing and after scanning two columns of ads, she had no idea what jobs she'd just read about. For the first time in those long months since the tragedy, all her attention was not focused on herself and her loss.

The next Sunday, Connie again attended the church for the sole purpose of trying to solve some of the mystery surrounding Reba and Sylvia Wahlen. During sharing time at the beginning of the class, Connie asked if anyone knew them. No one did. Connie supposed Reba could be in a Marrieds' Class or a Couples' Class. She also mentioned Sylvia, and got the same response.

The dark-haired leader asked, "Does she have a pet?"

Surprised, Connie glanced at him, then away. Others laughed, but Connie didn't get it and didn't bother to reply. She wondered if the class members all thought her questioning as inane as his remark made it appear. They went on to discuss other things and make prayer requests. Connie didn't think she would come back again.

After class, while everyone else bowed their heads for a closing prayer, Connie got up and slipped out the door. Halfway down the hall, she heard her name being called. Glancing over her shoulder, she saw the guy who'd made the quip. He caught up with her.

"Please," he said. "Let me explain the reason for my question. I should have explained why I asked about the little girl having a pet, even though the subject changed."

Connie stared into his dark brown eyes. *He looks sincere. He sounds sincere.* "You see," he said, his dark eyebrows drawing together and making a furrow in the middle of his forehead. "I'm a veterinarian. The class members are always joking about my knowing everyone in town who has a pet. Most everybody around here either buys a pet from me or brings theirs in to the animal hospital."

Connie nodded. "Thank you for your explanation, but I didn't see a pet."

"I could check my records," he offered. "What was the name again?"

"Wahlen," Connie replied. "I don't know the spelling. But don't go to any trouble."

"I don't mind," he said and smiled. "Are you going to the worship service?"

"No," Connie said abruptly, not wanting to deal with any man inviting her to anything—even a worship service. The Sunday school bell rang, signaling the end of class. Doors began to open. People started to spill out into the hallway. She turned quickly and hurried out a side door.

Her car was parked on the other side of the church and she had to walk around, passing people coming into the church. But she didn't look at them. The sense of panic followed her all the way home.

After taking off her stylish leaf-green suit, she slipped into jeans and a sweatshirt. Looking into the mirror to fluff out her short brown curls, she couldn't miss the look of a scared rabbit vivid in her green eyes and the unnatural flush on her cheeks. Inside was that fluttery feeling. She turned from the reflection, but couldn't ignore that small voice reprimanding her, saying she had been much more rude to the apologetic veterinarian than his quip had been—even though it turned out that his words were not a quip at all, but a serious inquiry.

She'd tried to steer clear of personal conversations, and certainly private ones with men. This one, whose name she didn't even know, had been kind and smiled and catapulted her into orbit. She couldn't have a normal conversation with a man who showed interest in her. That only served to confirm she didn't belong in that class—with that group. She'd been married and had a child. Acting single again was just not possible.

Late Sunday afternoon, a knock sounded on Connie's front door. She was surprised. She always parked at the back and hadn't used the front door since the day she rented the apartment. *Maybe it's Sylvia,* she thought, with a lift of her spirits. She hurried to the door, but felt like shutting it when she saw Betty Smith and a young woman a few years younger than Connie.

Not wanting to be rude again to people who only meant well, Connie invited them in and took their coats. Betty introduced Jolene, who was wearing a two-pieced outfit that looked like a maternity dress, although she didn't appear to be showing.

Connie led them into the kitchen. She hadn't yet turned the heat on this fall and the kitchen was cozier.

They sat at the kitchen table where Connie had been stuffing envelopes with her resume and cover letters. Connie served Betty and herself a cup of coffee and Jolene accepted a glass of ice water.

Connie set her paperwork aside and tried to relax. Jolene made a few general remarks, including the fact that she was in the Young Marrieds' Class. Betty didn't get personal either, but left her statements open-ended, such as saying she and her family had come to the church ten years ago, she had three grown children and two grandchildren. Connie was able to say she had been there two weeks, and neither woman pressed her for details. Betty had obviously picked up upon her reluctance to speak personally—or had she gotten that impression from the veterinarian?

She thought her question was answered when Jolene said, "Ken mentioned you're looking for a job."

"Ken?" Connie questioned, suspecting that was the vet's name.

Betty smiled. "He said you might not know his name. Dr. Russell. That good-looking man in our class that's got that thick wavy hair. Some men have all the luck," she quipped, touching her own fine hair that looked permed. "I believe he said he wasn't very tactful with you."

Connie hadn't registered whether or not he was good-looking. But, "our class," Betty had said, as if Connie were a part of things. Or was that just a general statement, an off-handed way of including everyone who had attended?

"It wasn't important," Connie said. "He seems very kind."

"He's the greatest," Betty said and smiled. "He owns the animal hospital a few blocks from the church."

Connie nodded briefly and looked down at her coffee cup, feeling that warm flush again and tried to remind herself that he was not being pushy, just kind. She really wasn't looking for kindness—or anything else, however—just to be left alone.

"I believe it was mentioned in class that the church

is looking for a part-time secretary. Why don't you let me take your resume to Pastor Grimes?"

I'm the last person a church needs. She answered honestly, "I'm not sure I'll stay in the area. I'm just testing the job market, really."

Both women smiled. "That makes you an ideal candidate for the job," Jolene said. "We're not sure how many hours you'd be needed, or for how long, or if it will be temporary or permanent. I'm the church secretary and I'm pregnant." She glowed with happiness but a concern touched her eyes. "I'm having difficulties with the pregnancy."

"Difficulties?" Connie asked quickly, feeling a jolt inside, not even thinking about whether or not she was being too personal.

Jolene nodded. "I'm five months along, but have gained only six pounds. My sister had problems with her placenta and the doctor thinks I may have the same. He says I have to cut back on my hours and may have to have complete bed rest later on." Her smile was uncertain. "We'll see what happens later."

Connie recognized the hope in Jolene's words and expression, but she also knew the fear that the unborn baby might not be perfect. That mother instinct had been stronger than anything she'd ever known. It would be so for Jolene.

Connie forced her eyes and thoughts away from Jolene. She didn't want the young woman to see the pain she felt. She mustn't frighten her with life's terrible realities. Looking down, she said, "I haven't been involved in church for a long time."

"That's not the requirement," Betty said softly. "They have a need and I have a feeling you could meet it."

Connie bit on her lip. She didn't feel she could do anyone any good.

Betty moved back from the table and stood. Jolene followed her lead. "Why don't you stop by in the morning around nine o'clock and talk to Pastor Grimes about the job?" Her voice was encouraging, as if she thought the two of them might get along well together. But Connie wondered if she could possibly relate to this woman who would be so joyful about expecting her first child. And yet. . .there were complications with the pregnancy. How frightening that would be. But at least, Jolene had a warning. Connie had never suspected her own life could be wrecked in an instant.

She nodded and handed Jolene a resume from the stack. Somehow, her heart wanted to hope.

Chapter 4

Walen, Wailing, Whalon Walon, Wallen, Wallon? Names kept going through Ken's mind all of Sunday evening after Betty called to say Connie might be interested in the church job. "But you were right, Ken. Something is bothering her that she's not ready to talk about. We'll just try and be her friend."

Monday morning he was in his office, turning on the computer to check the files starting with "W" when his receptionist Judy came in, apparently surprised that he'd arrived before her. Judy returned to the reception area, unlocked the front door and he heard her greet someone. Just as he brought the files up, something whipped over his head, then grasped his shoulder and fanned his face.

Wary of making a quick move, he turned his head slightly and his eyes as far to the side as he could. Perched on his shoulder was a big gray and white cockatoo looking straight ahead, but edging its big sharp claws closer to Ken's neck.

A vet shouldn't scream in front of his patients, he reminded himself. He wondered if he should chirp, but decided this guy no doubt could carry on a conversation. "A cracker?" he said low. The bird didn't respond, just edged closer to his neck.

Just then, Judy and a frustrated woman appeared in the hallway. "He does this every time I open the cage door. I'm so sorry."

The woman held out her arm and the bird jumped on. It spread its wings precariously and squawked "Whatsupdoc? Awk."

The woman and Judy laughed delightedly, then the woman explained, "I'm here to have TooToo's wings clipped."

Good idea, Ken thought. *I'll suggest TooToo get his nails clipped, as well.*

Before eight o'clock Connie was dressed in a conservative navy skirt and light blazer with a cream-colored blouse. The morning was cool with only a light breeze blowing the leaves that had begun to change colors. However, she opted to drive rather than walk the couple of blocks in her two-inch heels. The day Sylvia stood her up and she'd walked in heels had made her feet cramp—she still had a small blister on her left heel.

It's not like I have any interest in the job, she kept telling herself. *But since it doesn't matter one way or another, why not check it out?* she countered, the argument leaning heavily one way. Jolene had been so sweet to think they'd work well together. Since no one was expecting her to be permanent, why not help out a little? It would give her a chance to check the records and see if Reba and Sylvia Wahlen had at least visited the church.

Jolene, whose fair skin was complimented by the pink color of her maternity dress with a lace collar, greeted Connie warmly and ushered her right in to see the pastor.

Connie's concern about talking with a pastor disappeared as soon as he came around the desk, looking as glad to see her as if he were her long-lost grandfather. Pastor Grimes' warm blue eyes were kind behind his wire-frame glasses. His gray hair was thin and conservatively cut. His smile was pleasant in his lined face as he pumped her hand.

"Ms. Turner, please sit down. Betty and Jolene tell me they talked you into giving them one of your resumes and coming to see me for the secretary position. You know it's part-time and may be temporary, is that right?"

"Yes."

"Your skills and abilities on your resume are impressive. But please tell me about them in your own words."

"Well, I was a kindergarten teacher and I've done computer work for businesses from my home. I decided to come to a bigger town to try to reach a larger market," she added hoping it sounded credible. It was at least partly true. She wanted customers who didn't know her personal tragedy.

Pastor Grimes outlined the duties; Connie knew he realized she was more than qualified for them. His questions were general at first, ones she didn't mind answering.

"May I address you as Connie?" he asked, at last.

Connie nodded. "Please do." That was more comfortable than having him say "Miss" or "Mrs." She had written "Ms." on the Singles' visitor's card.

She knew the informality meant he was about to ask the question she dreaded. She wasn't prepared, although she knew what it would be, when he asked, "Would you tell me a little about your personal background?"

Oh, I don't want to. I don't want to say it, or think it, or feel it. She swallowed hard and looked down at her hands clutching her purse as if it might take flight. She would like to fly away. She inhaled deeply, wondering if she should just get up and leave. Before she could, he spoke kindly.

"I would not betray a confidence," he assured her in all seriousness.

"I was raised in the church," she began. "The rest, I don't want others to know."

"Of course."

"My husband and baby died in a car accident over two years ago while I was at a missionary meeting. Julie would have been three this Christmas. John was a wonderful father. It's still. . .so real."

"I'm sorry," he said. "I know how you feel."

Connie looked at him quickly, ready to say he couldn't possibly, but his eyes were moist. She knew that he, as a pastor, would have known many persons who had suffered loss. She would be honest with him. "I don't want to become a church member," she said, easing toward the edge of her chair, ready to make her exit, "or get involved with any church activity."

She rose to leave, expecting that he might say he was sorry but she didn't have the right attitude for the job—or that she was too bitter.

Connie started work Tuesday morning. As she arrived, many cars pulled into the church parking lot at the back. To her surprise, little children and adults poured out of the cars and entered through a door on the lower level. Connie entered on the ground level, near the offices.

Jolene explained that there was a preschool Monday through Friday from nine until noon. Connie's heart sank. Those were the hours she would be working. She wanted to avoid contact with children—now this.

Connie knew her chagrin must have showed, because Jolene was quick to explain. "We never see them unless there's some kind of emergency or something. They're well organized and it's entirely separate from our work, although it is a Christian class and most of the teachers belong to this church."

Seeing the children, Connie was reminded of Sylvia and took the opportunity to ask Jolene if she had seen Reba Wahlen in the Young Marrieds' Class.

"Not that I recall, why?"

Feeling odd again, Connie explained, "Reba and her daughter Sylvia were the ones who invited me to this church. I assumed they went here."

"Maybe she was in the Couples' Class," Jolene said with a slight shrug. The phone rang and the conversation was dropped.

On Thursday Ken had finally pegged it. At noon he jogged across the parking lot just as Connie was leaving. He waved his hand in greeting. "I've checked my files for the name of Wahlen. The closest to a name like that is Wheelon, an elderly man whose pet is an English Bull. But," he said quickly, seeing that she was about to step away from him, "I'll check first names. Last names can change, you know."

Oops! he thought. That remark was an unintentional double entendre, and a sure way to alienate a woman. Trying not to give her a chance to think about "changing a last name," he dove right in and told her about TooToo interrupting his computer search.

"When that bird sneaked toward my jugular vein," he said, narrowing his eyes ominously, "I suspected he was really a bat in cockatoo's feathers."

She didn't laugh, but she did smile and he thought a tiny light gleamed in those lovely green eyes for just an instant. "By the way," he said, "the Singles' Group Meeting is Saturday night at church. We'll be planning our holiday food drive. Would—?"

"Thank you, but I'm not getting involved in activities. I may not stay in the area."

"I hope we won't *drive* you away," he said and smiled broadly.

"Everyone here has been very kind," she said, without even returning his smile. She climbed into her car and drove away.

She tries awfully hard to keep her distance from people, he thought. *She must have been hurt awfully bad. There must be something I can do to reach her.*

By Friday, Connie and Jolene had settled into a routine. Since Connie didn't want to socialize, Jolene manned the telephone and typed the pastor's personal letters while Connie handled other office jobs, helped with the newsletter, typed Sunday's bulletin, and entered financial transactions into the computer. She had even searched the computer for Reba and Sylvia—with no luck. Connie actually enjoyed getting out and going to the post office, the bank, and occasionally running other errands, picking up office supplies, delivering a package to the visiting missionary, and on Friday picking up lunch for her and Jolene to eat together while they discussed the productive week.

For the first time in a long time, Connie felt she was doing something worthwhile. She smiled when Jolene said, "I'm so glad you took this job, Connie. I'd wouldn't mind leaving this job in your hands."

Connie knew Jolene was not at all jealous of her abilities. Jolene had already made it clear she wouldn't mind staying home and getting the nursery ready. She wasn't sure she wanted to work after the baby was born. Her husband, Tony, wanted her to be a full-time mom.

"Come have dinner with us on Sunday," Jolene invited. "Our house is little, but you might have some ideas of how we could fix up our spare bedroom and make it into a nursery."

"No, I really can't," Connie said quickly and turned to throw away her plastic salad dish. *Julie's nursery was so pretty.* It had had a Noah's Ark motif. All her and John's relatives had advised, helped, given new and used items. The animal border in Connie's mind swam before her eyes. "I have to leave," she said, getting her purse and heading for her sweater on the coatrack by the door.

This is all wrong, Connie was telling herself on the drive back to the apartment. *I shouldn't be where I can dampen the spirits of a young woman so eagerly anticipating the joy of expecting her first baby. Maybe I should quit the job.* That thought brought an unexpected stab of regret.

As she pulled into her parking space, another surprise confronted Connie. A moving van was parked outside the Wahlen apartment. She hurried up her steps and through the back door, then sat at the kitchen table with a cup of coffee, watching the truck that blocked her view of any activity except an occasional glimpse of a worker holding onto the end of a piece of furniture.

She watched until the truck left, and Connie finally saw an elderly man and woman get into a car and leave. There was no movement around the apartment until the couple returned a while later and unloaded several bags of what looked like groceries.

Where are the Wahlens? Connie wondered.

Chapter 5

Connie felt more at ease in the Singles' Class on Sunday morning, being able to say she had a job, rather than being afraid she'd be asked personal questions. The other members responded with genuine delight. That led into the sharing time when needs and blessings were mentioned. Lois thanked the class for their donations made at the Saturday night meeting. It enabled her to pay another month's rent for her and her two children. Now, she said, there was a plumbing problem in the bathroom and the plunger wasn't effective anymore. Her landlord said there was nothing wrong with the plumbing when she had moved in, so he refused to fix it.

Connie marveled at the honesty of some who bared their hearts. But it wouldn't help for her to do it. There was nothing anyone could do. Her family was gone forever.

With that thought, she bit on her lip and looked down. Suddenly, the door burst open. In rushed Ken, whom Betty had called good-looking. His hair was mussed this morning from the wind. She supposed the "really single" and divorced women would think him quite appealing in his dark blue dress slacks, light blue shirt open at the collar, and tweed blazer.

"Sorry I'm late," he apologized as he crossed the room, heading for the empty chair right beside her. *Why couldn't he take one of the other empty chairs?* But he plopped down, and she could feel the prickle of the air he stirred as he sat so close she feared they might even touch.

She didn't want a man that close to her. It wouldn't matter if it were someone like Pastor Grimes, the older grandfatherly type. But a young man, so exuberant that the air seemed to crackle with his energy, unnerved her. Then he said, "Sassy wouldn't let me turn off the Ricky Skaggs album until it finished."

Connie's questioning eyes flew to his, then she quickly glanced away. *Who was Sassy?*

A new guy in the class, Henry, posed the question. "Sassy?"

Ken leaned toward Connie and explained, "That's my golden retriever. You should hear her sing when I put on 'Achy Breaky Heart.' " He turned and smiled at Connie, who thought, *If he inadvertently brushes my arm, I'm leaving.*

He didn't.

When rainy, windy Monday morning rolled around, Connie was glad to roll out of bed and have a job to go to. She couldn't imagine spending such a morbid day alone at the apartment with nothing to do. And without the church job, she'd have to find something—somewhere. That prospect was even more morbid.

As soon as Connie arrived at work, Tony called,

saying Jolene had a bad night and morning. Her doctor wanted to see her at eleven. She wouldn't be coming in to work at all that day.

Tony's parting words, "Pray for her," left Connie speechless. Apparently, he didn't expect a response, but thought the request would be honored for he immediately said, "Bye."

I prayed for Julie—all kinds of prayers—thankful ones—hopeful ones—even about her future when she grew up. My prayers were unceasing. But my little girl is gone. Troubled, she buried her thoughts behind the enormous stack of work Mondays demanded, beginning with entering Sunday's offerings into the computer.

After the pastor came in at ten and hung his wet raincoat on the corner rack, Connie gave him Tony's message about Jolene, including the prayer request. Afraid he might ask her to join him in prayer, Connie quickly turned to the subject that had been on her mind. She knew the Singles' Class members helped each other out with baby-sitting, hand-me-down clothing, advice, and so on. She couldn't find Sylvia to help her and she felt a need to do. . .something.

"Pastor Grimes," she said. "One of the singles has a plumbing problem and no money. I'd like to help financially."

"That's wonderful, Connie. Just let Ken know. He handles the business for the Benevolence Committee that distributes the money and finds manpower for those in need at our church."

"I'd like it to be anonymous."

"You can trust him to keep it confidential," Pastor

Grimes said. He smiled warmly, went into his office, and closed the door.

It was past noon before Connie realized she had finished entering all the finances, written two personal letters for the pastor, and had the newsletter halfway finished. "You're a whiz, all right," Pastor Grimes said, after signing the letters and returning them to her to be mailed. "I have to run home, but as soon as I get back, I insist you take time out for lunch."

"Lunch?" In came a whiz of another kind. Ken appeared in the doorway wearing a glistening yellow slicker. "Somebody just said the magic word."

The pastor laughed, grabbed Ken affectionately by the arm, and while Ken shucked out of the slicker, the conversation turned to Henry, whom Ken intended to visit that evening.

Connie couldn't help but stare, transfixed by the irony of things. There stood a doctor, on his lunch break, dressed in a sweatshirt and jeans, his hair mussed, his face slightly flushed so that a few freckles she hadn't noticed before were apparent across his strong nose. She figured he had run the few blocks from his business, even in the rain.

How could a person be so vibrant and exuberant?

"Man, what a morning." He ran his fingers through his damp hair that tended to curl. "You ever tried to give a physical to a full-grown Great Dane who doesn't want one?"

Connie couldn't help but give a short laugh. "Not that I recall."

"Well, see, being the vet and the only man in the office, I'm elected to meet the beast at the front door and try to get a muzzle on him. He knows me and knows what he's there for, but no amount of pulling or offering food will get that dog inside the door—that is, until I step out onto the porch. Then the dog jumps inside. I come inside and the dog lunges for the porch. His eyes say, 'Ha ha, you can't outdo me' and I know he's telling the truth."

Connie smiled, imagining the incident.

Ken sat on the edge of her desk, turned sideways, watching her face as he related his experience. "We played that in-and-out game for about twenty minutes. Then I got the bright idea of letting him stay inside, while I ran around the building in the rain and came in the back door."

"Ingenious," Connie said, enjoying his story.

He nodded. "I thought so, too. But then, we went through the same fiasco trying to get him into the exam room. Did you know that you just can't force a Great Dane to do anything he doesn't want to do?"

"I'm sure you thought of something," the pastor said.

Ken nodded. "The owner finally managed to chain him to the hook we have outside the reception desk—which I expected him to pull over at anytime. Ultimately, I had to give his physical right there while a litter of kittens, two puppies, and a parakeet looked on."

They all laughed. "He wasn't the least bit embarrassed," Ken added. "Oh, yeah, there was a pig in there, too."

Connie blinked. "A pet pig?"

"Sort of. He's the defending champion in the annual greased-pig racing contest. That's another story."

"While you're entertaining my secretary," Pastor Grimes said good-naturedly, "I'm going to run home for lunch." Then he told Ken about Jolene, adding that Connie might have to put in her first full day of work. "By the way," he said, "Connie wants to talk to you about a Singles' matter."

"Is there something we can do for you?" he said in what sounded like a hopeful voice as the pastor left.

"No, I'd like to do something for Lois. She said she needs a plumber."

"Badly," he said. "I went by yesterday with Craig Mills, a member here who is a plumber. He'll cut down the cost as much as possible, but there are still parts to be bought and workers' wages to be paid. Craig said he can set up a payment plan, but Lois has trouble making ends meet as it is. She gets no help from her ex-husband or family. Her children get sick and doctor bills eat up her rent money. She can't afford insurance."

"Just send the plumbing bill to me," Connie said. "I'll see what I can do."

"Anything would help," he said.

Connie nodded. "But keep it between us."

"I will," he said. "That's very kind of you, Connie."

She looked down from the warmth in his eyes and shook her head. "Not. . .really. Writing a check takes little effort, and I'm. . .not in a bind."

"It's still kind," he insisted.

Connie shuffled the papers in front of her needlessly. She knew he sensed her discomfort, for he displayed his usual exuberant self. "What can I bring you for lunch?"

Connie opened her mouth to say she'd wait until the pastor returned, but promptly closed it, surprised when Ken said, "Dutch treat, of course. We've talked about this at our Singles' meetings and it works best that way."

"I don't expect you to buy my lunch, Ken. I was about to say I would go to my apartment for lunch, as soon as the pastor returns."

"Oh, I'm not questioning your intentions, Connie. I just believe in letting another person know where I stand about friendship or personal relationships. I've learned the hard way that sometimes a simple gesture of kindness or friendship is misunderstood."

Connie could hardly believe what she was hearing. Beginning only a few months after John's death, she'd had to tell guys back home that she wasn't interested, but they didn't seem to believe it. They seemed to think she wasn't interested in anyone else—but them. And this week, Bill from the Singles' Class had called and asked her to see a movie with him—go out as friends, he had said. She'd had to let him know she wasn't into dating right now. She couldn't imagine that she would ever "date" again. She thought she might have to let Ken know where she stood. Instead, he was letting her know he wasn't interested in her. Instead of relief, she felt a little disappointed. That didn't make sense at all.

Chapter 6

Ken didn't know how he would manage to keep Connie from knowing how interested he was in her. At least, she'd finally let him buy lunch for her—even though she tossed him a five-dollar bill.

From the moment he saw her something leapt into his heart and he knew she was special. Not just the physical, although she was a lovely woman, particularly those fascinating green eyes that seemed to speak volumes, like, "Don't come too close!"

Did she feel the same way about God? She must, otherwise, why did she always slip out of church right after Sunday school? She must have been badly hurt. But she had a caring and generous spirit, wanting to help Lois.

And why was she so concerned about the Wahlens—and a little girl named Sylvia? If the Wahlens had done something wrong to her, it wasn't likely she'd be looking for them in a church. Maybe she wanted to do something for them.

There must be something I can do for her.

That afternoon, after checking the appointment schedule and discovering it was a relatively slow day that his assistant could handle easily, he left the animal hospital at three o'clock and drove to the elementary school.

After school was dismissed, he went to the first grade class of Peggy, a teacher who had been in the Singles' Class before she married. He asked if she knew a Sylvia Wahlen who would be around five or six.

Peggy didn't need to think more than a second before shaking her head. "I don't know of a Sylvia in the entire school."

Ken sighed. "Her mother's name is Reba Wahlen. I suppose the child could have a different last name."

"Now that's possible," Peggy agreed. "But still, I don't know of a Sylvia anywhere. It's not a common name and I'm sure I would remember." Seeing his downcast look, Peggy added, "Ken, you know I trust you, but it's against the rules to give out such personal information."

"I wouldn't expect that. If there is a Reba Wahlen, the school could ask her to contact this friend of mine who's inquiring. Then Ms. Wahlen could decide what to do."

Peggy agreed to check the student roster of the past couple of years for a Sylvia, a Reba, and the last name of Wahlen.

"Incidentally," she said, before he left. "I have this friend, who has this cat. . ."

Connie sat at her kitchen table, eating a bite of supper, looking out the window. It was a beautiful fall evening, the temperature cool but mild, and a breeze teased the colored leaves beneath an orange-red sunset. The elderly couple across the way was talking to the lady in the apartment next to them.

Something occurred to Connie. Maybe the neighbors knew each other. If so, maybe the lady next door *had* known the Wahlens. Maybe they were even relatives and she'd let them stay in that empty apartment, which of course she wouldn't want to admit to Connie.

"I'll bet that's it!" Connie said aloud to herself as she washed the few dirty dishes, watching the lady rub her arms as if it were getting colder outside. She went into her apartment and the couple into theirs.

Connie wiped her hands, grabbed a sweater, and soon was knocking on the couple's door. The woman opened the door and the aroma of home-baked pineapple upside-down cake beckoned her inside. Connie introduced herself as the neighbor across the road and immediately regretted not bringing cookies or something to offer the newcomers.

"Please, dear, do come in. It's so chilly out there! I'm Martha Brown and this is my husband Frank. We just moved here from Minneapolis to be close to our son. Frank has rheumatoid arthritis and can't take care of things like he used to." Martha handed a warm piece of pineapple upside-down cake to her without even asking. "Now you take this, dear. You look hungry." It reminded Connie of her own grandmother's kind of cooking and hospitality.

"Did you know the Wahlens who lived here before you?" Connie asked.

"No, we never met them. It's my understanding that the family who lived here moved out weeks before we came. That's what Grace said."

"Grace?"

"The lady next door."

Connie nodded feeling awkward. "We've spoken,

but I didn't get her name." She felt guilty that she had intended to pump this sweet couple about the neighbor. Instead, she changed the subject, told them about her job and the church. Before she knew it, she was inviting them to church.

Connie had just made a fresh pot of decaf when someone knocked on her back door. She wasn't accustomed to company. *I hope it's Martha with some more of that pineapple upside-down cake.*

Smiling broadly, she opened the door.

"Well, it's nice to be greeted by such a happy face."

"Oh, I thought you were. . . I mean, Ken! What brings you here?"

"This." He held up a wire cage. "I need a favor."

Connie opened the door wider.

Ken set the cage on the table. Connie couldn't take her eyes off it. Curled up on a soft blanket was a little ball of white and gold fluff, no bigger than the palm of her hand.

"What. . .is that?"

"One of God's little homeless creatures," Ken said. "Her mother died. Homes have been found for all the kittens except this one."

Connie felt almost as frightened by this prospect as she had the day she saw Sylvia. She didn't want any small living things around her. With her hand to her throat, she shook her head. "Can't you. . .take it home with you?" she mumbled.

"I'm afraid this little one and Sassy would be devastatingly incompatible. Could you do me this favor,

Connie? For just one night?"

She glanced up, wanting to say an emphatic, "No!" But Ken's expression looked as helpless as the kitten. "I've written out all the instructions."

Connie already felt a lump in her throat and a weight on her chest. She thought she might even start crying if she said no. Instead, she blurted out, "Would you like a cup of coffee?"

While she poured, he set the cage on the floor. He told her he had checked with a school teacher who was checking the records for the Wahlens. "If there's some problem concerning these people, Connie, you know there are professionals who can help in every area."

"Oh, nothing like that," she said, setting his coffee in front of him. "Cream? Sugar?"

He grinned. "Black's fine."

Connie poured milk from the refrigerator into her own coffee and sat opposite him.

"I asked a friend at the grade school about Sylvia and Reba Wahlen, and she doesn't know of any Sylvia in the school," he added. "Do you mind if I ask why you're looking for them?"

She wondered if she should tell him about Sylvia—leaving out the part about being frightened by her. She had gotten nowhere trying to find the child and her mother. There seemed to be no trace of them and no one but her ever seemed to have seen them. It was making her wonder if Sylvia was real. Perhaps he could come up with an explanation.

"To be honest, Ken, I went to church because Sylvia asked me. They lived in that apartment across the road," she said pointing her thumb toward her kitchen window. "She wanted so desperately to get her gold star. . . . On Sunday her mother wouldn't let her go with me to church, which makes sense since I was a total stranger. But the next Monday they were gone. I've kept going to church, trying to solve the mystery surrounding them. So you see," she confessed. "I'm not as dedicated to church as it might appear."

"That's the best place to be, Connie," he said seriously. "Whatever the reason."

Connie didn't want to get into that. "So, do you think I imagined Sylvia?"

His eyebrows lifted slightly. "Unless you're accustomed to fanciful delusions—"

She laughed lightly. "I'm not. I had been. . .emotional," she admitted. "But not to that extent."

"Seriously, Connie. I think God deals with us according to our need. Whether Sylvia was imagined or real, it served to get you into church, and into a job."

She thought about how specific Sylvia and then Reba had been about *which* church they wanted her to go to. . . *the one up on the hill. If Sylvia wasn't real, what was she?*

Connie turned her attention to Ken. She couldn't help but be suspicious about his being there. From all indications he was a fine, Christian man. With a wonderful personality, happy, successful and helpful to others. The way the overhead light brought out that reddish sheen to his dark hair made her realize anew that he was quite a handsome man. If she didn't turn this conversation around she was going to tell him far too much about her life.

"So, it's your turn. You run an animal hospital, visit class members, you're in charge of the Benevolence Committee, attend Singles' meetings, and you rescue kittens and try to help strangers find imaginary people. No wonder you're not married," she teased.

"I nearly was once. It was in med school when I first became really serious," he said. "I picked out a girl who had everything—looks, personality, even money. She had to be right for me. She was, until her Mr. Right came along."

Connie could tell, although he was saying it simply, that one hurt him. Maybe he'd never forgotten her. Maybe he was like Connie, intent upon never being hurt again. But his next words belied that.

"For the next few years I concentrated on my career, and after that was underway, fear began to settle in. I was getting older. Most of my friends had married, even had children. Where had all the girls gone? Every time a new single came into class, my first thought became, 'Is she the one?' "

Connie nodded. She knew that was typical, even with girls she'd gone to college with. And it was natural. Who and where is Mr. Right?

"Finally," he continued, "I took another good look. Most of my married friends had troubled marriages, or were divorced, or on their second marriages. It was then I turned it over to God, told Him I wouldn't try and pick my mate, and gave it up to Him. If there is a woman for me, He will let me know." He smiled. "In the meantime, Sassy and I will live," he spread his hands and tilted his head, "happily ever after."

"I've heard a dog is a man's best friend." She looked over at the cage where the kitten was stirring.

"Not only dogs, Connie," Ken said seriously. "A pet can make a huge difference in a person's life. One can fill a void, ease loneliness, provide companionship. Not only can a pet be fun, it can be therapeutic."

Well, it would take more than a kitten to do that for me. "Maybe I can help find a home for this one—where it would make a difference."

She wasn't going to share her story with Ken. Perhaps. . .another time. He took the hint well and didn't ask her any questions. He gave her a few pointers on the care of the kitten, thanked her for the coffee and said good night.

After he left, Connie gazed into the cage. Surely. . . keeping one helpless little kitten—for one night—wouldn't matter.

It did matter. During the night Connie sat straight up in bed at the sound of faint mewing. She got up and the tiny kitten was whimpering. The printing on the label of the small bottle stated that the kitten should be fed an ounce of warm milk. *Surely the kitten could last until morning when I can call Ken and have him come get it.*

Then it began making a sound like a wee cry. Connie gently touched it, and felt its soft warm fur. Its little body trembled and the thought ran through her mind that it missed its mother. She warmed a little milk in the microwave and soon had the little kitten in one hand and was feeding it from the bottle. When it finished, it was sound asleep.

The memory of Julie going to sleep while feeding rushed through Connie. She wanted to fling away the cat and the memory from her mind, but instead she held the kitten to her chest and felt its little body vibrating with the beat of its tiny heart. Only a handful of softness, of warmth, and it was only a helpless kitten.

Holding it, stroking its head, touching its soft wet nose, its tiny mouth, Connie let the emotion spill over. It was like pouring water into a cup from a faucet and it kept overflowing. Her face was drenched and she feared she might crush the kitten, so desperately did she want her Julie. She laid it gently in the basket and it didn't stir. Julie had been like that—so content, so secure, so dependent. Connie lay on the bed and cried until the early hours of the morning.

Later at work, both Jolene and Pastor Grimes could tell by Connie's face that she wasn't feeling well. As soon as Connie was sure the work load wasn't too much for Jolene, she took their advice, and went home. All the time she was changing into jeans and sweatshirt, the kitten was mewing. *Poor thing, you haven't been fed since the middle of the night.* After warming the milk, she lifted the soft, fuzzy, warm body to her face and its tongue, like fine sandpaper, tickled her cheek.

"Don't try those tricks on me," she said affectionately. "I can't keep you. You make me cry." She didn't this time, however, but instead watched the hungry little mouth satiate its hunger.

After the feeding, she saw that Martha was sweeping off her back steps and Frank had come out to rake leaves. Holding the kitten close to her chest, Connie hurried over. They raved about the adorable kitten.

"I can't keep her," Connie said. "Would you like to have her?"

"Ohhh no," Frank said and walked to another spot with his rake.

Martha looked longingly at the kitten. "We've had animals before. They just require more time and effort than we can give anymore." She touched it. "But I'm sure Frank wouldn't mind if we cat-sat occasionally."

"I. . .do need a few things from the store."

"Well, then. Let me take this little thing in the house before it catches cold. Now, you scat and do your chores."

I'm not the cat, Connie mentally responded, grinning all the way to her car. *If Martha had her way, she'd keep the kitten. Maybe Frank will change his mind.* After buying a few groceries and a few personal items that could have been done another day, she returned to the apartment and put them away. Her eyes wandered to the empty cage. Surprisingly, the kitchen seemed a little lonely.

When she went over to get the kitten, Frank said, "There's your mama." Connie surmised he wasn't quite ready for a pet.

Martha reluctantly handed it over. "She wasn't a bit of trouble. You just call on me anytime."

Before returning the kitten to its cage, Connie stood inside her kitchen door, feeling its little heart beat fast. Maybe she had thought she'd abandoned her—like her real mama had done. "I'm not going to get attached to you, you fluffy little thing," she whispered, as she brushed her cheek against its soft fur.

Chapter 7

Connie. Am I glad you're not a three-hundred-pound middle-aged man!" Ken said, the moment he came into the church office the following day.

She stared, unable to fathom such a remark.

"Lois made me promise to hug her benefactor, who paid her complete plumbing bill. She has water pressure, can use the bathroom, and is so grateful. Stand up."

Connie felt so relieved that this encounter with Ken was not awkward, that she laughed and stood, then his arms enfolded her in a brief embrace. Automatically, Connie's arms came up and around him. She quickly dropped them to her side and they both stepped back.

While unwanted emotions stirred in Connie, remembering her aching, empty arms of the past two and a half years, Ken seemed perfectly at ease. But she knew the singles often hugged. They were a close, caring group. Ken launched right in with one of his animal stories, ending with, "Your kitten will need to be examined and started on its vaccinations soon. You might want to make an appointment."

That afternoon, after work, wanting to see Ken's

place of business, Connie stopped by the animal hospital. When she stopped up to the desk to say her kitten needed shots, the receptionist asked its name.

Name? She hadn't named it. Her thoughts flew. There was only one name for it. "Fluffy," she said, then smiled. *Yes, that was perfect. Fluffy!*

The receptionist filled out an appointment card. "Dr. Russell can see your kitten next week. Is this date all right?"

Connie said it was.

My kitten! Connie thought on the way home. Ken had called it hers, and so had the receptionist. She hadn't really admitted to herself that she was attached to the little ball of fluff until now. But as the days passed, she found herself looking forward to having the little animal in her apartment after she got off work. She could tell it anything, and Fluffy didn't mind what it was, but looked at her with adoring, trusting eyes, licked her fingers, and sometimes lay on her lap.

She laid the basket beside her bed and in the middle of the lonely night when a cold gust of wind rattled the window, Connie could reach down and touch the warm, living animal, then go back to sleep. She began to remember Julie with joy instead of only despair.

When her mom and dad called, they were pleased that she was working more hours, going to church on Sunday mornings, and now attending an occasional singles' meeting to hear about financial needs that she could help with.

Each time she helped, she tried not to wonder if Ken would embrace her again and she gave herself a mental shake to think such a thing, and added to herself quickly, *It would, of course, be only a friendly embrace.* She saw him every workday, on Sundays and at the weekly meetings. She even found herself missing him when she didn't see him on Saturdays.

Now, she turned off the noise-maker TV, put the kitten on her lap to purr softly while she read biographies first, then mysteries, then inspirational romances. Upon occasion, the hero reminded her of Ken and she thought of him. Against her will she remembered the touch of his hand, the feel of his arms when he had held her, his entertaining stories, his quick laugh, his unfathomable eyes, his caring ways.

These unwanted thoughts are not for me, she reminded herself. *I'm not the heroine here!* But she wished Ken's dream could come true. He was a great guy, and when she took Fluffy to him, she was impressed with the gentleness of his touch, his caring ways with animals and with their owners.

In early November, Connie decided it was time to tell Ken he was right. The kitten had been therapeutic. It was time she told him about losing her husband and daughter. He had been very kind and she was not being honest with him.

The next evening Ken arrived for dinner at Connie's apartment wondering why she was being so mysterious when she invited him. She said she had something important to talk to him about. He was hoping it wasn't a new job somewhere else. He had been afraid to let her know how much he enjoyed her company and looked forward to seeing her. He even made up lame excuses to see her and he now wondered if she had seen through him. Of course she had. The last one, stopping by to check the density of Fluffy's winter fur growth, had evoked a wry smile from Connie and he was sure his ruse was over. She was going to call him on it and he wasn't sure what he was going to say. Ken sure didn't want to scare her off, but he couldn't read her feelings about him and didn't know if she would appreciate him stating his feelings. She had been very careful to keep him at arm's length.

Hesitating at the door, hand in mid-air ready to knock, he said a silent prayer.

Connie opened the door, smiled, and invited him in.

"Hi, Ken. Come on in. I'm just getting the food out of the oven," she called as she headed for the kitchen. "Would you like some coffee or cocoa?"

"Cocoa would be great. It smells great in here." He glanced around the room. *Something is different.* There were pictures on the wall. Two photo frames and a package of snapshots were stacked on a photo album on the end table. He walked over to the table.

"My family," she said from the doorway, startling him.

"I didn't mean to snoop," he said.

"It's okay. That's what I wanted to talk to you about." She picked up the photos and sat down on the couch, motioning him to sit beside her. "These are photos of my husband John and baby girl, Julie. They died almost three years ago in a car accident. Julie would have been three this Christmas."

"Oh, Connie. I had no idea. I'm so sorry." His mind whirled as he pieced everything together. Her reluctance to be close to people, to participate as a "single," to help Jolene with the nursery. It all made sense. She had a lot of healing to do. "Thank you for telling me."

"You were right, Ken. Fluffy was just the therapy I needed—along with your patience and understanding. You've been a tremendous help and I want you to know how grateful I am."

Quietly she showed him the photos and unburdened her heart to him. They talked over dinner and she told him of her childhood, her hopes for her daughter, and her irrational fear of Sylvia.

After dinner, as they washed the dishes, she told him, "I'm not ready for others to know about this yet. The main thing that drove me away from home was the pity I felt from everyone. I don't want that now, either. I just felt I had to be honest with you since you've been so kind to me."

"One step at a time, Connie," he told her. "I understand you not wanting this to color your new friendships, but eventually you'll be ready to tell others. You've already told one person."

"Two. Pastor Grimes has known since he interviewed me."

"See, two people."

When Ken left, he knew he had a lot to think about. He smiled as he walked to his car. *She trusts me.*

"How's the personal life coming?" she asked the following day when he brought her lunch.

"Didn't I tell you? There's been a major breakthrough," he said. "I hope it's just a matter of time."

She nodded but couldn't help but think, *Time—it's supposed to work wonders. And I suppose it has for me. I have a life. I can live a reasonably useful life of giving to help others. That brings great satisfaction. But anything personal—I can't allow myself to hope. But if I could, it would be someone like Ken.*

Decisions were gnawing at Connie. Jolene would have her baby in January. If she came back to work full-time, then Connie would have to go out and find a job elsewhere. She did not want to do that. She felt reasonably comfortable and secure at the church. That is, until the next Thursday, when right after she arrived at work, Pastor Grimes called her into his office.

"We have a situation, Connie," he said seriously.

The look on his face told her it was serious and he seemed reluctant to speak. "Connie, I would never break a promise if I could possibly avoid it. But I know you have a background of teaching kindergarten children."

It took all her strength not to rise from the chair and fly out the door. "You. . .told someone?"

He held out his hand, his eyes wide. "No, no. I wouldn't do that, Connie. You asked me not to talk about the past and now I'm bringing up this one point. That's all I mean. We have an emergency, and that's the only reason I mention this."

Connie nodded, waiting. It must be terribly important.

He leaned back in his chair as he spoke and folded

his arms across his chest. She recognized that as a defensive sign that he thought she might verbally attack him and she felt ashamed that she had doubted that kind man.

"You know we have the tutoring of first graders today."

Connie nodded.

"Katherine Mims, one of the tutors just called. Her son was hurt on the playground and she had to rush to the hospital. Aware of your background, I naturally thought of you. I'm sorry. I did not even consider this invading your privacy. I thought only of Ben needing his tutor and I will need to go to the hospital to see Katherine and her son. We'll just have to double up, that's all."

She felt so self-centered then. The tutoring was for one hour only. Often, children passed through the hallways and occasionally a parent brought one into the office. She could be around them now without going into a complete panic. Surely, for one hour, she could forget her phobias and concentrate on one little boy having difficulty in life—a first grader who's only just begun.

"No, it's not asking too much, Pastor Grimes," Connie said, ashamed to even meet his eyes, lest he see her doubts. "I. . .will try. Are there some materials I can review?"

"We can't get the materials from Katherine, but I can give you the phone number of the director. She will be able to tell you what they've been doing."

Connie called the director, Jan Claud. Then she put

the phone on answering machine and went to the church library next to the office and looked for children's books that a little first-grade boy might like.

When Mrs. Claud came, she filled Connie in on the boy's background. He seemed bright in many ways and had artistic ability. However, he'd been subjected to a bitter family dispute and divorce when he was only three years old. Apparently that had been quite traumatic, according to his dad, with whom the boy lived. After he accepted that situation, his dad was planning to remarry and Ben had to begin adjusting to a different situation, now fearful he would lose his dad, like he'd lost his mom. That seemed to have affected his concentration and motivation. It was too soon to diagnose whether the boy had attention deficit disorder, dyslexia, emotional problems, or merely inner rebellion against his frustration and hurts life had dealt him.

By the moment, Connie was feeling less sorry for herself and more concerned about this child who'd been through so much in such a few years. Childhood years should be fun and happy. Hers had been. Going downstairs, Connie had to fight back her emotions about entering a room filled with young children. Soon, she concentrated on the beautiful little boy with big soulful brown eyes, dark curly hair down over his ears, a babyface not smiling, as if he were more afraid of her than she of him.

For an hour, Connie gave of her herself, of her caring and her expertise, to Ben. When it was over, she praised him and he literally beamed as if he had accomplished something great. He didn't know how great. He had given her an entire hour free of emotional trauma. He had given her more confidence than she had given him. She could not help but hug him and tell him how proud she was of him. He was not stiff nor did he try to wriggle away from her, but she felt his little arms eagerly accept the embrace.

After the session, and the children had gone, Connie did not feel ready to involve herself with children in any permanent way, but volunteered to substitute and help with organization or even teaching tutors if needed. Mrs. Claud was more than eager to accept her offer.

Like a light turning on, it occurred to Connie that perhaps Sylvia had been part of this special group, and not a member of the church. That would explain why she was not part of the church records and no one knew her.

However, Mrs. Claud, who had tutored before becoming director three years ago was positive there had been no Sylvia in the group.

And there had been no gold stars—no stars at all.

Chapter 8

During their lunches together, Connie had come to trust that Ken would not pry into her past beyond what she had told him that evening in her apartment. Some days she even called to say she was bringing lunch for the two of them. He continued to invite her to singles' outings, but he never pressured when she always said, "Thanks, but no."

"I always have Thanksgiving dinner at my house," he said a couple of weeks before the holiday, when they sat on the couch, eating lunch. "There are several who have no place to go and it's just more homey than going to a restaurant. Want to join us?"

"Thank you, I'd like that," Connie said.

He nodded and took the last bite of a sandwich she'd brought. After swallowing, he commented, "If you change your mind, even at the last minute, let me know."

She stared at him as he picked up his coffee cup. Then saw it stop near his lips and his head turned toward her with a unbelieving expression on his face. "What. . .did you say?"

"I said I'd like that."

His coffee almost slopped over as he plunked it down on the table. He turned toward her and his hands came up and grasped her shoulders. His face was so close. "You said yes?" He moved back immediately and stood. Then threw his coffee into the trash can. Didn't he know he hadn't finished it?

Connie stood, ready to get back to work.

Ken faced her. "Where's my coffee?"

"In the trash can."

"Oh. Well, it's time to go anyway. I'll let you know details." He hugged her quickly, awkwardly.

The real reason she had readily accepted his invitation was because she didn't feel ready to go back home and face her family and all their children just yet. This presented a perfect excuse. They all would be glad for her to be involved with people again, having friends, facing life. But Connie knew it was just another form of escape.

That afternoon she parked at the back of her apartment, then hurried up the back steps, aware of the cold wind striking her face.

Upon closing the door after stepping into the kitchen, Connie's eyes lit upon the kitten and her hands reached for the warm ball of fur that she snuggled close to her face.

She felt its warmth. She remembered the warmth of Ken's hug. *I'm not going* to *get attached,* she reminded herself. The thought took her breath away. *That's exactly what I said about Fluffy that first night.*

Since Lois didn't have a car, Connie offered to give her and her two young children a ride to Ken's. Lois was so grateful, Connie felt a stab of conscience. "You're really doing me a favor, Lois," she admitted. "You may know I don't mingle with the group. It's easier, having you go in with me."

Lois smiled knowingly and nodded. "I know how that is. I have to force myself not to run away and hide somewhere in my poverty, feeling guilty because my marriage didn't work, feeling self-conscious because my own relatives can't or won't help out. But I try to keep my eyes on Jesus, and it makes all the difference."

Connie couldn't respond to Lois' comment. It must appear to the singles' group that she had faith like they did. That made her feel all the more hypocritical and she would have turned back had Lois not been with her.

"This must be it," she said, seeing the number 11 over the door and several cars parked in the driveway and on the street in front of the house. The houses were close together, like many older homes. The two-story, white frame house looked cozy and inviting, with smoke curling from the chimney into the overcast sky.

Lois steered her children up the walkway and to the front door located to the left of center, which gave character to the house with its big picture window across much of the front. Two white columns reached upward to of the pointed roof, forming a cover for the concrete entrance.

Connie held back, taking in this home of Ken's, thinking it suited him much more than a contemporary or ranch-style house. He opened the door and enthusiastically greeted them. Connie thought he looked particularly appealing in his navy-blue jeans and rust-colored sweater. Stepping inside and closing the door behind her, she noticed a stairway directly ahead, along the left wall.

While Lois was getting the coats off her children, Ken took Connie's coat, giving her a special warm look of welcome and a broad smile. Feeling that her eyes inadvertently lingered on his lips, she looked quickly away and he turned to hang her coat in a closet under the staircase. She still remained in the entry, behind Lois, holding onto the couch that separated the space from the living room section. Others began greeting them, however, and Connie wondered if she could handle it, hearing children's lilting voices and laughter somewhere beyond.

As Ken led them around the couch to where others were sitting on the side couch and on another one across the wall in front of the picture window, they all greeted her and Lois equally, as if she'd always been a part of their group. Maybe, like Lois, they had assumed she was a part of them, just because she attended Sunday school and worked in the church office.

There were five women in the living room and three men, two she recognized from the Singles' Class and a middle-aged, pleasant-looking man Ken introduced as his dad, Richard Reeves. They didn't have the same last name. And there was no resemblance, with the older one being shorter than Ken, his thinning hair was dark brown, and he had brilliant blue eyes behind his eyeglasses. Ken led Lois out with the children to see Sassy. Richard patted the empty space beside him on the couch, indicating she should sit there, which she did, and gazed into the cozy fire burning in the fireplace across from them.

He began to talk about the weather, how cold it was, and that it might snow. It rarely snowed in Greenfield, but that was the forecast. That remark triggered stories from several of the others about blizzards, ice storms, and just the sound of it gave Connie the shivers, until she again focused on the cozy fire.

Soon, Ken returned with a woman he said was his kitchen assistant. The woman slapped his arm with a dish towel she had hanging over her shoulder and threatened to leave the dinner to him, which brought his quick apology and his pretense of cowering like a scared rabbit. It was obvious the spirited red-headed freckled-faced woman was a close relative. Then he introduced her to Connie as his mom, Irene Reeves.

"Have you met Sassy?" Irene asked.

"No, but I've heard a lot of stories about her." Everyone agreed that seemed to be Ken's favorite subject.

"Come on," Irene prompted and Connie followed the jovial, slightly plump woman through the house. They passed through the dining room, dominated by a large table that could seat at least a dozen people. A buffet was along one wall and a hutch in a corner. Irene led her into the kitchen, where a narrow aisle lay between a cozy booth on the right wall and cabinets on the left.

Behind the booth and cabinets was another narrow aisle and beyond that was a compact kitchen of upper and lower cabinets and appliances. Irene turned to the left before reaching the compact kitchen, led her past a bathroom and into a room with the most surpising sight.

"Oh, my," Connie gasped as soon as they stepped into the room. No wonder the children were laughing and squealing, even applauding at times, as they sat on the floor. Lois and Betty Smith sat in folding chairs against the wall, watching a beautiful golden retriever entertain them. It reminded Connie of a dog show she went to with her parents and siblings when they were little. There had been steps, hoops, tunnels, and jumping rails. This room was obviously equipped for training or playing with an animal.

"I've got to get back to the dinner," Irene said. "Just make yourself at home."

Connie stared at the activity before her, while she eased along the wall to a chair next to Betty, trying not to disturb the children's entertainment.

"It's okay," Betty said. "Sassy is well-trained. So is my husband." She laughed, gesturing toward the man in a costume of a long-tailed black coat, a red bow tie, and a black top hat with a red band. "That's T. J. And the outfit belongs to Ken. T. J. can't resist doing this every chance he gets."

Connie was as fascinated as the children. With simple commands, and a lot of theatrics from T. J. waving his long white gold-tipped baton, the dog was fantastic, climbing steps, crawling through the tunnel, jumping through hoops, stopping and staying on command. The most amazing was her standing and bouncing on one leg. Connie knew dogs could be trained, but this was unbelievable. Sassy had only one back leg. She was a three-legged dog.

When Ken came to tell them dinner was ready, he

had a bowl of dog food for Sassy. During dinner, Sassy came to the dining room doorway. Ken said, "Go home." Sassy turned and Connie saw her disappear in the direction of the playroom.

She sat between Lois and Greta, a divorced mother of one little girl. Connie felt more comfortable with the children sitting in the kitchen booth, except for a toddler, whose mother held him. The dinner conversation was light, centering on the superb traditional turkey dinner, complete with cranberry sauce and pumpkin pie that Ken insisted he made.

After several comments about the remarkable Sassy, the upcoming football game was mentioned and that was the end of any other subject matter. As soon as dinner was over, Connie offered to help clean up. Others did too, but Irene said there was only room for two in the small kitchen. The children and a couple of parents returned to play with Sassy. A couple of singles with small children needed to leave. Others settled in the living room to watch the ball game on TV.

Connie felt comfortable with Irene, and more relaxed helping clear the table than in the other situations. "I like this house," Connie said. "It's the kind of place that makes one feel right at home."

"That's exactly what Ken wants it to be," Irene said, with an affectionate sound to her voice upon mentioning her son. "It belonged to my parents. Mom died in a fire at the factory she worked in; Dad lost his will. He suffered a stroke six months later and was in a rehab center for several years.

"Dad was released, but confined to a wheelchair. In

his teen years, Ken came to live with Dad. That boy took care of him. He loved that old man so, even when Dad was so bitter. But Ken never gave up. It took years before Ken got through to him. He's dead now, but Ken always felt more at home here than. . ." She paused for a deep breath. "Than with Richard and me."

"You don't have the same last names," Connie said, rinsing and placing in the drainer the dishes that Irene washed.

"Ken's dad had a fatal heart attack when Ken was ten years old."

Connie knew this kind of information didn't come easily and wasn't the kind of thing one said in casual conversation. "Did Ken tell you about me?" she asked.

Irene looked over at Connie, who saw the moisture in the older woman's eyes. "He would never tell anything specific without another's permission. So, no, I don't have details. He did say, as he has said about many of the singles, that you have had a hard time that's difficult to deal with. We've prayed for you, Connie. I have a good feeling about you."

Connie almost dropped the dish she was rinsing and quickly looked down at it, away from the warmth in Irene's eyes. This woman was opening her own wounds because she cared. They'd prayed for her. How could she pray, when God had allowed her husband to die a tragic death? Connie really wanted to know.

"My husband and baby died in a car wreck," Connie managed to say.

Irene nodded and Connie's glance revealed that the moisture in Irene's eyes was overflowing down her cheeks. "How did you. . . ?" Connie heard herself say, and could not voice any other words, but Irene knew what she meant.

"I almost drove myself crazy. I was young, with a ten-year-old boy who needed his dad and suffered even more than I did."

How difficult that must have been for Ken. Connie could be grateful that Julie didn't have to grow up without her dad. *The two of them are together—in heaven. Heaven? I do believe that. God was merciful in letting them be together.*

"I questioned how God could let it happen," Irene was saying. "Only when I gave it over to God, was I able to stand it, forgive myself, go on, deal with it."

Connie nodded, as if agreeing. But her thought was, *I don't know how.*

Chapter 9

The apartment seemed lonelier than usual when Connie woke up on Friday morning, realizing she had three days off, with nothing to do but minor cleaning and one load of laundry, all of which could be done in about an hour.

When the phone rang and Ken asked if she'd do him a favor, she laughed. "What kind of animal this time?" She realized she had completely forgiven him for trying to help her by giving her a kitten. In fact, she appreciated it.

"A talking cockatoo, a golden retriever puppy, a Great Dane puppy, a Great Dane adult, two kittens, and Sassy, of course," he replied, with laughter in his voice.

"Ach," Connie gasped. "You must think I'm in really bad shape. But I'm afraid they would be incompatible with. . .me!"

He chuckled. "I'm not looking for a home for them. My assistant has the flu and I have a big meeting tomorrow afternoon at the children's hospital, talking to parents who are considering getting a pet for their children."

"What would I have to do?"

"Just put the animals back into their cages, and help

me carry them. Simple."

Simple! She suspected dear ol' Ken was just trying to make her be more sociable. But it might be better than facing the apartment all weekend. Besides, she'd thought about Irene's conversation about Ken's early life and was curious about it.

"Yes, Ken, I'll do what I can."

She heard his intake of breath, and thought he was about as surprised as he'd been when she accepted his Thanksgiving dinner invitation.

The following evening, Ken gave a brief talk to parents only, telling them that his own personal experiences with animals led him into the veterinarian field. He said that an animal can be a friend and of great psychological value to some who have lost a loved one, or have permanent or temporary physical handicaps, whether emotional, mental, or physical. He encouraged them to acquaint their children with animals, whether at a pet store, a zoo, or dog shows.

He didn't go into detail about himself, but gave illustrations of others. Some who needed a seeing-eye dog, others with paralysis who found a monkey to be indispensable. Then he told of a personal incident.

"After my grandfather had a stroke and went to a nursing home, I'd take my shepherd with me and tie him to a tree outside. The residents would walk or wheel over to the windows to see the dog. I began to notice they'd perk up whenever Shep was there. The workers noticed it too and asked if I'd bring the dog inside. They told me later that Shep lifted the spirits of those patients more than anything they'd been able to do." His voice lowered as he said seriously, "It was the beginning of recovery for my grandfather. It gave him something to relate to and he eventually returned to his home."

Connie realized that Ken had an even greater depth of character than she had thought—and it had been there when he was very young. There was so much more about him that she wanted to know. But he began to tell about the problems one could have with a pet, the constant care, the space needed for a large animal.

Connie helped him bring the cages closer then, grateful that the larger ones had wheels on them. As the huge dog stood and shifted its weight, she lost her grip on the cage. The image of people scattering like bowling pins rushed through her mind as the cage lunged toward the audience perched on folding chairs. Ken grabbed the back of it, nearly sat down backward, and pulled it to a stop beside him.

"Whoa! See what I mean?" Ken laughed as he stood back up.

The audience chuckled good-naturedly at the near disaster while Connie, flushed with embarrassment, brought the puppy over to Ken and took him out of his smaller cage.

He showed the adorable Great Dane puppy, then the adult Great Dane. "The little one grows to be like this," he said, standing by the cage of the older dog who almost drowned out Ken's words with its barking and scratching in the cage. "He belongs to a friend of mine, but isn't too keen on anyone else, especially me, since I'm the one who gives him his shots."

The audience laughed at that, but was getting the point that the adult animal had to be considered, particularly where children were concerned.

"And finally, remember that animals do not live forever. Although they make a difference, and certainly have in my own life, I needed something more permanent, and that was a personal relationship with Jesus Christ. Now, while the aides bring your children in to pet the smaller animals, are there any questions?"

One woman stood and asked what kind of pet might she consider for a girl who had a fear of dogs and cats.

"How old is she?" Ken asked.

"Sylvia is five."

Ken and Connie exchanged glances. *Sylvia? Could this be. . .my Sylvia?* was all Connie could think about and she hardly heard the rest of the question and answer period. Was Sylvia a patient here at the hospital?

Her heart beat faster as children were brought in, some in wheelchairs, others walking with casts on arms or legs. A little dark-haired girl with her arm in a sling, and "Sylvia" written on a nametag, went over and sat on the woman's lap.

Ken looked expectantly at Connie, who shook her head.

Ken wheeled the big Dane out of the room so the children could pet the puppies and kittens and listen to the cockatoo. Connie watched as Sylvia joined in, much to her own and her mother's delight.

When he came back in, Ken introduced Sassy. "Sassy was found by her owner in an old bear trap in the woods. We weren't able to save her leg, and the owner didn't want a three-legged dog. So Sassy lives with me now. As you can see, she does more than most dogs with four legs," Ken told them proudly. Then Sassy proved it.

It was as if the dog drew energy from her enthusiastic audience, children with broken limbs, missing limbs, bandaged heads, and some obviously medicated. But for a while, Connie could see that their problems vanished and so did the problems of the parents. All eyes were on the dog, whose handicap made her more of a star of the show than if she'd had all four limbs.

After Sassy performed and the children and parents left, Connie and Ken loaded the animals into the van.

"That was very impressive, Ken. And very inspirational. It looks like your program for those kids is well thought out." She had told him about John and Julie, but she was embarrassed she had never bothered to show any genuine interest in his past. "How did you go through your loss and still become such a joyful person?"

Connie almost wished she hadn't asked, hearing the sadness in his voice as he remembered when he was a ten-year-old boy whose dad would never come home again. "I turned to my collie, who became my best friend. I told him everything. When I yelled, when I cried, he stuck by me. We even ran away together till I got cold and hungry and ended up at my grandparents' house."

Ken looked over and in the shadowed van, with passing car lights, she saw the deep sadness of a little boy in his eyes, even though he smiled. "I'm so sorry, Ken. And sorry I thought you couldn't understand my grief. It must be worse, when you're just a child."

"I don't know, Connie. But it seems that whatever difficult situation we find ourselves in is the ultimate trial. For my grandfather, it was the loss of his wife, then his stroke. It seems we all have our trials. But the important thing is how we handle it. What kind of attitude we have toward it."

"And it was your collie that got you through," Connie said.

"To a great extent. The collie was my friend and confidant when I needed to say things I couldn't say to my mom or to my grandfather. When I thought I was handling things well, my mom started seeing Richard. That plunged me right back into the past. I accused her of never having loved my dad. I was awful."

"It's hard to believe that, Ken."

"It's true. I escaped to my grandfather then. It was he who turned me toward the Lord. It really didn't sink in though, until after he had a stroke and returned from the nursing home. I began to remind him of what he had taught me. It became real to me, Connie, and I saw how all the events of my life were leading me toward being a veterinarian that reached out to others with my animals and my life."

When Ken pulled into the parking space at the back of her apartment and switched off the engine and the lights, Connie turned toward him. She'd felt so close to him, hearing about his childhood suffering. "You're the finest man I know, Ken," she said with feeling and reached up to touch his face. She didn't want him to suffer.

Why or how it happened, she didn't know. It was totally impulsive and irresponsible, but there in the dark, hardly able to see his face it was as if their eyes met and held and she could feel his warm breath against her face in the van that was becoming quite cold and then their lips met. It must have been some subconscious effort on her part to let him know he was attractive, desirable, and that any woman should want him.

She knew she had taken the initiative and lifted her face to his, and then felt the warm gentle pressure of his lips on hers that increased with intensity and she felt herself wanting to respond and forced herself to move away.

"I'm so sorry," she whispered, her head dropping with shame, although he couldn't possibly see her flushed face in the dark.

"Don't be, Connie," he said gently, lifting her chin with his fingers. "It's natural, normal. We connect, Connie. You know that. And by now, you should know you can trust me."

She could only shake her head. If she could love again, it would be someone like Ken, but she doubted there was another like him.

"Connie, I wanted to kiss you."

"But I started it, Ken." She turned and put her hand on the door handle. "You deserve someone who can share your religious beliefs. I would not want to do anything to come between you and the woman you believe God has chosen for you."

She opened the door and the dome light came on. She clearly saw the seriousness in his eyes when he replied, "You're the only one who could, Connie—the only one."

Chapter 10

Not wanting to face Ken just yet, and afraid she couldn't be "just a friend" to a man she had deliberately kissed, a man who as much as admitted to being tempted by her, Connie didn't go to Sunday school. Later, deciding not to answer the phone, she listened as Ken left a message, saying he missed her, hoped everything was all right, call if she wanted to, and if not, he'd see her Monday.

Betty Smith called too, saying they missed her and to call if she needed to. Lois called too, to say she hoped everything was all right.

That afternoon, when her mom's voice came on the answering machine, Connie picked up. Her parents encouraged her to come home for Christmas.

"I might," Connie conceded, wondering if she should return to her hometown, or leave here for someplace new. She dreaded the thought of starting over again. It had begun to seem perfect here, had she not messed it up by being. . . "normal!"

She knew her absence made it hard on her parents and relatives who loved her. She'd like to go home, but feared her lack of enthusiasm would be detected and it would spoil things for everyone. She could relate better to strangers, or to those with whom she had no binding responsibility.

But that night, instead of sleeping well, Connie kept remembering Ken's intimating she had the power to come between him and the woman he thought was God's choice. Oh, she must never have such a thing on her conscience. Surely, she was becoming a hindrance to a wonderful man who tried to live by God's rules. Connie felt guilty and wondered if she should leave here rather than do any damage to anyone—and maybe. . .even to her own heart.

When Connie pulled into the church parking lot the next morning, she saw Ken's van parked at the basement door. Then she remembered he'd said he would be bringing some animals for the Day Care Center as part of their last class activities until after the first of the year. She pretended not to see him, but he called her over, saying he could use some help.

She held the basement door open while he took the cages in. He seemed like the same Ken as always, as if nothing had happened. Perhaps she'd made too much of it. It hadn't been more than a normal thing for him. But for nearly three years now, she hadn't engaged in anything that normal.

But, she determined, she would not go around kissing her "friend" again!

After helping Ken, she went through the fellowship hall and up the steps to the church office.

Jolene was there, saying she felt better that morning than she had in a long time. She and Connie caught up on past events and talked about Fluffy and Ken's animals down in the Day Care Center and how much of a blessing animals can be to people—something neither had ever seriously considered.

"Ken learned by his own experiences and puts that to use," Connie said, and as she said it, the thought occurred that she had no idea that she could ever bring good from the devastating experiences that happened to her. And yet. . .Irene's sharing her own experiences had helped Connie know that someone could understand. Irene was able to regain her faith in God. Even able. . .to marry again.

Jolene had just hung up the phone and Connie was typing Sunday's program on the word processor when a loud explosion sounded and screams were heard. Then the deafening sound of the fire alarm throbbed in Connie's ears. After a startled instant of the two women staring at each other, each jumped up out of their chairs. The pastor rushed from his office.

"I'll call the fire department," Connie said.

"The alarm rings in at the station," Jolene reminded her.

Yes, Connie had been told that the first day at work, but who ever really expects such a happening? The odor came first, then smoke began curling up the stairs and into the hallway. Pastor Grimes and Connie were almost neck and neck, running down the stairs and Connie looked back to see Jolene hurrying after them.

Day Care workers were filing the children out in an orderly manner as they had obviously practiced. Smoke was fast filling the room and a terrific fire was blazing in the kitchen area.

Seeing that the children were under control, Connie began helping Ken get the animals back into their cages and took them outside, having to make two trips.

Finally the pastor came out, having made sure all the children were outside and accounted for. "Where's Jolene?" Connie's voice was trembling.

The pastor called her name loudly, but got no response. They could hear the fire trucks coming. Two of the kitchen workers came out; one woman's clothes were smoldering. The other pointed inside in response to the pastor's call for Jolene. Ken made a mad dash for the door where the woman pointed, with Sassy right with him. Smoke was pouring out. Connie opened her mouth to yell, "No" but knew she mustn't say the word aloud. Of course, Ken must try to find Jolene. She must be saved.

Ambulances arrived as the firemen jumped from their trucks. Two of the paramedics went to the woman whose clothes were burned. The pastor told the firemen Jolene and Ken were inside. Sassy was inside barking. Connie watched the smoke and flames at the door, expecting them to emerge at any moment. But they didn't. Firemen rushed inside. An eternity passed. Finally, two firemen appeared with the limp bodies of Ken and Jolene in their arms. They were immediately put on stretchers and carried away in the ambulances.

Connie felt so helpless. Like Sassy, who was shoved out of the way so the ambulance doors could be closed. The ambulance drove away and Sassy started to run after it. Connie called her back. Sassy came to her, whimpering and she saw that her fur was singed in many places. Connie knew Sassy would have stayed by Ken. . .no matter what.

"He'll be all right," Connie soothed, caressing the dog's ear that was not singed. "He has to be." How could she lose him too? *Oh, please. . .* Her thoughts stopped there. She wasn't a praying person.

Connie was vaguely aware of neighbors and parents arriving to help, of herself moving the panic-stricken animals in their cages further away from the burning building, of firemen and hoses and endless streams of water and smoke. Then Jolene's husband, Tony came. The pastor talked to him. He looked frantic as he ran to his car and sped away. Oh, what would that young man do without his wife and baby? Tears scalded her cold face. Then she realized she was shivering. The temperatures were below freezing. And only a few feet away a building was burning.

She didn't know how long she stood there by the cages with a singed three-legged Sassy beside her as if she were the dog's protector. Or maybe Sassy was trying to protect Connie. Her eyes followed a last billow of smoke upward and her gaze went further. *Why a church? Why would God let a church, of all things, burn? Why would He take away everyone she got attached to?*

"Thank God the children got out safely," Pastor Grimes was saying. "And Ken's animals." Connie realized most of the people had gone. Now, after this terrible tragedy, Pastor Grimes was thanking God. She stared at him, bewildered.

"I need to go to the hospital, Connie. Can you take care of the animals and be available for the fire investigators?" Before she could answer a fireman walked up to the pastor.

"The damage to the building will have to be assessed and an investigation done before we can allow anyone inside, Pastor Grimes. Where can we reach you this afternoon and evening?"

"I'll be at the hospital with the families of the injured. This is our secretary, Connie Turner. I've asked her to be our contact person. You can let her know what you need us to do and when we can go back inside. I'll be in touch with her from the hospital later."

Pastor Grimes excused himself, and left for the hospital. Connie vaguely remembered answering the fireman's questions about what she saw and heard and gave him her phone number.

"Do you need us to call someone to help you with those animals?" the fireman asked. Connie realized she had no keys to Ken's van.

"No, thanks. I'll put Sassy and the smaller cages into my car and take them back to the animal hospital. I'm sure Dr. Russell's staff will have a key and can help with the rest of them. Poor things. They're terrified."

After Sassy was treated for her burns and the rest of the animals and van had been picked up, Ken's assistant assured Connie the dog would be all right. Connie took Sassy home with her to wait for the fire investigator and Pastor Grimes to call.

Irene! Had anyone let her know? Connie looked up

her number and called. Irene hadn't heard. "I'll go directly to the hospital," Irene said. "I'll let you know when I find out anything. Thank you, Connie."

Hours passed without word from Pastor Grimes, Irene, or the fire department. "I'll just have to call the hospital myself," she told Fluffy.

"Are you a family member?" the woman asked.

"No, I'm—"

"I'm sorry, we can't give out any information to nonrelatives for the patients' privacy."

"What are your visiting hours?"

"I'm sorry, visitors for emergency patients are limited to immediate—"

"Family only. Thanks anyway." Connie hung up the phone to wait.

Chapter 11

Mid-morning the following day, the phone finally rang.

"Connie, I'm so sorry It's taken me so long to call you," Pastor Grimes fatigued voice told her. "I've been with the families of Jolene, Ken, and Helen at the hospital."

"I understand. I know you probably haven't had any sleep either," she said, trying not to sound impatient. "How are they? What happened? Why didn't they come out?"

"Jolene went to help put out Helen's burning clothes. She was overcome with smoke and fainted before reaching the doorway. Jolene is in a coma, and because of the toxicity in her blood, the baby was taken. Both are in intensive care. Helen is fine with only minor burns, and Irene is right here and wants to tell you about Ken. I'll pass her the phone is a moment."

"Thank you, Pastor."

"Again, I'm sorry we didn't call you sooner. Here's Irene."

"Hi Connie. I feel awful not calling you last night." Irene sounded stressed, but calm.

"That's okay, Irene. How is he?"

"Ken is in a decompression chamber because of the smoke inhalation and carbon monoxide poisoning. He apparently went into the kitchen area and something fell on his head, possibly a beam. He has a terrible headache and his throat is raw from the toxic fumes. He's not allowed any visitors just yet, but I know he will want to see you as soon as possible. It looks like he'll be here a few days at least. I promise I'll keep you posted."

"Thanks for filling me in, Irene. Call any time. Bye."

Connie hung up the phone, picked up Fluffy and gave her a quick nuzzle as a small tear of relief ran down her cheek.

The sanctuary was not damaged and the pastor taped a voice message to be sent to all the members, letting them know there would be a special prayer service for Jolene, her baby, Helen, and Ken the following morning.

Connie didn't want to attend. She knew how close to death each person was—only a breath away. It could happen in an instant, and even to an infant. She had not prayed since those desperate days when she begged God to bring back her beautiful family—to let it all be a bad dream. But He had not. Then she had prayed He would take away that awful aching pain. But He had not.

But she was the church secretary. Jolene was her friend. She cared about her and the baby now in intensive care. Ken was her friend. She cared that the business of the church continued. Maybe the pastor would have her stay in the office and answer telephone calls that would inevitably be coming in.

She offered to do that when she arrived at the church, but he wouldn't hear of it. "You should be in the service, Connie," he said. "You've worked closely with Jolene these past months and I know you want to be in there."

But she didn't. She wanted to stay away from those haunting, gnawing memories and reality and awareness of possibilities. The baby could die. Jolene could die. Ken could die. And her prayers wouldn't make a bit of difference.

She had told the pastor about her past. Didn't he care? Didn't he know how she felt? Didn't anyone? No! All those people coming into the sanctuary would pray for the healing and recovery of the three injured persons—and maybe God would even hear their prayers.

Then Jolene's husband, Tony, came into the hallway from the side door. His eyes were shiny, like a fever had touched them. Hope, that's what it was. Oh, she didn't want him to lose his wife and baby.

After Irene and Richard came in, Connie walked with them into the sanctuary and they sat near the front next to Mary, the pastor's wife.

Connie felt as if she were doing it all over again. She knew the feeling of walking into a sanctuary and sitting with family members, feeling hands on your shoulders, touching your arms, whispered words of condolence and sobs of sympathy. But none of that helped. If God didn't care about your problem, or didn't want to do anything about it, you were sunk. And that's where she was, sunk into the depths of despair, lost in the labyrinth of disappointment.

"I don't know what causes every act in this world," Pastor Grimes began. "God didn't cause that fire in the kitchen. He could have put it out, but where would He draw the line? When God doesn't do what we want Him to do, or act like we want Him to act, we get upset with Him. It's easy for us to say: 'If I were God, I'd put an end to evil. If I were God, I'd heal all the sick. I'd never let a sinner prosper. If I were God, I'd never let anyone get hurt. I'd turn this planet into heaven on earth. I wouldn't let the sinners have free will to hurt others. If I were God. . .'

"But that was the mistake Adam and Eve made. The evil one said, 'Eat of this fruit and you will be like God.'

"We are not God. We are His created beings. He has a plan and purpose for this world. I doubted all that when Mary's and my little unborn baby died."

Connie's head came up and her eyes fastened on Pastor Grimes. *He lost his baby?* Mary was sitting beside her. *She lost her baby? This woman who glows with joy, is involved with all the organizations, presides over meetings and dinners. Mary felt. . .what I feel?*

Connie couldn't take her eyes from the pastor as he continued, feeling he wasn't talking about Jolene, her baby, and Ken at all. He seemed to be talking directly to Connie.

"But through that experience," he was saying. "I learned what sorrow is, what pain is, what suffering is, what blame and hurt is, and what it is to turn from God and resent Him because He has the power to work magic or miracles, but He didn't give me one. Or did He? Yes, that baby has been saved from any hurt or suffering. And through it, He gave me a heart to feel for others. A joy that my baby is safe and happy. A compassion and understanding that only pain can bring.

"So I cannot pray for healing, or even for life. You pray as you feel led, but I pray for God's will to be done and for our grace to accept it. I pray for courage, for strength, for hope, for compassion, and to tell God what we think is best—and that is for the complete healing and recovery of our loved ones, Jolene and the baby and Ken.

"God knows what it's like to suffer. He came to this earth in the form of Jesus—suffered and died."

The pastor's words began to drift farther and farther away. Connie became lost in her own thoughts, which included the puzzlement about the Wahlens, the strangeness of her life, wondering what she was even doing working at this church, helping out with children, and now sitting with a congregation who was praying for the lives of three people near death. Phrases began to leap into her mind like, *Train up a child in the way he should go and when he is old, he will not depart from it.*

Well, Connie thought, *I am the exception. My parents' faith has not helped me, nor their teaching. My pastor's faith had not saved me either.*

Saved me? The words rang through Connie's mind. *Saved me from what? From sin? Me, a sinner?* That startled her. *Not me. I always was a good girl, raised in the church. The word sinner denotes one in darkness, though doomed, hopeless, alone, even dead. Doesn't that describe me?*

"Jesus died for our sins." What a simple statement.

Connie had heard it all her life. She had believed it. She had confessed it because she had believed it.

Then what was wrong?

The phrase, "The devil also believes and trembles," jumped at her. How could she have missed it?

I don't have the Holy Spirit in my life, she realized, and trembled. He had never been real or personal. She had been taught what she should do, and did it. She had believed *about* Jesus, but not *in* Him.

She hadn't known it was for her, personally, that He died. Suddenly, it was as if she were the Roman soldier who drove the nails and mocked Him.

Slowly, it penetrated her thinking that it was not even for the sins she had committed during the past few years that He died. She was a sinner before committing a known sin. She was a sinner because she lived in a world dominated by Satan and his powers, where, since the beginning of time, humanity had yielded to the Evil One and rebelled against God. From that day forth, each and every person must deliberately choose God or forever be condemned.

She had heard words like that for years, yet it seemed as if this was the first time they ever had any deep and personal meaning. Perhaps it was because somewhere in her subconscious she was reaching out for anything to save her.

Shouldn't I at least give God a chance? she asked herself. *I have tried living apart from Him since the tragedy. Shouldn't I give Jesus a chance to see what He can do? If nothing happens, I will not have lost anything. I have nothing to lose.*

The service was over. Connie hadn't even heard most of it. But she was moving with other people down the aisle, making her way to the front of the church, falling on her knees at the altar where some still prayed. Her heart was praying, not for Jolene, the baby, or Ken. *I don't know what you want of me or my wasted life. It has counted for nothing. It is over. Yet, Jesus, you said that I am the kind of person You died for. If it is true, if for some unknown reason You want me, You can have me. It would have to be a miracle. But if You want to try, here I am.*

Connie didn't know the moment it happened. Perhaps it was when she gave her life up as useless and gave it to Jesus. Perhaps it was when she saw Mary go into the pastor's office and close the door and Connie followed. Mary was searching for a clean tissue, but Connie already had a box in her hand. The two women looked at each other. Their eyes met. Their lips trembled. Mary came to Connie and embraced her.

"Oh, honey," Mary said. "I knew there was something—but I didn't suspect you might have such a loss. Oh, my dear." They clung to each other, sharing pain, experiencing joy of release. Mary didn't ask for details. It wasn't necessary. They communicated because they both knew each had experienced a devastating loss. Connie was strengthened by knowing Mary had lost, and yet she was a useful Christian whose faith was obviously intact.

Perhaps it was when the pastor understandingly counseled with Connie the next day. He cried too, and Connie knew his scars had become an open wound again. But his would heal, as they undoubtedly had done time and time again. And for the first time, Connie could be glad John had not been left to deal with such hurt.

Maybe it was when the pastor asked, "Did you love John and Julie more intensely before or after their deaths?"

Connie couldn't believe he asked such a thing. Then she began to see his point. She had loved John and Julie completely when they were alive. But it was after their deaths that John and Julie consumed her being. They became top priority—her loss of them, her grief, her suffering, her pain, her self.

"I've been. . .selfish," Connie admitted.

The pastor scooted his chair closer to her and reached out to hold her hands. "No, Connie. You've been hurt. You're only human. That's why we need God so much. We can't handle life alone. John and Julie were not yours. They're God's. They are together with Him. We cannot know the mind of God, but perhaps God thought Julie needed her dad with her. Maybe He thought you were strong enough to stay here—for a reason. We're not here just to enjoy ourselves, although a lot of that is possible. We're not put on this earth for fun and games. God created us. He loves us. He has eternity prepared for us, but we must get the ticket, get on board, get back on the tracks when we get off, make the journey. While on board, there are a lot of wrecks, delays, detours, and getting off track. But the Bible is our roadmap so we get back on track and keep going until we reach our destination in heaven."

Maybe it was when she sincerely sobbed into her

pillow and prayed for Jolene, the baby, and Ken. Or perhaps it was not in a moment at all. She couldn't say. But she knew she had gained a new quality of life. There was an underlying strength, a Presence, a sense of well-being.

Connie began to realize this "new life" that the New Testament pictured was not something one demanded from God, but was a simple act of faith. It was so simple she had almost missed it—simply offering her life to Him, to use to guide, to give purpose and meaning.

She knew her problems had not vanished. Many questions remained unanswered. Some were so much a part of her that they would remain forever. But she also knew that Someone was with her, telling her everything would be all right. She felt a peace that she hadn't felt since her personal tragedy.

Chapter 12

"Tis the season to be jolly," sounded over the car radio as soon as Connie pushed the "on" button. She didn't feel jolly, however, fighting back her emotions after she parked her car at the hospital and neared Jolene's room. Would she be able to face Jolene and whatever was happening with her and her baby? All she knew was, Jolene could now have visitors.

Connie slowly opened the door, while holding onto the pot of red poinsettias that wouldn't mean a thing if Jolene's baby was not safe. Then the most amazing sight was before her. She set the plant on the dresser and walked closer.

Jolene, her face aglow with joy, was sitting up in bed, holding her precious baby, bundled up in a soft pink blanket.

"Would you like to hold Marietta?" Jolene asked.

Connie wasn't sure she could. But she wanted to. This was the first time, since Julie, that she wanted a baby in her arms. Carefully taking the child, she felt its warmth, breathed in its baby odor, looked at its perfect face. Her heart and mind overflowed with the memory of her own baby and she handed Marietta back to Jolene, afraid she might tremble and drop the child, or that she might crush it to herself, never able to let go.

Connie could only nod as Jolene talked about her wonderful blessing, and how she never dreamed she could feel such love, or such a burden of responsibility for this perfect, helpless infant.

With tears in her eyes, Connie encouraged Jolene. Maybe she could tell her someday about Julie. But not now—not while this new mother was filled with such perfect love and looking toward the future. *Maybe, if I stayed in Greenfield, I could be friends with Jolene—maybe I could reach out—somehow.*

After visiting with Jolene, Connie found her way to Ken's room in another part of the hospital. Irene had called earlier, saying that only family was allowed to visit, but she knew Ken would be thrilled to see her. She could go directly to the room during visiting hours.

Connie tapped lightly on the door, then peeked in. Irene immediately came to her and Richard stood. "We'll run down and have a cup of coffee," Irene said. "And we won't hurry."

"Thank you," Connie said. She greeted Richard as the couple walked out. Connie focused on Ken. "Oh, you look wonderful," she said. A doubtful look crossed his face as his eyebrows shot up. He held out the neck of his hospital gown, indicating he wasn't exactly dressed in the latest style.

She had to laugh and he grinned. There he lay with his head bandaged. His rust-colored curls were spread in disarray above the bandages, looking as if they could stand a good shampoo. Freckles across his nose stood out like sprinkles of red clay in his pale face. He had a cut on the side of his face and bruises on his arms.

"I mean," she said, feeling herself blush, "it's wonderful that you're sitting up and recovering." Afraid she was mistaking the affection in his eyes for something she was feeling herself, she sat in the chair he motioned at. She pulled it closer to his bed. He'd probably been told about Jolene and the baby, but she wanted to tell him anyway. "They're going to be fine. I held the baby," she said. "For me, that was a major breakthrough."

He reached for her hand and grasped it firmly and he blinked slowly, indicating he agreed and was pleased.

"I have something else to tell you, when you're better." She knew it would mean so much to him, knowing she had experienced the Holy Spirit coming into her life, helping her cope, giving her hope.

He looked at her for a long time, making her wonder if he could read her mind—his eyes seemed to be searching hers so deeply. Could he fathom how much she appreciated his befriending her? How much it meant that he broke through her reserve? That he had persisted in being her friend when she thought she wanted none? Her own eyes closed against the emotion threatening to spill from her eyes. Then she felt his hand squeeze hers and realized he'd held it for such a long time.

She moved her hand away from his and looked toward the door. When would Irene and Richard come back? "I'd better go and let you get some rest. Oh, I'm taking care of Sassy."

He nodded again and mouthed "Thank you."

When she stood to go, he lifted his hand as if she should wait. He reached over to the bedside table for a pad and wrote on it, then handed it to her. She read, "Promise to visit me as soon as I get out of here."

On the drive back home as darkness settled in, Connie noticed a world transformed by colored lights. Businesses were outlined, some blinking. Leafless trees seemed to have arrayed themselves with color, dancing in the cold wind. In neighborhoods, light shone from windows. Yes, it was beginning to look like the season to be jolly!

I should be, Connie lectured herself. *Although I can never forget my loved ones, I know the Lord is healing my grief. I could become closer to Jolene, her family, and Ken. But, I should have taken Ken's warning when our conversations first began. He had warned about friendship being mistaken for more. I am grateful he's made me feel again, hope again. So, perhaps it's time. . .to go home again.*

Two days later, Irene called the church office to tell Connie that Ken was home.

"I'll bring Sassy over right after work," Connie promised.

As soon as she arrived and Irene opened the door, Sassy made a mad dash for her master. Ken was putting decorations on a Christmas tree in the corner next to the couch. Nearby, the fireplace was burning with a cozy fire.

"Ken can whisper now," Irene said. She took Connie's coat and hung it in the closet, then put on her own. "I've got to get home and see what Richard cooked me for supper," she said, then gave Connie a word of advice. "When your man cooks for you, never be late!"

They laughed and after Irene left, Connie walked over to the fire and warmed her hands, then watched as Sassy and Ken began to settle down. The three-legged wonder appeared only to be trying to lick the skin off Ken's hands.

"She hasn't had her supper yet. We've been eating together after I get home from work. By the way," she said with a triumphant grin. "Sassy and Fluffy *are* compatible."

"I'll feed her," Ken whispered. "Make yourself useful." He smiled and pointed to the boxes. Connie was fascinated with the decorations, obviously handmade. Several were tiny cardboard frames with pictures of a collie and a shepherd. Others were apparently family members, for she recognized Irene and Richard. One was a miniature Bible. There were pieces of a nativity set. None were flashy baubles.

"I'd say each of these has a special meaning," Connie said when he returned to her side.

He looked at her fondly. "I'd like to tell you about each one, when I have a stronger voice."

I don't think I'll be around then, Connie thought, quickly looking down at the empty box, wishing there were another ornament to hang, lest Ken suspect her thought and detect a trace of regret in her. He had served a wonderful purpose in her life—and that was all.

Ken took the empty boxes into the kitchen, then

returned to the couch, where Connie sat, staring into the fire and thinking how cozy this house was, especially now that the golden retriever had come in and lay on the hearth.

"What's been happening with you, Connie? In the hospital you said there was something you had to tell me."

Connie nodded. She wanted him to know this. She told him about how losing John and Julie had made her angry with God, about her past heartaches, and about her disappointments with God. Then she told him about her newfound faith and feeling God's presence in her life. He moved to the edge of the couch then, closer to her and she looked at his face. His eyes were moist with emotion and so full of caring. She felt an overwhelming desire to fall into his arms and tell him how much he had meant to her these past months. But she mustn't. "I think perhaps I should go back to Columbia."

His hands were on her shoulders. "Why, Connie? You've just indicated you're ready to face life now—go on."

How honest could she be? There were so many things to sort out, she wasn't even sure of her feelings. Had she mistaken her gratitude to Ken for. . .something else? "But things here have changed, Ken. And someday that special woman God has for you will come along. My relationship with you will. . .end."

He threw another log on the fire, then walked over to the Christmas tree and plugged it in. Tiny lights spread a colorful glow in the corner. He then reached underneath the tree and brought out a small box she hadn't noticed.

It had her name on it. "Go ahead and open it," he encouraged.

Connie untied the bow and slowly removed the wrapping paper. His giving it to her now must be his way of saying she was right, she should go home, and he didn't expect her to be here for Christmas.

She stared for a moment at the red-velvet jewelry box, then lifted the top. Lying on white satin was a twinkling star, full of diamonds and outlined in gold. "Oh, Ken. This is beautiful. But I can't accept something so—"

He touched her lips to shush her. "Yes, you can," he said. "I went looking for something like this the day you told me about Sylvia. I suspected there was much more to the incident than your imagination. I felt God brought that little girl into your life, marking a new beginning for you. It has been that, hasn't it, Connie?"

"Oh, yes," Connie agreed. "But—"

He shook his head. "Please let me do this, Connie. It's my way of saying thank you for meaning so much to me these past few months. I've watched you continue on in spite of your doubts and hurts. I've watched you trying not to reach out to others, but being unable to hold back. You've been caring and generous and. . . wonderful."

He took the pin from the box and leaned closer to pin it on her sweater. "Please keep this, Connie. To remember me by, if you cannot open your heart to me beyond friendship."

Connie searched his face that seemed to hold the kind of longing she felt within herself. But she shook her head. "I can't allow myself to come between you and—"

"Connie!" he said loudly and put his hand to his throat as if that hurt. Then his voice became a whisper again. "Don't you know? The woman I believe God intends for me is you, Connie. You're the woman I love."

Connie stared and blinked.

He leaned close to her ear. "This is the part where you tell me how you feel," he whispered. Then he sat back pretending he hadn't coached her.

"Oh, Ken. I never thought I would feel this way again." His eyes sparkled with emotion and Connie leaned toward him, her love for him overflowing her heart.

"I was beginning to wonder if you were ever going to kiss me again," he teased, as he wrapped her in is arms, his kisses warm and gentle.

While "Oh, holy night, the stars are brightly shining," was playing on the stereo, Connie stood at her kitchen window, fingering the gold star on her sweater, looking at the snow falling, Fluffy paced across the window sill. Connie had taken all weekend to think, to absorb all the major changes that had taken place within herself. So much had happened in spite of herself. Even falling in love with Ken—something she never intended to do. But before she could make any kind of commitment to him, beyond friendship, she had to ask, *What would John want me to do? What would I want John to do if he were in this situation?*

Her eyes lifted higher, to lacy white flakes falling

from a black sky. *More important than that*, she thought, for the first time in her life, *what would God have me do?*

Lowering her eyes to the ground, covered with a blanket of snow, with the street light casting an eerie glow, a shadow caught her eye.

Connie couldn't breathe—or move. *Sylvia!* Sylvia, bundled up, playing about in the snow, stopped and waved. Connie rushed outside, down the steps and to the spot where Sylvia had been playing. She looked all around but couldn't find her.

Then, Connie realized there was only one set of footprints in the snow—her own. Slowly realization dawned. Sylvia had drawn her here, had opened her heart to a child, had guided her through the darkness of despair to hope, to search all because of a gold star. She didn't know if Sylvia was imaginary or an angel, but now she was sure God had spoken to her through Sylvia.

She whispered, "He loves me."

She said it louder, "God loves me."

She sat down in the snow, and fell back laughing. Then she did something she hadn't done since she was a child. Spreading her arms, she made a snow angel in the white blanket covering the ground.

Her kitten, and maybe the neighbors, could be watching and think she'd gone crazy. But she didn't care. She lay there, the gold star glistening on her sweater in the soft light, while she was seeing anew the wonder of the beautiful, gold Star of Bethlehem.

Yvonne Lehman

As an award-winning author from Black Mountain, North Carolina, in the heart of the Smoky Mountains, Yvonne Lehman has written several novels for Barbour Publishing's **Heartsong Presents** line. Her titles include *Drums of Shelomoh, Southern Gentleman, A Whole New World, Hawaiian Heartbeat,* and *Mountain Man,* which won a National Reader's Choice Award, sponsored by a chapter of the Romance Writers of America. Yvonne has published more than two dozen novels, including books in the Bethany House "White Dove" series for young adults. Her novel *Gomer,* a reprint of *In Shady Grove,* is being published by Guideposts. In addition to her writing, Yvonne teaches an occasional adult class at Montreat College.

Whispers from the Past

Loree Lough

Dedication

To my dear daughters, Elice and Valerie,
who taught me what true love was all about.

Chapter 1

But Victor," Hanna pleaded, "if you sell the land, what'll become of all those kids!"

Smirking, Victor Powers walked a fat, unlit cigar from one side of his mouth to the other. "That ain't my problem, Mrs. Marsh."

Mrs. Marsh? Not one of his customary insulting nicknames, like "gorgeous" or "sweetie" or "honey"? The formality told Hanna things weren't going well.

Victor winked one ice-blue eye. "Aw, don't be upset, pretty lady. I'm not *totally* heartless." And as if to prove it, he chuckled good-naturedly.

Hanna didn't like the fact that he'd read her mood. With a man like Victor Powers, a woman had better keep her emotions in check. She'd often likened him to a lion studying a herd for signs of fear or weakness; one hint of vulnerability, and it was all over.

"I know it won't be easy, finding a new place for that many young'uns, so I'll give you 'til the first of the year." He ignited a fancy, gold lighter.

Under other circumstances, Hanna might have told Victor exactly what she thought of him. But she owed it to the children who called The Kids' Place home to try to change his mind, and she couldn't do that by calling him a greedy, self-important fool. Softening her tone, she plastered a pleasant smile on her face. "That's barely more than six months, Victor. Can't you give us just a little more—"

Victor's face all but disappeared behind a thick cloud of smoke. When it cleared, his smile was gone. "I'm being more than generous, considering. . . ."

She stifled a cough and, with a dainty hand, waved the smoke away. "Considering what?"

"That land has been zoned commercial for over three years, Hanna. It'll be worth a good sight more with a shopping mall on it than with an orphanage sittin' there."

"Children's shelter," she corrected politely. "More than half the kids have parents."

"I don't know much about young'uns," Victor drawled, "but I know it takes more than calling folks 'parents' to make mothers and fathers of 'em."

Victor almost seemed sorry for The Kids' Place children, but then he bristled, as if he regretted letting his true emotions show. *So,* Hanna thought as an idea dawned, *the lion has a weakness of his own. . . .*

Straightening to his full six-foot height, Victor inspected the glowing tip of his cigar. "I have a big fish on the line, and soon as I—"

"A fish?"

"A buyer," he explained. "And soon as I reel him in, it's a done deal." Smiling, he let silence punctuate the sentence for him.

In a desperate attempt to lighten the mood, Hanna laughed. "Oh, Victor," she teased, "you already have more money than Scrooge. What do you need with more?"

He took a step closer. "Don't *need* more. . ." He wiggled his blond eyebrows suggestively. "But that's not the point, is it? It's my land, to do with as I see fit. And as I see it, I've taken a loss on that parcel for too long already."

"But. . .surely we haven't exhausted all the possibilities. I could arrange more fund-raisers. Then you can raise the rent, and—"

"Hanna, darlin', much as I enjoy jabber-jawin' with you, I don't owe you any explanations." He used the cigar as a pointer, "I'm doing you a favor, telling you about the deal so far in advance. The law says I only need to give you sixty-days notice; I'm giving you three times that."

Victor settled onto the seat of an oversized leather armchair, tapping his cigar against a massive crystal ashtray. "Now, unless you'd like to make. . .uh. . . 'other arrangements,' I suggest we change the subject."

"Other arrangements?"

He propped his cordovan Italian leather loafers on the glass-topped mahogany desk, inspected his fingernails and casually said, "Well, Stella's been dead nearly five years now." He gave an indifferent shrug. "Man gets lonely." Victor's dark eyes now flashed with intensity. Hanna looked quickly at the floor. "Now, if you were to become the second Mrs. Victor Powers, I might be convinced to reconsider selling the land. Call it a. . ." He squinted, searching for the right words. "Call it a wedding present."

A wedding present? She wanted to turn and run, but

her shoes seemed nailed to the floor.

Victor misread Hanna's silence to mean she was actually considering his crude proposal. He put both feet back on the floor, swiveled the big chair so that he faced her head on. "I've had my eye on you since high school," he said, his smile dimming, "but you were way out of my league back then."

He set the cigar on the edge of the ashtray and steepled his fingers under his chin. A dry chuckle escaped his lips. "Fact is, you're way out of my league now. Which is exactly why we'd be a good match." He gestured toward the blood-red leather wingbacks facing his desk. "Please, Hanna. Sit."

He's. . .he's not joking, she realized as her heart hammered and her pulse pounded. Hanna sat, but only to keep from keeling over.

She had had no idea that he felt this way. She'd always been nice to him, but surely he hadn't misinterpreted her simple acts of Christian kindness. . . .

When the other kids in school had teased him because he lived in a ramshackle old house down by the river, Hanna had gone out of her way to treat him with respect. While others had stared and snickered at his rumpled, out-of-date clothes, she had looked into his *eyes,* so he'd know it didn't matter to her that his outfits had come from the secondhand store.

Then as the rest of his classmates were headed for the altar, or college, or the military, Victor won the million-dollar lottery. He'd never had money before, and at first everyone figured he'd probably fritter every cent away. But as it turned out, Victor had a natural talent for making savvy investments, and within a few years, he more than tripled his net worth. Hanna hadn't treated him differently when he moved to Knob Hill, but others in town had. . .as though money had made him suddenly socially acceptable.

"You're a wonderful woman, Hanna. . . ."

There was no mistaking it: He was gearing up to ask her to marry him. . .for real this time.

Hanna thought of all the times he'd pretended not to notice when the rent checks for The Kids' Place came in late for lack of donations, and how quickly he would get a repairman out to the house if the furnace broke down or the water heater leaked. He was gruff, rough-and-tumble, sometimes coarse and uncouth. But a good heart beat under all that bluster and blow, and she owed it to him to spare his dignity.

"Being married to Paul pretty much ruined me—" she began.

Victor's dismissive wave cut her off in mid-sentence. "If the sailing accident hadn't killed him, I might have done it myself. . .seein' the way he made you do everything while he was off playing his rich-boy games."

Hanna sighed. She hadn't been aware that Victor had even *noticed* how she and Paul had lived. "Well, for all his faults, he gave me Paige and Pete. . . ."

"And that's about *all* he gave you," Victor continued his cynical tirade. "I heard how he left you with a mountain of bills, how he cashed in his insurance policy to buy that sailboat." He paused, narrowed his eyes and said, "Live by the sword, die by the sword. Seems fitting he died in his toy."

Hanna was dumbstruck. It was true that Paul had been a self-centered boy who never grew up, and neither marriage nor fatherhood had given him the incentive to accept the responsibilities of adulthood. But he was Paige and Pete's father, and she would not speak disrespectfully of him, not even to spare Victor's ego.

"Victor, I don't know what you're saying, but I made myself a promise the day I buried Paul." *Please, Lord,* she prayed, *help me find the right words.* "I vowed as they lowered him into the ground that I would never get involved with a nonbeliever again."

There. It was out. Victor wasn't a Christian. . .and seemed quite proud of it. "Bunch of Bible-thumping weaklings who use God as a crutch," she'd once heard him say.

"So there's no hope for me then," Victor muttered as he jammed the cigar firmly in the corner of his mouth.

"Well, that all depends on what you mean by hope, Victor," Hanna said sweetly. "You know there's always hope in Je—"

"Don't start that with *me,* Hanna. We both know how I feel about religion."

Victor escorted her to the door, and once again turned on his oily charm. "It's been nice talkin' with you, sweetie. If you have a problem finding a place for those kids before January, give me a call."

As she sat at the traffic signal at the corner of St. Paul and Main, Hanna mentally replayed the scene with Victor Powers. Could she have handled things better?

Differently? Was there something she should have said. . .or shouldn't. . .that might have changed his mind about selling The Kids' Place? *No. . .no, I think I did everything that—*

The blare of a car horn broke into her thoughts. Startled, her gaze darted to her rearview mirror. A man in a blue pickup behind her was pointing straight ahead. Hanna read his lips: "Move it!" he commanded. Move it? She looked ahead and saw that the light had turned green. Embarrassed, she lurched her car forward, whispering a sincere "Sorry!"

At the next stoplight, she remembered Victor's marriage proposal and murmured a prayer of thanks that she had gotten out of there without insulting Victor. He had a good heart, but he could be ruthless, too. If she'd riled him, even in the slightest, it wouldn't have surprised her if he had reneged on his January 1 deadline.

Again, the blast of a horn startled her.

She glanced at the mirror just as the driver of the blue pickup—again!—was mouthing, "Hello?!"

He'd caught her in the middle of yet another daydream! *This hasn't been your day, Hanna Marsh.* Easing the car forward, she made a right onto Rogers Avenue.

The blue pickup was still on her tail.

Hanna gripped the wheel tighter and refused to let his persistent prodding rattle her further. Victor's announcement had already shaken her quite enough. She had two errands left before returning to the bookstore, and she wasn't about to let the impatient old grouch behind her darken the rest of her day. *He probably thinks you're a typical, dizzy blond anyway,* she thought. Hanna smiled into the rearview mirror, waved expansively, and continued heading north to Route 40. She reached the next intersection just as the light turned red.

Here we go again, she sighed, but this time the blue pickup pulled up *beside* her. *At least now he can't honk at me for not moving fast enough!*

Hanna resolved not to look over at him. *Not so much as a peek!* It was humiliating enough being caught woolgathering—twice—by the same driver. He'd been well within his rights to be impatient, but in Hanna's opinion, he'd carried it to an extreme. Still, she had no intention of giving him the satisfaction of knowing how effective his "wake-up calls" had been.

As the seconds ticked by, temptation got the better of her, and Hanna cut a quick glance in his direction. He was staring right at her with a crooked smile on his face. He tossed his head and snapped off a smart salute. *He's actually sort of cute,* she thought, noticing a thick mustache slanting above his flirty grin. She was about to return the friendly smile when he raised one dark eyebrow and gestured for her to roll down the window.

When she did, he called out, "Three's a charm."

She wrinkled her nose in confusion. "What?"

He pointed in the direction of the traffic signal. "You're three for three. The light's green. . . ."

Hanna didn't know if she was more angry at herself for looking, or at him for his sarcastic scolding. Sitting rigid in the driver's seat, her cheeks now burning, she faced forward for an instant. Then to his wide-eyed disbelief, she looked back, stuck out her tongue, and drove away.

Chapter 2

Mondays, experience had taught her, usually meant fewer customers. Hanna took advantage of the slow morning by placing phone calls to try to generate some leads to find a new home for the children at The Kids' Place. After leaving messages all over town, she tore into the storeroom. Out-of-print books, file folders, index cards, and empty cardboard cartons that had been accumulating over the past month were driving her to distraction.

She cleared out the worst of it, and the dust and grit streaking her face and clothes were evidence of her hard work. Stiff and sore from hefting heavy boxes and rearranging the desk and shelf units in the sparsely furnished space, Hanna stretched the kinks from her neck and shoulders.

The bell above the front door jingled, alerting her that a shopper had entered the bookstore. Hanna had been so busy in the back room, she hadn't noticed that Missy, one of two part-time employees, was late for work. She had no choice but to greet the customer herself. She gave herself a quick once-over: Blue jeans and a dusty T-shirt that said "You Can't Judge a Book By Its Cover." *How ironic,* she thought, laughing to herself.

Darting into the bathroom, Hanna peeked into the mirror and tried to tuck in loose tendrils of escaped hair. "It's useless," she told her reflection. Shrugging, she added, "So much for Mom's proverb, 'Always look your best; you never know when opportunity will come knocking.' " One last sigh and she headed for the front of the shop.

"Hello," she said to the customer's back. "May I help you?"

"Yeah," he muttered into the book resting on his palm. "I'm looking for something about how kids need their parents."

She knew her inventory well. "You've already selected the best book on that subject."

Without looking up, he nodded. "Good. Good. I've got a custody case coming up, and I need some good 'psyco-babble' to bolster my argument. It always helps to have the latest authority on your side."

"Oh, are you a lawyer?" Hanna asked innocently.

"No, I'm Huckleberry Finn," he replied as he continued to riffle through the pages of the book. He still had not so much as glanced in her direction.

What is this guy's problem? she shook her head at his snide comment. As she waited to see if he had any further questions, she noticed that this lawyer was tall, six-foot-two at least. She knew because the top of his head aligned with the top bookshelf, and the unit stood six feet tall. He had broad shoulders and dark, shining waves that curled gently over his white starched collar. A good-looking man. . .at least, from this angle. . . . She wondered what he looked like from the front.

Glancing at her watch, she wondered how long he intended to stay; she'd promised Paige and Pete dinner at the local pizza parlor, and it was nearly closing time. "The lighting isn't very good over there," she said. "I'm sure you'll have far less eye strain if you take the book home to read it."

He chuckled. "I'm just trying to make sure this thing is worth $29.95. Pretty hefty price tag for a book that's only a hundred and twenty pages. That's two bits a page." Another chuckle. "Aw. . .well. . .why not? I'll buy your two-bit book. If I'm gonna win this case, I have to prove that kids without fathers are nothing but tragedies waiting to happen."

Hanna gasped. *Her* kids didn't have a father. . . . She looked back in time to see the man finally turn to face her. *He's the man who kept honking at me!* He was nodding and smiling, looking like the proverbial cat who'd snagged the canary.

They stood—he in the aisle, she behind the cash register—staring each other down like two gunfighters in the Old West.

"Don't tell me you disagree," he snorted. "Anyone with two functioning brain cells knows most women need a man to give kids a proper upbringing."

"For your information," she began, hands flat on the counter, "my husband died five years ago, leaving me alone to raise my son and daughter. They were six and four when it happened. *And,"* she spouted, "they're both in the Gifted and Talented Program at school."

"I didn't mean—"

Ignoring him, she counted on her fingers: "Paige

plays basketball and soccer, and Pete is on the pee-wee football team. Pete plays trumpet in the band, and Paige is in the choir."

"But—"

"They're well-behaved, well-rounded, and well-adjusted, *despite* having been raised by a woman. What do you think of *that,* Mr. Smart Lawyer?"

"I'm sor—"

She trembled visibly as her finger jabbed at the air. "And as for the cost of that book. . .I don't set the prices!"

Sometime during her tirade, the lawyer had closed the book. He looked as though she'd struck him with a stick. . .several times. Slump-shouldered and red-faced, he tucked the book under his arm and ran a hand through his hair. Hanna couldn't remember a time when she'd lost her temper that way. He'd stepped out of line—there was no getting around it—but certainly not far enough to earn a tongue-lashing like that.

"I, ah, don't know what to say, except. . .I'm sorry. Honest. I never meant. . .I, ah. . ."

It was surprising how quickly a six-foot man could cross a twenty-foot space. Hanna watched him shove through the door without so much as a backward glance or a by-your-leave.

It was only as the door swung shut behind him that she realized he had left without paying for the book.

Mitch couldn't get her off his mind.

Having upset her that way, he felt like a heel. And he *had* upset her. The evidence was written all over her pretty, big-eyed face. Ordinarily, he was tight-lipped.

He usually saved his snappy retorts for the courtroom. *If you'd kept your big yap shut at the bookstore,* he complained, *you wouldn't be feeling lousy now.*

"What's the matter, boss?"

Mitch took a deep breath. "One of these days, I'm gonna fire you. . .ya nosy old biddy."

Rolling her eyes, his secretary shrugged. "Don't make promises you can't keep."

"Wasn't a promise," he fired back. "It was a threat."

"There are laws against things like that, you know."

"So sue me."

"Do you know where I can find a good lawyer?"

They'd been "having at it" this way at least once a day for years.

"Seriously, son," Marge said sweetly, ruffling his hair, "what's bugging you? You've been a bear all evening."

Mitch's mother had come to work for him soon after he'd hung out his shingle. She had dropped by to visit one day and, true to form, started tidying up his cramped, cluttered office. Before he knew it she was answering the phone, typing his motions, setting appointments, and paying the bills. Helping out seemed to cheer her up. He hadn't seen her smile much since his dad's funeral. It was a blessed sight; it had seemed like the perfect solution to both their dilemmas: He needed an efficient secretary who'd work cheap, and she needed to be needed. It was strictly temporary, they'd both agreed, just until he could afford full-time help and she got her "widow" act together.

A decade had passed since then, and in that time, Mitch and Marge had forged far more than a solid mother–son association. They were friends, the very best. He could read her moods, and he was an open book to her. By the look on her face now, Mitch knew there was no point in denying that something had been bothering him. Heaving another sigh, he said, "Got myself into some hot water today, and for the life of me, I don't know how to get out of it."

Marge plopped herself into one of the upholstered chairs across from his desk. "Stop beating around the bush. It's a waste of time, and not very good for the bush, either." She crossed both arms over her chest and said, " 'Fess up."

Ignoring her semi-scolding expression, he explained how he'd behaved in traffic, then told her how he'd gone into the bookstore and compounded things.

"You must love the taste of shoe leather," she teased, shaking her head, "the way you keep putting your foot in your mouth." It was Marge's turn to sigh. "You're so much like your father it's scary."

Chuckling, he tapped the psychology book. "I'm going over there first thing in the morning and pay for—"

"You stole the book?" Marge was incredulous. "You mean to tell me you insulted her, hurt her feelings, *and* stole from her? I guess that makes you three for three." Covering her face with one hand, she groaned, "What's a mother to do?"

"I didn't *steal* it," Mitch insisted. "I just forgot to pay for it, that's all."

"I'm not the lawyer here," Marge said with a laugh, "but I don't think that would stand up in court."

"Very funny, Mom, but I'm being serious. I've always

lived by the Ten Commandments, so first thing tomorrow I'll pay for the book. . .and apologize for acting like a caveman."

"Well," Marge said, leaning forward to straighten a stack of papers on the corner of Mitch's desk, "I guess there's hope for you after all." Grinning, she added, "So. . .what's she like? Is she pretty? Is she sweet? Is she every mother-in-law's dream?"

He pictured the wide smile she'd flashed at him at the intersection, her shining blond hair, big eyes that were neither green nor brown. She sure didn't have the figure of a woman who'd had two kids. But then, what would he know about a thing like that? "She's way out of my league, Mom."

"Nonsense. She didn't have wings and a halo, did she?"

"Didn't notice," he said distractedly, "but I wouldn't be the least bit surprised. . . ."

Hanna didn't like working weekends. For one thing, there was the matter of baby-sitters, and shuttling Paige and Pete around town. Hanna had often joked that it was probably easier setting up the route for the Pope's visit than arranging her kids' assorted music lessons and sports practices. For another, she relished those leisurely Saturday mornings, sitting at the kitchen table with the newspaper and a cup of coffee, watching the birds and the squirrels that gathered at the feeders.

But here she was, in the bookstore. . .on a Saturday.

Missy, as it turned out, had discovered she could earn ten cents more an hour working at the fast-food joint up the street and had quit without notice. Jolie,

Hanna's assistant, couldn't handle the workload alone. Though Saturday usually wasn't one of their better days, the past several weeks had been phenomenal.

Hanna busied herself straightening shelves. At ten o'clock sharp she went to the front door to open for the day. No sooner had she unlocked the door than in walked her friend the lawyer.

What a difference a day makes, she thought, taking note of his clothes. He'd traded his chalk-striped suit and polished wing tips for jeans and a polo shirt. She hadn't noticed yesterday that his sideburns were beginning to go gray.

She'd fallen asleep thinking about the humiliated expression he'd worn out of the shop the night before. Not that she blamed him. If someone had blasted her for making a simple statement, it would have unnerved her, too.

He walked up to the counter and laid the book beside the register.

"I'm sorry about yesterday," they said in unison.

Silenced by the harmony of their words, their mouths opened simultaneously again. . .this time to welcome a gale of laughter.

Chapter 3

"What-say I buy you a sandwich. . .to make up for my miserable behavior yesterday."

Hanna hoped he couldn't see the flush that was heating her cheeks. "Really, that isn't necessary. I'm the one who—"

He glanced at his watch. "It's nearly noon. You have to eat eventually." Using his chin as a pointer, he indicated the back room. "Ask your boss. I'm sure it'll be okay."

She smiled thinly and understanding suddenly flickered in his dark eyes.

Something akin to a groan escaped his lips as he clapped a hand to his forehead. "Don't tell me. . .you *are* the boss, right?"

Hanna nodded.

"Well, never let it be said I don't make a good first impression." He stuck out his hand. "Pleased to meet you. Name's Riley. Mitch Riley. But you can call me by my nickname. . ." He assumed the pose of a cigar store Indian and deepened his voice. ". . .Big Fat Foot in Mouth."

"I'm Hanna," she laughed as he wrapped her hand in his. "Hanna Marsh. And really, I'm as much to blame for yesterday as you are."

He paused, pocketed both hands. "Have lunch with me anyway."

"I'd love to," she said, "but—"

"We'll go 'dutch' if it makes you feel better. . . ."

"We're shorthanded today, and as you can see," Hanna gestured toward the milling patrons, "I can't leave Jolie alone with all this traffic."

Mitch wiggled his eyebrows. "If memory serves. . . you like to daydream in traffic. Are you sure you'll be safe?"

"Oh, don't worry about me," she rebutted his teasing with a joke of her own. "I can always count on someone to blast me back into consciousness if my mind wanders too far."

"I really am sorry about that. You have to let me make it up to you." He didn't wait for an answer. "What time do you close?"

"Five."

"Since you're too busy for lunch, I'll take you to dinner. I'll be here at ten minutes to five."

She bit her lower lip, considering it. . . . The kids were spending the night at their grandparents' house, but her in-laws wouldn't be picking them up until six. . . .

Have you lost your mind? You can't go out with a man you just met yesterday!

"Quarter of? Five after five?" he pressed.

He seemed harmless enough, what with those big, innocent brown eyes and that boyish shock of dark, wavy hair. *Lord, give me a sign. If You don't think it's a good idea, I won't—*

"By the way," Mitch said, thumping the psychology book. "I, ah, I kind of walked off without paying for this thing yesterday."

"Mm-hmm?" She narrowed her eyes in mock suspicion, but she was grateful for the change of subject. "Well, Mr. Honesty, will that be cash, check, or charge?"

He tucked in one corner of his mouth. "I don't want to buy it; I'm returning it."

Hanna feigned a stern expression and pointed to the sign taped to the register.

" 'No Returns Without Receipt,' " he read aloud. His thick, dark mustache slanted above a flirty grin. "Well, call me Jelly, 'cause now I'm really in a jam."

Jelly?

Smiling, she acknowledged the warm, giddy feeling that spread throughout her being. *We're a fine pair,* she thought, grinning as she pictured a storefront-type sign: Jelly and Giddy, Professional Association.

"I can't meet you at five. . . ."

His slight pout reminded Hanna of the way her son sulked when she scolded him for watching a scary movie on cable. . .but Pete was only nine!

What do You think, Lord? Should I have dinner with him? Her heartbeat doubled as she looked into Mitch's disappointed eyes. She took that as a go-ahead from God. "Seven would be better."

His eyes widened, and so did his smile. He fished a business card from his wallet. "In case you have second thoughts," Mitch said, handing it to her. "But keep in mind that I'm very sensitive and don't take rejection well."

Suppressing a giggle, Hanna turned the card over, wrote her home phone and address on it, and handed it back to him. "If you need directions, feel free to call."

Mitch slipped it into his shirt pocket and, backpedaling, headed for the exit. "Thanks, but I have a map. I'm outta here," he added, waving good-bye, "before you change your mind."

Change my mind? Fat chance! she thought. *This is the first time I've actually looked forward to going out with a man since Paul died!*

Before the door closed behind him, Hanna knew she'd be recalling that mischievous, slanting grin for a good long while.

In the five years since Paul's death, Hanna had dated a few times.

She owned one evening gown, and had worn it to the Morris Mechanic when the Moscow Ballet performed the *Nutcracker.* Wore it again to enjoy the Baltimore Symphony Orchestra at the Meyerhoff. She had several Sunday dresses that doubled nicely for the movies, and jeans and T-shirts were perfect for cheering the Orioles at Camden Yards.

Her escorts—some quite handsome and successful—had been Christian gentlemen, every one. But Hanna had never gone out with the same man twice. When her confused Cupids asked why, the answer had been simple: God had not given her a sign that she *should.*

Tonight, her companion would be a handsome, successful gentleman. But was he a Christian? Had he ever been married? Did he have children? The answers to those questions would determine the path of their relationship.

Relationship! Hanna chided herself. *Just listen to you, considering a future with a man you barely know. If Mom were here, she'd say, "Hanna, get real!"*

Sighing, she surveyed the mess in her room. It didn't appear she owned the proper attire for 'getting real.' But since she didn't know where Mitch would take her, how could she decide how to dress? Flats or heels? Hair up or down? Stylish earrings or classic pearls? She'd never had this problem before, so why couldn't she make even the simplest decisions tonight?

For one thing, Mitch had asked her out directly, and she'd said 'yes' because. . .*because I wanted to!*

What a switch to be going on a date that hadn't been arranged to help a friend entertain an unmarried brother visiting from out of town, or to balance the "male–female" seating arrangement at a dinner party, or as a favor to the pastor's wife, whose recently widowed cousin had no one to accompany him to a corporate function.

Yes. . .tonight was going to be different, all right, and if her children had been around to see *how* different, she'd have a lot of explaining to do. . . .

If Paige and Pete had turned their rooms upside down this way, she'd have scolded them soundly. Clothes, shoes, and accessories were strewn across the once-tidy bed, the carpet, on the chaise beside her bed.

And she'd lost an earring between the wall and the bathroom vanity, run her panty hose, stubbed her toe stepping into her heels. She could almost hear Pete now: "Calm down, Mom; if he doesn't think you're pretty, he's nuts!" And Paige, who had decided on her last birthday that "Mom" was passé, would say, "Oh, Mother, don't be nervous; you're *beautiful!*"

They were good, sweet children, and Hanna thanked God for them every chance she got. Because they deserved only the best life had to offer, she would always seek the Lord's guidance in matters—no matter how inconsequential—that involved their well-being.

Mitch seemed to have a lot going for him. . .a stable career, a vigorous sense of humor, and good looks, but, as Hanna had acknowledged during her what-to-wear worry-fest, she knew very little about him.

Dear Lord, she prayed, closing her eyes, *don't let my loneliness make me do anything foolish. . . .*

Suddenly, a great calm washed over her, and Hanna took a deep breath. How silly to worry about what kind of a man Mitch Riley was. God had protected her well before, and she'd trust Him to guide her tonight.

Mitch arrived at precisely seven, bearing no gifts, and wearing neatly creased brown trousers, a camel sports coat, and a cream shirt. He'd stood on the porch a second or two, assessing Hanna's outfit. . .two-inch black heels and a long-sleeved navy sheath, adorned by a plain gold chain. "Wow," was all he said.

To hide her flush, Hanna gathered her sweater and purse and locked the front door.

"You look way too pretty for the place I had in mind," Mitch continued. Pressing a hand to the small of her back, he guided her to the driveway, where his blue pickup was parked. "Too pretty to ride in this rattle-trap, but. . . ." Shaking his head, he opened the passenger door. "Well, m'lady, your sad old chariot awaits."

When he slid in behind the steering wheel, Mitch continued to make excuses for the vehicle. "Sorry it's such a mess," he said, scooping newspapers and magazines, fast-food bags, and soda cans into a plastic grocery bag he'd found on the floor. "The plan was to run her through the car wash, but I got myself knee-deep in some legal research." He grinned apologetically. "I get a little single-minded sometimes."

Hanna didn't want him thinking she was one of those women who judged a man by the kind of car he drove. "Stop apologizing," she said. "When you get to be my age, you learn to appreciate 'firsts.' "

"Your age?" He chuckled. "I'll just call you Gran for the rest of the night."

She rolled her eyes.

"So. . .what's all this stuff about 'firsts'?" he asked, backing down her driveway.

"This is my first pickup."

"No way! Good-lookin' woman like you? I'll bet guys try to pick you up all the time."

It was a waste of time putting on rouge, she thought as her cheeks burned with a blush. "Not that kind of a pickup," she defended. "I meant—"

His quiet laughter told her he'd been teasing.

"This ought to be a very interesting evening," she observed.

"Well, it isn't going to be boring, that's for sure!"

They drove in companionable silence for a few

minutes before Mitch said, "Where are your kids tonight?"

"With their grandparents. Paul's mom and dad live across town. It's only an hour's drive around the Beltway, but they like to use the distance as an excuse to keep them overnight." Hanna laughed softly. "Paige and Pete just love them. . . ."

"Paige and Pete," he echoed. "Nice names."

"Thank you." She couldn't think of a better time to ask: "Do you have children?"

"Nope."

"Why not?"

He looked straight ahead. "I just always figured my mom would prefer that I get married first."

"Just your mom?"

Mitch nodded. "Dad died the year I graduated law school."

"Siblings?"

"Two brothers and a sister, but they're scattered all over the country. . .Illinois, Wisconsin, California. . . ."

He'd answered all her questions, save one: Was he a Christian?

Pointing, Mitch said, "Terrific, there's a parking space right in front of the place." He winked at her. "I have a feeling you're going to be good luck."

She started to say "I don't believe in luck." But when Hanna realized where he'd taken her, the words froze in her throat. Tersiguel's, housed in one of Ellicott City's oldest buildings, boasted a fancy French cuisine and equally fancy prices. She supposed he must be trying to awe her with the menu since he felt he hadn't done it with his vehicle. "Mitch," she began, "I don't think I'm dressed for a place like this. And besides, you're not wearing a—"

Motor off and seatbelt unfastened, he leaned across her to reach into the glove box. "Voila!" he announced, withdrawing a burgundy tie. After fastening a perfect Windsor knot, he cocked the rearview mirror his way, adjusted the tie at his Adam's apple. "Like they taught me in Scouts, 'Always be prepared.' "

He hustled around to Hanna's side of the truck, yanked open the door. "Ready?" he invited, offering her his arm.

Ready as I'll ever be, she thought wryly as he led her up the restaurant's wooden steps.

Chapter 4

They discussed everything from politics to pelicans during their three-hour dinner. Halfway through the dessert course, Hanna heard loud, boisterous laughter coming from a nearby table. Identifying the source was easy: Victor Powers had a one-of-a-kind voice. She gritted her teeth and sat up straight. How can he enjoy himself in a fancy French restaurant, she wondered, when a house full of needy kids will soon be homeless because of—

"What's the matter?" Mitch asked, laying a hand atop hers. "Looks like you've seen a ghost."

She sniffed indignantly, casting a steely glance in the direction of the raucous conversation. "Actually, in a lot of ways, I'd prefer a ghost."

Mitch followed her gaze. "Which one of those three do you know?"

"The guy with the foghorn for a voice," she sniped. Then, in a lighter tone, "You know them?"

"I should say so." He wadded up his napkin and tossed it onto the table. Eyes blazing as he focused on Victor Powers, he said in a grating whisper, "I had one of the biggest battles of my legal career with that—" He paused, as if finding an acceptable term was a difficult thing. "He's ruthless." Softening, he returned his attention to Hanna. "What's a nice girl like you doing associating with a cutthroat like that?"

"I suppose he does have a reputation for being a hardnose. But he isn't all bad. I've seen his softer side."

"Yeah, well, you must be the only one then. . . . But you haven't told me how you know him."

Hanna sipped her coffee and, shoving a forkful of cheesecake around on her plate, told him the story of how, years ago, she got involved in The Kids' Place. "The county was stacking kids like sardines into that old place down on Main Street. They were always sick . . .or bickering about one thing or another because of overcrowding." Knowing that Victor owned a small farm at the far edge of the county—complete with a huge old house, outbuildings, and a stream—she'd gone to him, Hanna explained. "That land was just sitting there idle, and the house was falling down from neglect. Every time I passed it to take the kids to a softball game or a soccer practice, it just broke my heart. . .seeing all that waste."

"Whoa," Mitch injected, a hand in the air and a smirk on his face, "are you telling me that Victor Powers *gave* you that land?"

"No. He's been renting it to us for the past four years." Hanna sighed heavily. "But now he says the land is worth more with a mall on it than The Kids' Place."

"I hate to say it, but he's right," Mitch said. He inclined his head to forestall her objection. "That doesn't mean selling the land is the right thing to do, mind you. . . ."

"Especially not for those kids!" Hanna proceeded to tell him about the children who inhabited the old farm house. . .kids who were orphaned, abandoned, neglected, abused. . .all of the above. She told him about the dozens of calls she'd made, trying to find a new home for them. . . . "They're like one big happy family, with the live-in counselors acting as surrogate parents. They go into that house a mess—bad grades, bad attitudes—and after just a few months of stability, they improve. More than half of them go on to college, some join the military, others apprentice to become electricians, plumbers. . . .

"I just don't know what's going to become of them if they're separated. . .if they're shuttled into foster care. . . ."

Mitch felt helpless to comfort her, to ease her obvious distress. What could he say, besides a sincere "I'm sorry"? And that wouldn't provide the kids with what they needed. . . .

An idea began bubbling in his mind as he listened and watched her absent-mindedly push her dessert back and forth on the plate. He couldn't help but notice the way her eyes flashed as she listed the shelter's successes, dimmed when she spoke of the possibility that the "family" would be disrupted. She really cared about those kids!

And the Good Lord knows she has plenty of other things to worry about, what with a business to run and two kids to raise.

She was lovely, and not just in a physical sense. Oh, there was no denying her outer beauty, not with that shoulder-length blond hair, those big eyes, and—

What color are *her eyes, anyway?* he wondered. In

the candlelight, they seemed almost brown. But in the shop earlier, under the bright florescent lights, he would have called them green.

Mitch suddenly realized he was leaning so far across the table, he and Hanna were practically nose to nose. *Close enough to kiss,* he thought.

Immediately, he sat back. Re-wadded the napkin. Rearranged the placement of his cup and saucer, his water glass, the tiny silver pitcher of cream. Among all this busyness, he heard her voice, soft and sweet, yet lilting and lively.

"She doesn't have wings and a halo," his mom had teased. And he'd said, "I wouldn't be the least bit surprised." After hours in Hanna's company, angel adornments seemed all the more likely.

She'd awakened something in him with her animated gestures, her adorable facial expressions, her unique way of phrasing things. Hanna had a sense of humor like no woman he'd ever known, and a wit to match his own. She'd positively glowed with maternal pride when she talked about her own children, with personal pride when she told him she'd managed to get roses to thrive in a place where not even dandelions had grown before.

She'd made her position on feminism clear: "God has a plan," Hanna had said, "and when husbands and wives tinker with it, they're bound to have miserable marriages. Besides," she'd added with a wave of that dainty hand, "equality isn't about paychecks and job titles, it's about love and mutual respect."

She's quite a woman, he acknowledged, nodding. *Quite a—*

". . .and the price of bee eggs is fourteen dollars a dozen."

Her voice came to him as if it had rolled in on a fog. *Bee eggs?* he scrunched his eyes closed and shook his head to reorient himself.

"I've heard the price is so steep because, well, think about it," Hanna said, "imagine how difficult it must be, for the egg gatherers, I mean."

Mitch's brow furrowed with confusion. . .and suspicion. From the playful glint in her eyes, he had a pretty good idea that she was pulling his leg. . . .

"Honk, honk," she said, her impish grin reminding him of their first meeting.

Mitch chuckled good-naturedly. "Touché," he said. "But you can't blame me for getting distracted." His smile faded and, reaching across the table, he took her hand. "You're the most lovely woman I've ever met. And I mean that right down to the soles of my holey socks."

He'd leaned in close enough to see his minuscule reflection in her pupils. At six-foot-one and two hundred pounds of solid muscle, Mitch had twice earned the army's heavyweight boxing title, and though a decade had passed, he could still probably hold his own in the ring. Yet women had always made him feel small, vulnerable, weak. Not Hanna. The way she looked at him and hung on his every word, made him feel like he didn't even need the red cape to take on the world! *Funny,* he thought, *how strong a man can feel. . . when he's with the right woman. . . .*

He wanted to kiss her. Right here. Right now.

Hanna had tilted her head slightly, causing her

long, lustrous hair to fall over one shoulder. Her eyes flashed in the glittering candlelight. And her smile, small and wistful, gave her mouth a pretty, almost pouting look. "Um, Mitch? There's something I need to ask you."

Mitch smiled and looked her straight in the eye. *She's not pulling her hand away; that's got to be a good sign,* he said to himself. "Fire away," he said to Hanna.

"Well. . . ," she paused, trying to gather her thoughts. "Remember earlier when I was telling you about my friends from church? Um, well, I just want you to know that church is an important part of my life—I mean, God is important to me—and I promised myself that I wouldn't go out with guys who don't. . . well, you know. . . . What I'm trying to say is, where do you stand with. . .you know. . ."

"Do you mean, am I a Christian?" Once again he had been so busy watching *how* she was talking that what she said took him off guard.

"Yeah," she said and then immediately looked down at the table.

"Well, yes. I accepted the Lord as a boy. I don't get to church maybe as often as I should, but my parents were solid Christians, and they gave me a good basis to build on."

Hanna released a large breath, then hoped Mitch hadn't noticed her obvious relief at his answer. "That's great, Mitch," she said. "Isn't the Lord wonderful?"

Before he could answer, a booming voice echoed in his ear. "Well, if it ain't Mitchell Riley," said Victor Powers. "Didn't know you hung out in places like this."

Mitch gave Victor a businesslike nod. *You have horrible timing.* "How's it going?" he asked.

"Can't complain. How 'bout yourself?"

"Same."

Victor faced Hanna. "You look pretty tonight." He squeezed her shoulder. "But then, you always look pretty."

Mitch sat back, crossed both arms over his chest and watched through narrowed eyes as Victor stuttered and stammered, shifted nervously from one big foot to the other, pocketed then unpocketed his hands. *The man's nuts about her,* Mitch thought. Not that he could blame him. . .she had everything any red-blooded American man could possibly want. . .beauty, brains, breeding. . . .

Hanna, much to Mitch's relief, simply sat there, smiling and nodding politely, making small-talk.

"I didn't know you two were, uh, acquainted," Victor said to Mitch.

And I didn't know you knew words like "acquainted," Mitch countered silently. "Oh, yeah," he said emphatically. "We're old buddies. . .go *way* back." Grinning, he met Hanna's eyes. "Isn't that right?"

Once, when he was eight, Mitch put a frog in the collection plate. His father grabbed it and tucked it into his suit pocket before any trouble started, and made a "wait 'til you get home" face. The expression on Hanna's face now reminded Mitch of that look.

"You're a lucky fella," Victor was saying. "I've had my eye on this pretty little lady for years." His smile never made it to his eyes. "But she's way out of my league."

Hanna frowned. "I wish you'd stop saying that, Victor.

What have I ever done to give you that impression?"

Victor ran a hand through his blond hair. "You've been you."

The comment had come straight out of Victor's soul, and for an instant, Mitch felt sorry for him.

Victor must have seen the flash of pity that crossed Mitch's face, because he straightened in an attempt to hide his embarrassment. "Well," he said in a very loud voice, "I'd better get back to my, uh, guests." Facing Hanna, he said, "The guy in the blue suit? He's thinking of buying the farm."

"But Victor, the kids are—"

He held up a hand. "I promised to give you 'til the first of the year. If we strike a deal tonight, I'll make that clear. You have my word."

Her shoulders slumped. "I wish there was something I could say to change your mind."

Victor raised one eyebrow. "There is."

Her demeanor changed completely, from calm and serene to fidgety and frightened. *What sort of agreement had Victor suggested?* Mitch wondered. *Must have been something pretty rotten, to make her blush like that.*

"I'll keep you posted," he told Hanna. "Good to see you, Riley." And then he was gone.

Mitch signaled the waiter for the check as Hanna rose. "I'll just be a minute," she said softly as she headed for the ladies' room.

The minute she was out of sight, Mitch walked over to Victor's table. He gave each man a cursory nod, then handed Victor his card. "In case you lost my number," he said through clenched teeth. "I want you to call me, first thing Monday morning."

Victor laughed. "Call you? For what?"

"Because we have business to discuss."

"I had a very nice time," Hanna said once they got on the road.

"Until Victor Powers walked up."

She sighed. "He's a piece of work, all right."

"Don't worry about him. All bluster and blow, no bite."

"I've learned never to underestimate him. He can be tame as a kitten, or vicious as a tiger." She turned toward him. "How do you and Victor know one another?"

"It's like I said, we had business once."

"Unpleasant business, from the sound of things."

"You could say that."

Hanna faced forward again. "It's a beautiful night. Would you mind turning off the air conditioner, putting the windows down?"

Mitch did as she asked. "Never had a woman ask me to do *this* before."

"I can't imagine why not." Closing her eyes, she took a deep breath of the summery night air.

"I guess they were worried the wind would muss their hair."

Hanna only smiled.

As he watched her, head leaning against the seat, eyes closed, the urge to kiss her washed over him again. Mitch cleared his throat. *Get a grip, Riley. She's not the type to let you get that close on the first date.*

Then he remembered how, just before Victor

Powers had hulked up to their table, she'd seemed willing (if not eager) to accept his lips. Shrugging, he thought, *What have you got to lose?*

"I believe in giving a person fair warning," he said, breaking the comfortable silence.

She opened her eyes and smiled sweetly at him.

Cut that out! he silently scolded. *Or I'm liable to crash into the nearest telephone pole.*

"Who are you going to warn, Mitch?"

"You."

"And what are you going to warn me about?"

"Well," he began haltingly, "I hope you won't be insulted—because believe you me, I mean this in a very complimentary way—but I like you, Hanna. I like you a lot."

She giggled. "I like you, too." Then, "Why would that insult me?"

"Not *that*. . . ." He took a deep breath. "I don't believe in beating around the bush. As my sweet mama always says, 'It's a waste of time and unnecessarily hard on the shrubbery.' "

"Okay. . .?"

"Okay," he echoed. "When I get you home, I'm going to take you in my arms and give you a long, lingering good-night kiss."

Mitch thought for a moment that he'd made a terrible tactical error, saying it straight out like that. But when Hanna shrugged nonchalantly and said, "Okay," his heart turned over in his chest.

He glanced at the speedometer.

Thirty miles an hour.

He peered through the windshield.

One mile to go.

He glanced at the dashboard clock.

Two minutes, tops, before they pulled into her driveway.

"I forgot to leave the porch light on," she said softly.

"You mean so you can find your key? I have a flashlight in the glove box."

"Thanks anyway, but I have a mini-light on my key chain."

Tucking in one corner of his mouth, Mitch frowned.

"June bugs," she said as he pulled into her drive.

"June bugs?"

"I hate them. They're like Japanese Beetles. . .all those little barbs on their feet and legs that allow them to stick to things. . . ."

He turned off the truck. What *was* she going on about? She hadn't seemed afraid of his announcement about the kiss, but—

"How do you feel about slugs?"

"Slugs." Mitch scratched his head. "Never really thought about 'em." Maybe nonsensical chatter was her way of screwing up her courage to do new things, to take risks.

"We'll have to watch out for slugs. With the light off, we won't have to contend with moths and beetles, but the slugs don't seem to mind—"

"Hanna?" he interrupted.

"Hmmm?"

"Shut up and kiss me."

Chapter 5

Mitch wasted no time in shuffling his calendar to make room for Hanna. The morning after their dinner at Tersiguel's, he surprised her by showing up at church. It happened to be the same day as an after-church social celebrating Flag Day, so they were able to spend the entire afternoon together. Over the next couple of weeks he managed to squeeze in another dinner, a last minute trip to the movies, and a midweek lunch with Hanna, but still he hadn't met her kids. They been away at their grandparents' house that first weekend, and had already gone to bed the two times he had dropped Hanna off at her house. Finally, one weekend, Mitch dropped by just to meet Paige and Pete. Paige, a romantic at heart, seemed to decide at first sight that Mitch was a perfect match for her mother.

Pete hadn't been as easy. . . .

Having been de facto "king of the house" since Paul's death, Hanna's son had no intention of abdicating his throne without a fight. He seemed determined to make the man prove himself, every step of the way. Mitch, sensing the boy's fears, let Pete win every contest, whether real or contrived. And each time Hanna called the boy to task for what she termed "smart-mouthing his elders," Mitch came to his defense. "He didn't mean it that way. . .did you, Pete?" or "He was only kidding. . . right, Pete?"

By the time Labor Day rolled around, Pete had surrendered, and ended his one-sided war. "Bobby Jensen always wins the treasure hunt," he'd started. "If I want that trophy this year, I need a partner with brains. So how 'bout it, Mr. Riley?"

Mitch had cleared his throat and stroked that thick mustache of his and distracted them all by saying, "Well, now. . .that seems like the kind of thing you'd ask a buddy to do."

Grinning, Pete had hooked both thumbs in his belt loops. "Yeah. So?"

"So I'll do it, on two conditions."

The boy's eyes narrowed slightly as he waited for Mitch to spell it out:

"One, you'll have to keep the trophy in your room, 'cause frankly, I don't want to dust it. And two, 'Mr. Riley' is way too formal. . .for a pal." He'd held out his hand. "Call me Mitch, and it's a deal."

Later, Mitch made the same offer to Paige, whose bright blue eyes had gleamed with girlish glee.

As summer turned to fall, Mitch had helped Paige do the research for a paper about First Amendment rights. He helped Pete earn four Scout badges, taught Paige to throw a curve ball, and taught Pete to tie his own fishing flies. He'd become the male role model Hanna had been praying for. And he hadn't missed a Sunday at church. . .or so he had said. . . .

Still, Hanna had been careful not to lead Mitch on about her own feelings. *It's one thing to be a "big brother" to Paige and Pete,* she mused as she chopped onions for the Thanksgiving stuffing, *but it's something else entirely to take responsibility for raising them.*

The jangling of the phone disrupted her thoughts.

"Do you mind setting an extra place for dinner?" her mother asked.

"Of course not. There's always room for one more." Hanna paused. "Anybody I know?"

"As a matter of fact, yes. You went to school with him. I ran into him in the mall the other day. Honestly, honey, it's amazing how time can turn a boy into a man."

Hanna frowned. Her mother was a dear, but she could dance around a subject until her listeners were dizzy.

"Did you know his mother died last month? You'd think I would have heard about a thing like that, being on the Ladies' Auxiliary and all. Well, anyway, I felt sorry for him, knowing he doesn't have any family at all now that Gladys is gone."

Gladys? The only Gladys that Hanna knew was Gladys Powers. Laughing to herself, Hanna rolled her eyes. Ellicott City wasn't the biggest town in the state of Maryland, but surely there had been at least one other Gladys on the list of Centennial High School parents. . . .

"Mom," Hanna said, "what's his—"

"He's quite the big shot now, you know. And I have it on good authority that he's had a crush on you since the eighth grade!"

"Mom, who is—"

"He's not as handsome as your Mr. Riley, but then, Victor Powers would marry you in a heartbeat, and I'll just bet *Mitch* hasn't—"

"You invited Victor Powers to Thanksgiving dinner?"

"Of course I did. And you'd have done the same thing, if you'd seen the look on his face when he said he was having dinner at the Westview. No one should eat Thanksgiving dinner alone in a restaurant!"

She sighed. Her mother was right. But something told Hanna that matchmaking, and not Christian charity, had been the reason for the invitation. "I have a feeling it's going to be a very interesting afternoon."

"Interesting? How so?"

Mentally, Hanna counted her guests:

Mitch was bringing his mother, and Sarah was bringing Victor Powers. Paige had invited her English teacher—a young woman who'd just transferred to the Baltimore area from Chicago—and Pete had asked his soccer coach to join them. The couple next door (whose children lived on the West Coast) were coming over, and so were Pastor and Mrs. Rafferty.

"Well, let's just say it's a very good thing I'm not superstitious," she explained, laughing, "because counting Victor, there will be thirteen people seated at my dining room table!"

"Dinner was delicious. And where did you learn to make stuffing like that?"

She lifted one shoulder. "Here and there, trial and error." Hanna giggled. "Just be thankful you weren't around for what the kids now call The Year of the

Clove, and The Sagebrush Year."

"Huh?"

Lifting the other shoulder, she explained. "I used to clip recipes from women's magazines, then double the ingredients so I wouldn't have to make up two separate batches of dressing." Another giggle. "But the kids were always underfoot, asking for cookies, or needing help with something, and I'd get distracted. I'd forget whether or not I added sage, or cloves, or whatever. . . and put it in twice. Spice is nice," she concluded, "in the right amounts."

"Well, you turned out okay, so I guess a little kitchen rebellion can be forgiven."

"Enough small talk, mister, you've got some explaining to do."

Chuckling, Mitch held up sudsy hands in mock self-defense. "Explaining? Why? What did I do?"

Hanna dried the plate he'd just washed and added it to the stack. It had been Mitch's suggestion to let the dishes soak while they drove their mothers home. It had also been his idea for him to wash, since, as he'd so aptly put it, "You know where everything goes."

"It isn't what you did," Hanna explained, sliding the china onto a shelf in the hutch, "it's more what you didn't do."

His dark mustache slanted above a rakish grin. "Wait. . .I'm in trouble. . .for something I *didn't* do?"

"You aren't in trouble. I'm just curious about something."

"Okay. . .what?"

"You didn't say more than a dozen words to Victor,

and he didn't say ten to you. Now I understand that old cliché."

"What old cliché?"

" 'The tension was so thick, you could cut it with a knife.' " She shook her head. "I realize he caused you some serious headaches in the past, but it was Thanksgiving, for goodness sake." She paused. "You'd think the two of you could put your nasty business on the back burner, during dinner, at least." Resting a fist on her hip, Hanna wagged a maternal digit in his direction. "Something tells me there's more than your legal wrangles behind what went on. . .or should I say what *didn't* go on. . .here today. 'Fess up. What's with you two?"

One brow rose high on his forehead. "Don't you narrow those big eyes at me, missy." It was a tone and a phrase he'd heard his father use on his sister hundreds of times. If his fingertips hadn't started to shrivel from being immersed in hot water for so long, he might have added his dad's raised forefinger into the mix. "As long as we're on the subject. . .I've been dying to ask you a question *for months*."

"Okay, but I'm a mother, don't forget. . .I'm not easily distracted. . . ."

"Yeah, and I'm a lawyer," he countered, laughing; "if traffic lights and turkey stuffing could talk, you'd have witnesses to that fact."

She waved a playful hand under his nose. "Ask your question, before I show you what *else* moms are good at."

"What color are your eyes?"

"Hazel."

"I thought that was a TV show in the seventies."

"Very funny. We ought to take you down to that Water Street comedy club. You could make big bucks. . . ."

He leaned forward, placed a kiss on the tip of her nose. "Don't roll those eyes. . .those gorgeous *hazel* eyes. . .at me."

Standing on tiptoe, she kissed his chin. "Okay. . .I answered your question, now you answer mine: What's *really* going on between you and Victor?"

Mitch's brow furrowed and his lips formed a taut line. "I don't know what you're talking about."

"Oh, yes, you do."

"It's nothing. Really."

"Then why can't you look at me when you say it?"

He dried his hands on a terry dish towel, rested them on her shoulders. "Look, I'm sorry our behavior put a dent in your dinner. I'll make it up to you, I promise."

She shook her head.

Lord, did You make a stubborn woman when You made Hanna! "It's business, plain and simple."

She inclined her head. "But what kind of business do you have with a man like Victor?"

Mitch stuck his hands back into the foamy water, brought out a handful of silverware. "Sweetie," he said, scrubbing the utensils, "I'd give you a kidney if you needed it—"

"I know that. And I'd do the same for you."

"—but that doesn't give you snooping rights into every area of my life."

Hanna gasped, lay a hand against her chest. "*Snooping!* I wasn't snooping."

"Okay. You weren't snooping." He rinsed the clean knives and forks, stuffed them into the drainboard cup. They hadn't had a disagreement, minor or otherwise, since that day on Rogers Avenue, and Mitch didn't want to spoil their record.

"There's no need to patronize me, Mitch."

"You're right. I'm sorry." He hoped his apology didn't make her think she could continue the inquisition. There were some things she was better off not knowing, at least for now. And the details of his relationship—and present business dealings—with Victor Powers was one of them. He thrust his hands back into the sink in search of more silverware.

"Yeeoouch!" he hollered, sticking a bubbly fingertip into his mouth.

Alarm widened her eyes. "You're bleeding! Let me see that." Gently, Hanna cradled his hand in hers and inspected the cut. "It's not too deep, but we have to rinse out the soap." With her free hand, she turned on the faucet, tested the water temperature, and when she felt it was warm enough, stuck his hand under the stream.

"I know this stings," she said. "You're being very brave."

He thrust out his lower lip. "Does that mean I get a Band-Aid?"

"In fact," she assured, a maternal gleam in her eyes, "I might just have some with cartoons on them."

"Disney characters?"

"Flintstones. . .because despite all your horrible pain, you've been steady as a rock."

"Flintstones? Really?"

Hanna nodded.

"Wow!"

It had been one of the first things Mitch had ever said to her. She didn't know why, but hearing his innocent exclamation again brought tears to her eyes. "I'll . . .I'll just be a minute. . . ."

Mitch tried to grab her wrist, but she was too quick. "Where are you going?"

"To get some antibiotic ointment." She swallowed, to hide the sob aching in her throat. "And a bandage, of course."

"Hurry back, 'cause I'll miss you."

Nodding as she went, Hanna headed for the downstairs powder room, where she kept the first-aid kit. Only when the door closed behind her was she able to admit the real reason his little "wow" had affected her so deeply:

He was keeping something from her—which wouldn't be important, except. . . .she had fallen in love.

Chapter 6

The bandage had been slipping and sliding for two days now, curling at the edges and grungy from thumbing through musty files, but Mitch couldn't bring himself to take it off. Hanna had wrapped it around his finger with such tenderness that he wanted it to stay there, to remind him how much she cared about him.

In the months he'd known her, Mitch had learned that, despite her keen sense of humor, Hanna was a serious-minded woman. And was it any surprise? he asked himself. In addition to her normal motherly duties, the responsibilities that normally fell upon the shoulders of husbands and fathers had been heaped upon her narrow ones. The only way she could carry the added weight steadily, uncomplainingly, Hanna seemed to have decided, was to dot every "i" and cross every "t" before she was allowed to have any fun.

Leaning back in his desk chair, Mitch remembered the day after their first dinner at Tersiguel's, when he sent her *Peppermintland*, a children's game. He'd bought one of those "blank inside" cards and wrote "Learn to play a little!"

Two days later, Hanna had sent a package to his

office. Inside, he found the word game, *Unscramble*. The card attached said, "Play to learn a little!"

And that's pretty much the way it had been between them ever since. . .Mitch trying to lighten her load. . .Hanna making it clear she didn't feel comfortable accepting his help.

Except where her children were concerned. Hanna had confessed during that first dinner that both Paige and Pete were sorely in need of a male role model. And once he'd met them, Mitch had been more than happy to fill the position.

Hanna had needed a man every bit as much as those kids. Not to make minor repairs around the house (he'd learned early on that she could fix a leaky faucet or a jammed garbage disposal with the best of 'em). No. . .Hanna needed a man *to make her feel like a woman*.

She reminded him of that philodendron his college roommate had brought into the dorm. Unwatered, unfed, deprived of light, it began to shrivel, turned brittle and brown. When Mitch took it upon himself to give it a shot of fertilizer, regular doses of water and sunshine, the plant changed. It had taken time, and some patience on his part, but before long, it grew big, shiny-green leaves. . .would have grown *miles* of them if he hadn't pruned it from time to time.

A month or so into his relationship with Hanna, when frustration at her arm's-length attitude threatened to make him throw in the towel, Mitch remembered something else about that philodendron: Before his careful tending could do any good at all, he'd first had to remove all those dried-up, dead leaves.

He likened Hanna's marriage to Paul to those leaves. If he wanted a future with her—and he'd known from the start that he did—he would have to exercise patience, give her time to shed the whispers of her dead past.

"Why the long face, son?"

"Aw, I've got myself in hot water—"

"Again?" Marge interrupted. "Who turned on the heat *this* time?"

"Hanna."

She sat across from him, wagged a warning finger in his direction. "You better not do anything to hurt that girl, or you'll answer to me!"

Mitch's eyes widened with mock shock and hurt. "Wait just a minute. You're *my* mother, and you're warning me not to hurt *Hanna*?" Grinning at the irony, he added, "What's wrong with this picture?"

"She's such a sweetie. I've been to the bookstore. . . even the name she chose for it is cute. . .the Bookworm Emporium." Marge giggled girlishly. "She works so hard. A real trouper, that one. Everybody says she's worked her fingers to the bone for those precious kids of hers. Why, if your father had died while you kids were little, I don't know what I would have done."

He was still reeling a bit at the support his mom had put behind the new woman in his life, when always before, she'd given him a verbal laundry list of their faults. . . . "You would have done fine."

She shook her head gravely. "You don't understand. Your dad was a *man*. Not like that Peter Pan that Hanna married. . .always playing, leaving her to carry the ball. . . ."

"How do you know so much about it?"

"His mother is with the Ladies' Auxiliary, too. She used to come to the meetings, bragging that her Paul was off sailing with the governor, or her Paul was on the golf course with Senator So-And-So, or her Paul—"

"Sounds like he invented the cliché 'All work and no play. . . .' "

Marge huffed. "Your father was nothing like Hanna's husband. He never would have left me with a pile of unpaid bills." She shook her head. "I'm not saying you kids wouldn't have been clean and fed; of course I'd take care of things like that. I'm talking about being put in the position of having to make major decisions—on the heels of funeral arrangements, mind you—like whether or not you can afford the house your kids were born in, and having to find a job with a salary that could support a family, and being the only one to see that there's gas in the tank and oil in the furnace."

"Mom. . .it's not like you to be this serious." He grinned. "At least, not for this long. . . ."

Marge met Mitch's eyes. "Maybe because this is no joking matter. I don't think I would have had that kind of strength, son. We're not *all* Hercules."

Hanna Hercules. Mitch's grin grew, because despite her Lilliputian size, the name fit.

His mother took a deep breath. "Hanna Marsh is a prize, and if you let her go, you're plumb loco."

Chuckling softly, Mitch leaned both elbows on his desk. "I know she's a find, Mom, and I've thanked God for her every day since we met. And if I have anything to say about it, you're going to be calling her Hanna

Riley some day. And maybe, if you behave yourself, I'll let you play Cupid. . . ."

She pretended not to hear his invitation to help him seal the deal with Hanna, but Mitch knew she had, because her familiar teasing grin was back in place.

"Well," she said, "that's the first smart thing I've heard you say in months."

"Oh, I don't know about that. I said 'lipotropic' and 'diplopia' just the other day."

She crossed both arms over her chest. "What did you say to hurt Hanna, smart guy?"

"I didn't say anything to hurt her."

"Then why are you in hot water?"

Mitch rolled his eyes and sighed heavily. "She wanted me to tell her about the business with Victor Powers, and—"

She leaped up and gasped. "You didn't tell her, did you!"

"Calm down, Mom. Of course I didn't tell her. I don't want to spoil everything."

"Thank goodness! Can you imagine what she'd say if she knew?"

The idea made him frown. "Yeah. I have a pretty good idea." Then, "Maybe it was a mistake to involve you in this."

"Don't be silly. You needed a witness." She reached across his desk to tweak his cheek. "And who does my widdo Mitchy wuv and twust more than his Mummy?"

Wrinkling his face, Mitch held up his hands in mock self-defense. "Cut it out, Mom. The door's open . . .what if a client walked in here and—"

Straightening, Marge patted her coifed hair. Her accent was oh-so-British when she said, "I'd just tell them to step into the outer office, and close the door behind them, thank you veddy much." She stuck her nose in the air and strolled from Mitch's office.

"Close the door behind you," he said, echoing her English imitation.

When Marge shot a "be careful what you say" look over her shoulder, he quickly added, "Thank you veddy much."

Alone again, Mitch had to admit that no amount of tom-foolery was going to get his mind off the deal he'd struck with Victor Powers. It had been difficult, hiding the truth from Hanna during their after-Thanksgiving conversation.

He ran both hands through his hair, knocking the bandage off. Heart aching, he scanned his desktop for it, and when he stood to widen his search, the tan plastic-and-gauze cylinder fell from his lap and onto the floor. The cut badly needed a fresh bandage by now, but he slid the old dressing back in place anyway.

Yeah, hiding the truth from her had been difficult.

"You ain't seen hard *yet*, Riley, m'man. . .*keepin'* the truth from her. . .*that's* gonna be the hard part."

Danny was doing a fine job. Better than Missy on her best day, though he was a full year younger than Hanna's former employee. A rabid reader, her new part-timer borrowed almost daily from the "Used Books" table. By the time he'd been with the Bookworm Emporium for a month, he'd read, among other things, the biographies of

Abe Lincoln, Booker T. Washington, Alexander Graham Bell, and the Wright Brothers, quite an eclectic reading list, and she said so.

"They have a few things in common," he told Hanna as they hung decorations for the pre-Christmas sale, "but one thing stands out."

She had asked for the Lord's guidance in choosing Missy's replacement, and the moment Danny walked up to the counter, bright dark eyes flashing, she'd liked him. It wasn't until more recently, after she'd had a chance to get to know the boy behind the smile, that Hanna understood *why*: He reminded her of Mitch. "And what would that be?"

"They knew it would take long hours of hard work to get what they wanted, and none of them were satisfied with doing a job halfway." He'd just hung the last ornament on the tabletop tree, and stood back to admire his handiwork. "It's like my dad always says. . . if more people did their best, instead of settling for 'good enough,' this country wouldn't be in the shape it's in."

" 'All or nothing at all,' eh?" she quoted the age-old cliché.

"Exactly!" Danny nodded, his dark curls bobbing. "Your boyfriend reminds me of Lincoln and the rest of 'em, way he throws himself into everything a hundred and ten percent." He gave a confirming nod of his head. "But he's got an edge over those guys."

Hanna didn't know which she was more curious about. . .the fact that Danny had called Mitch her boyfriend, or Mitch's so-called "edge" over men like

Abraham Lincoln. *You're too old for a boyfriend!* she told herself. But the flutter in her heart at the mere mention of Mitch's name told her otherwise.

"That's the kind of man I want to be some day," Danny continued, "one who always gets the job done . . .but has a good time doing it." He gave Hanna a smile of approval. "You're lucky, Mrs. Marsh. He's a real cool guy." Then, looking almost embarrassed, he quickly added, " 'Course, Mr. Riley is lucky, too. . . ."

Hanna smiled as the bell above the door signaled a customer's entrance. "You lookin' to 'up' your Christmas bonus, Dan?"

Laughing, he shook his head. "No." Doing his best Simon Legree imitation, he rubbed his hands together and said, "But now that you mention it, I've been meaning to thank you."

"For what?"

"For being the smartest, nicest, most understanding, best-lookin' boss a guy ever had."

The boy's words stopped Mitch in his tracks. It didn't make a bit of sense. . .being jealous of a kid half his age. "Goodness," he heard Hanna say, "with all that going for me, maybe I don't need to pay you at all!"

"Well," was Danny's response, "let's not get carried away. . . ."

Good advice, Riley, Mitch thought, relaxing his clenched teeth and doubled-up fists.

Hanna had been on his mind all week, in one way or another. How he'd managed to get anything done was a mystery. Because no matter how tedious or trying the task, Hanna managed to slip into his thoughts.

Even in the middle of the pastor's sermon, some sweet thing she'd said would echo in his brain. Or he'd picture that way she had of tilting her head when she talked. Her lilting laughter might tinkle in his memory, or he'd recall the wide-eyed attention she paid to every word he uttered. Or maybe instead, he'd recollect something she did, like packing lunches and sneaking in when no one was around to leave them on his desk. It was always the same when he called to thank her: "Now really, when would I have had time to do a thing like that?" And what about the time he'd stopped by her shop unannounced, and she'd noticed a button missing on his sleeve. Needle and thread and a button seemed to materialize like magic. . . .

With all she had to do, Hanna always made him feel that he was the center of her world (or, at the very least, that he shared it with her kids). She had done so many small things for him, thoughtful things that made him completely forget the slights of other women. She was an incredible, amazing, one-of-a-kind woman, and. . .

You're beginning to sound like Danny, he chided, grinning to himself.

He could hardly blame the kid, because Hanna really *was* all those things Danny had listed, and more!

You're out of your ever-lovin' mind, avoiding her. . . .

Since Thanksgiving—afraid he might spoil everything by spilling the beans about the Powers' deal—he'd been making excuses to keep his distance. At least until Christmas, he'd told himself. But he hadn't counted on missing her this much.

Mitch stood near the door, content for the time

being, to watch and listen. If Hanna had known she was the object of such intense scrutiny, her cheeks would have reddened and her eyes would have widened; stammering and stuttering and a hand to her chest, she'd have demanded to know what he was looking at. The idea made him chuckle.

"Mitch Riley, what on earth are you staring at?"

She looked, when his mind returned to the here and now, as he'd pictured her. Except that the real, live Hanna had propped both hands on her hips, blinked up at him, smiling sweetly.

She looked lovely in her sensible, short-jacketed blue suit, from the top of her ponytailed blond head to the soles of the navy flats on her tiny feet. He'd long ago stopped questioning the source of this incredible craving to kiss her—an urge that unexpectedly erupted when in her presence. It was as plain as the big eyes in her face that Hanna had never set out to elicit such a reaction in him. But there he stood, his heart hammering and pulse pounding, despite his best efforts. What sense did it make, fighting it?

And so he didn't.

When Mitch came up for air, he looked into her enchanting face, watched as those heavily lashed eyes fluttered, opened slowly, and met his. "Good to see you, too," she said, her voice barely more than a warm whisper. "I was beginning to think you were avoiding me."

"I was," he admitted quietly. "It was a test, to see how long I could go without you. . .without *this*." Mitch kissed her again.

"It's been six days," Hanna began, glancing at her

watch, "twelve hours and fifteen minutes."

"Gee, I've missed you."

"Missed you, too."

When the bell above the door tinkled, Hanna disentangled herself from his embrace, attempted to tuck a loose tendril of hair back into place.

"Looks like I've interrupted something. . .maybe I oughta come back some other—"

"Don't be silly, Victor. What can I do for you?"

Mitch watched her, hands clasped primly in front of her waist, brows raised innocently, and admitted it in plain English for the first time: *I love her*.

Powers' wrathful laugh punctuated Mitch's thought. "I'll tell you what you can do for me," he answered, angry eyes on Mitch, "You can give me the same welcome you gave *him*."

Chapter 7

Mitch walked through the rooms, nodding and smiling at the counselors and kids he passed in the halls.

The Kids' Place was everything he'd expected. . . and then some. Hanna had called in all favors, and arranged for the children to move into the old junior high school building on Route 40. Fortunately, he'd been able to head that one off at the pass, telling the contractor she'd hired not to start the reconstruction process. . .and swearing the man to secrecy.

He'd spent the past week poring over musty, dusty records in the courthouse, accumulating facts about this estate's rich and colorful history. The mansion was designed and built by William Wadsworth Wentworth in the mid-1800s with one purpose in mind: To entice one Mary McCarthy to become his bride. Wentworth had spared no expense. Italian marble lined the foyer floor, and teak, imported from Malaysia, paneled the library walls. Stained glass, crafted by French artisans, adorned the windows, which, like the doors and floors and cabinets, had been carved from rich, West Indies mahogany. There were brass and crystal chandeliers and sconces in every room, a hand-inlaid black-and-white tiled floor in the kitchen, intricately etched copper ceilings. The roof was slate. . .each shingle chiseled and engraved to look like seashells, so Wentworth's sweet Mary wouldn't be too homesick for the beaches of her homeland on Ireland's rugged west coast.

But Mary had said a terse and intense "no" in a letter to Wentworth. The letter, along with Wentworth's journals, had been found just two years ago beneath the attic floorboards by one of The Kids' Place residents. "You are one of them who put my father out of his home," she'd written above her fanciful signature; "I'd sooner go to my grave starving and poor than live a minute in your fancy house in America." Wentworth's response, the last entry in his diary, would resound in Mitch's memory forever: "If not Mary, than no one, for what's the point?" Rumor had it Wentworth wrote that line, then holed up alone in his fancy house, and mourned himself into an early grave.

Mitch knew all too well what the English had done to his ancestors, but Irish or not, he was a *man* first and foremost, and understood the Englishman's pain.

If he asked Hanna to marry him and she said no. . . .

It was too late for Mitch. He was in deep. Real deep. He loved her, as he'd never loved a woman before, and if he had to spend much more of his life without her, well, he might just end up like old Wentworth.

"What're you doin' here, mister?"

Mitch faced the waist-high girl who'd asked the question and smiled. "Just looking around, is all."

"You the rich man who bought this house?"

Chuckling, he said, "Well, I'm far from a rich man. . . ." In truth, he'd inherited a considerable sum from his grandfather. But since he'd always preferred to live the simple life, only the tellers at Maryland National Bank knew how much he was worth. "But I did buy the place." And it had cost him a pretty penny, too.

She ground her sneaker into the hardwood, looked plaintively up at Mitch. "You gonna make us leave? Miz Johnson—she's the lady who runs this place—she says the new owner might make us pack up and move out."

"Well, I'll just have a little talk with 'Miz Johnson'. . . set her straight."

"You mean. . .you mean you're *not* going to make us leave? We can stay here?"

Mitch nodded. His smile dimmed a bit when he asked, "How long have you lived here?"

The little girl shrugged. "I dunno. Five, six years maybe."

"How old are you, sweetie?"

"Seven."

His heart skipped a beat as pity and disgust panged within him; pity for the children who called this place home, disgust for a world that made their living here—instead of in houses of their own—necessary.

He got onto one knee, making himself child-sized. "What's your name?"

"Marjorie. . . ."

"Well, how 'bout that? Marjorie is my mother's name." Mitch winked. "But folks call her Marge. What do they call you?"

"Marjorie." And grinning, she added, "What's yours?"

"His name is Mr. Riley."

He stood, turned to face her. The dark mood of this place lifted at the very sight of her, standing there in her crisp little business suit, wearing a smile as bright as the sun.

For him?

A man can hope, he told himself, smiling back.

Mitch had seen her just that morning, had held her tight and kissed her soundly, and yet it seemed they'd been apart for months. If it meant she'd marry him, Mitch would gladly build her a house like this one, complete with wrought iron porch rails and a three story turret.

But he had to bide his time, just a little while longer, anyway. . . .

"What are you doing here?" Hanna wanted to know.

The warm light shining in her eyes was for him, he knew. And the tiny spark of fear and mistrust. . .that was for him as well. . . .

"Just looking around," he said again.

She tilted her head, lifted one brow. "Why?"

He shrugged. "Snooping isn't just a woman's prerogative, you know."

The intended joke backfired, big time. Her smile vanished like smoke. "I wasn't snooping. How many times do I have to say it?"

"Hanna," he began, reaching out to grasp her hand, "I'm sorry. I never meant—"

She slid her hand into her pocket, took a careful step back. "Miss Johnson tells me you're meeting with

Victor here this evening."

He straightened his back, pocketed his own hands. "That's right."

Lifting her chin, she said in a tightly controlled voice. "I can't imagine why." Her left brow rose and her eyes narrowed slightly when she added, "Birds of a feather?"

She couldn't have hurt him more if she'd hit him with a stick. *A big one*, Mitch added, *with a sharp, splintered end*. Victor Powers wasn't all bad—and since they'd struck their deal, Mitch knew it as well as Hanna—but the man never made a move without first determining how it would affect his financial security. That fact more than any other made Victor a ruthless businessman; for proof, one need only look at his decision to sell The Kids' Place. But once he'd learned he'd get more than his asking price for the property from Mitch, Victor had been more than willing to deal.

His own silence, Mitch knew, was responsible for making Hanna think he had anything in common with Victor Powers. But he couldn't tell her what she wanted to know. Not yet.

He couldn't—*wouldn't*—risk it.

Instead, Mitch endured her disapproving, disappointed stare, and sent a quiet prayer heavenward: *Just a little while longer, Lord. Just a little longer. . . .*

She couldn't forget it, and no amount of prayer or work would erase Mitch's expression from her mind. Hanna took it to mean God didn't *want* her to forget it.

Mitch's shoulders had slumped as he hung his head

and stared at a spot between his feet. That smooth, handsome brow had furrowed in deep concentration, those full, manly lips thinned as he'd nodded. No, he seemed to be saying, not birds of a feather.

Paige and Pete adored him. Why, just last night, her son had called Mitch at home. "Hey, buddy," she'd heard him say, "can you do me a favor?"

Mitch must have agreed to do it, because Pete's blue eyes had sparkled and his smile grew to twice its normal width.

"My Scout troop is having a father-son thing, two weeks from Saturday."

Having been just four when Paul died, Pete's memories of him were dim. He seemed to miss him most at times like these, when school or church or Scouting functions required a boy to be present with his dad.

"Cool," Pete had said. "Thanks, Mitch! You want I should have Mom pick you up at nine?"

The boy's full attention had been on whatever Mitch was saying into the phone. Nodding and grinning, he repeated, "Cool. I think your truck is neat. Okay. Yeah. Sure. Whatever you say."

Another pause, and then, "When are you comin' over?" Pete had put his back to Hanna to add in a rough whisper, "I think Mom misses you. . . ."

And it was true, after all. But that wasn't the issue. The point was: Pete had grown quite fond of Mitch. So had Paige. The children, like herself, had been drawn to his steady strength, and had come to depend upon it. And his gentle playfulness had added much-needed warmth and fun and a sense of family that hadn't been there, even when Paul was alive.

She had prayed, long and hard, before allowing herself to get close to Mitch. . .before introducing her children to him. He had turned out to be a good, decent God-fearing man who cared about her and her children. But why was he suddenly acting so cagey? If he couldn't trust her with the truth about his meeting with Victor, maybe her relationship with Mitch wasn't what she thought it was. What if, because she was lonely and tired of doing everything all by herself, she had mistaken Mitch's tenderness, his thoughtfulness, as God's "go ahead"?

They had come to love and need him, Paige, Pete, and Hanna—especially Hanna—and if he wasn't everything he appeared to be, they all stood to be hurt, deeply.

Especially Hanna.

On her knees beside her bed, Hanna bowed her head and folded her hands. "I am laying it all at the foot of the Cross," she prayed softly, biting back the dread that prickled in her mind. "I'll trust You to see to our happiness, Lord Jesus."

Opening her eyes, Hanna looked at the ceiling. "And if he should leave us," she added haltingly, "bless me with strength to cope. . . ."

Only a week to go until Christmas, and Mitch was as ready as he'd ever be.

His idea of decorating consisted of draping a strand of colored lights around the front door. The shopping had been done for weeks, too. Marge had never been difficult to buy for. Long about Thanksgiving, she'd start dropping not-so-subtle hints. . .such as leaving catalogs lying around. All Mitch needed to do was open them to their dog-eared pages, and look for the things she'd outlined in red.

In a Smithsonian catalog, she'd circled a silk scarf. The one from L.L. Bean identified a turtleneck with tiny mallard ducks all over it. And in J. Peterman's fun-filled book, she'd drawn an arrow to a long-sleeved denim dress. He'd been careful to tell the lady on the phone exactly which colors and sizes his mother had underlined. Three gifts, one for each of the important roles she played in his life: secretary, mother, and friend.

He'd wrapped each and stood them among the *Anne of Green Gables* and *Louisa May Alcott* collections he'd bought for Paige, and the fishing rod and reel he would give Pete. He couldn't wrap Hanna's gift. . .

. . .just yet. . . .

Standing in front of the foyer mirror, he tucked his shirt collar into the sweater Marge had given him for Christmas last year, tied his running shoes, and jammed an Orioles cap onto his head. The grandfather clock struck nine, telling him he was already ten minutes late, thanks to a power outage that had occurred during the night. The Scouts and their fathers would be gathering in the parking lot of the railroad museum at nine thirty. If he caught all the green lights, he might just make it to Hanna's, then to the end of Main Street, on time.

Grinning, Mitch slid behind the wheel of his pickup, remembering that a green light was responsible for his initial meeting with Hanna. Something told him he'd never feel quite the same about traffic signals again. Now, if only Hanna would send him a signal. . . .

It was at that moment that Mitch realized the long line of cars ahead wasn't responding to *this* green light. Stepping out of the pickup, he ran toward the intersection, and saw in the distance a man in a suit, kneeling beside a boy. Beside them, the mangled remnants of a bicycle. Cell phone resting on one shoulder, the man dug around in what appeared to be a doctor's bag. "Need any help?" Mitch asked. "I'm a volunteer EMT here in the county. . . ."

"Get an ambulance to Frederick Road and St. Johns Lane, stat!" he barked into the phone. "Tell 'em the victim is a boy. . .maybe nine or ten. . .knocked off his bike by a car." Hitting the phone's 'off' button, the doctor faced Mitch. "Thanks," he said, "but there's really nothing we can do 'til the ambulance gets here; can't move the kid 'til we know what sort of injuries he's sustained."

Mitch took another step closer, to get a better look at the boy, and sent up a prayer on behalf of the child and his family.

He caught another glimpse of the bike. . .one hundred percent shiny blue. Just last weekend, Pete had spent hours in the garage, spray painting the frame, handlebars, and pedals of *his* bike. . .silvery blue.

Chapter 8

A wan smile flickered across Pete's little-boy features when he saw Mitch hovering over him. "Mitch," he whimpered, grabbing his hand.

He was holding on as if for his life, and Mitch's heart thudded with fear. "Hey, buddy," he said, gently brushing blond strands from the boy's forehead. "You just relax and lie still now, you hear? There's an ambulance on the way; you're gonna be fine, just fine."

Nodding, Pete groaned, and then his smile was replaced by a grimace. "Guess I shoulda waited for you, huh?" he whispered. "I'm sorry if I caused any—"

Pete never finished his sentence, because he passed out.

"This your boy?" the doctor asked, packing up his bag.

"No. . . ." What definition should he give his relationship with Hanna? "He's my girlfriend's son."

The wail of a siren punctuated his statement. "Finally!" He'd assisted the EMTs and fire fighters at nearly a hundred emergencies, and without exception, he'd been as patient and reassuring as he knew how to be. But Mitch had never been on this end of an accident before; now that he understood how painfully frightening it was to wait for help to arrive, he'd be even more understanding in the future.

Two uniformed EMTs leaped from the vehicle, life saving gear in tow. "Hey," said the one with "Walsh" on his nameplate, "you look familiar. . . ."

Mitch nodded. "You were my instructor in the Basic Life Support class I took a couple years back."

Nodding, Walsh gave Pete a quick once-over, then strapped the blood pressure cuff around the boy's arm. "He's stable," Walsh told his partner. "But let's get him out of here. . . .head injuries can be tricky business." Together, the EMTs eased Pete onto a gurney and into the waiting ambulance.

"Where do you think you're goin'?" Walsh asked as Mitch climbed in behind them.

Reaching into a box near the door, Mitch snapped on a pair of rubber gloves. Then, from the IV bar above his head, he removed one of the three-inch lengths of surgical tape placed there by the guys on the previous shift. "I know the boy," he said, holding the tape out to Walsh. "We haven't been able to get in touch with his mother yet."

Walsh nodded as he inserted an IV into Pete's arm. "Yeah," he said, hanging the bag from the bar above, "guess it'll be better if there's a familiar face nearby when he comes to." Grabbing the tape stuck to Mitch's thumb, he used it to secure clear plastic tubing to the boy's wrist. Walsh signaled his driver with one hand and depressed the transmit button of his two-way radio with the other.

Mitch listened as Walsh rattled off the vital statistics. . .blood pressure, pulse, basic inventory of Pete's condition. . .to a doctor at the other end. Mitch hadn't worked on this particular ambulance before, and because he knew each crew set things up inside to meet their own self-specified requirements, he took a quick look around. Not that knowing where things were would do him any good; as a volunteer, he'd been trained to assist, and nothing more. He wished he'd gone whole hog, studied to become a full-fledged EMT instead of taking the "basics" course. But he hadn't, and frustrating as that was right now, Mitch had no intention of complaining. These guys didn't have to let him ride along, and he knew it.

"So what's your take on this?" Walsh wanted to know as the vehicle sped toward Howard County General.

"Witnesses said an elderly lady drove through the intersection. . .didn't see Pete." Shrugging helplessly, he added, "It appears he didn't see her, either. . . ."

Walsh nodded. "You want to call his mother, have her meet us at the emergency room?"

Call Hanna? It was the first time Mitch had given a thought to his truck, still sitting in the line of traffic, driver's door open, keys in the ignition. "I have a car phone," he grumbled, "on the front seat of my pickup." Scowling, he shook his head. "Fat lot of good it's doing me there."

Walsh handed Mitch a cellular phone.

"Thanks."

"Hey, we take care of our own." He paused. "I don't recall your name."

"Mitch Riley."

Nodding in acknowledgment, Walsh barked more information about Pete's condition into the radio.

Phone in hand and forefinger poised to begin dialing, Mitch froze, gaze glued to the keypad. What would he say when she answered? He punched the "on" button, and when it beeped, Mitch met Walsh's blue eyes. "What do I tell her about his condition?"

"Ain't much to tell. . .yet. He's got a head injury, but we won't know how serious it is 'til we get him into x-ray."

Mitch dialed Hanna's number. Four rings later, he hung up.

"Nobody home?"

"Nobody home." He'd been around the Marsh house enough to guess what had probably happened: Impatience had likely driven Pete to distraction, and distraction had driven him to the garage to fetch his bike. He could almost hear the boy: "It's only a few blocks to Mitch's house, Mom. I'm not a baby; I'll be fine."

He patted Pete's hand. "You *will* be fine, son, if I have anything to say about it." *Lord*, he added silently, *don't let anything happen to him*.

Hanna had told him she'd lost her uncle during the Vietnam war, that her dad had died shortly afterward. Paul's accident took him from her before their seventh anniversary. She'd had to sell her house to get on top of the bills he'd left unpaid. There ought to be a law: Just one tragedy per lifetime.

How many disappointments and losses could one woman bear—even a strong woman, like Hanna—before the weight of them broke her?

She'd come into the house, bag of groceries in each arm, humming happily. Paige was busy at school, packing up goodies for the family that would be this year's recipient of the Secret Santa project. Pete was off with Mitch and the rest of the Scouts, racking up ten cents a mile toward food for the homeless shelter. And her mother was at the church, baking sweet treats for the Christmas Eve festivities.

It had been a long time since all was this right with her world, and Hanna praised God for every blessing great and small.

Whistling now, she pressed the blinking red button on the answering machine. Her smile widened the moment she recognized Mitch's manly voice:

"Hanna, honey. . .it's me. . .Mitch. I'm, ah, I'm at the hospital. . . ."

During the brief pause, she stopped unloading groceries and stared at the recorder. Goosebumps raised on her flesh at his tone. He'd tried to mask it, but she knew him well enough to recognize his "all business" voice. "The hospital?" she whispered, hands over her heart. "Please, Lord, let him be all right. . . ."

"Call this number when you get home, so I can fill you in. Okay?"

She grabbed a pencil and scribbled the number on the back of an envelope. Then, with trembling fingers, Hanna dialed the hospital.

It seemed to take hours before someone knew where to find Mitch. She relaxed a bit the moment his steady voice sounded in her ear. *Thank You, Lord; he's all right!* "What happened? Sprain an ankle? Is Pete there with you? Do you want me to—"

"Easy, sweetie," he interrupted. "I'm fine, and I think Pete's gonna be fine, too."

Pete's *going* to be fine?

"You okay to drive, or should I come and get you?"

"Of course I'm okay to drive." Her heart began to beat like a parade drum. "Why wouldn't I be?"

"It's just that I think it's best if I stay put, 'til you get here, anyway, in case he comes to, I mean. They say it could happen at any—"

Comes to! Pete is unconscious? "Mitch, what happened?"

He rattled off the facts so quickly and efficiently, she couldn't help but feel calmer. "Probably just a minor concussion," he was saying, "but they'll know more when the x-rays come back."

Chewing her thumbnail, Hanna nodded. "I'll call Mom at the church, have her pick Paige up at school. I should be there in fifteen minutes."

"Okay, sweetie. Now you drive safely, y'hear?"

She promised to be careful, and hung up. And the moment she'd finished explaining things to her mother, Hanna left for the hospital.

Mitch had spoken in a soft, reassuring tone. And yet there was an unnerving edge in his otherwise smooth voice that stood the hairs up on the back of her neck. He'd chosen his words carefully, but he hadn't told her the whole truth. *He thinks you'll drive like a maniac, crash into a telephone pole if you know everything. Where was his faith in God?* she wondered. Mitch needn't have worried, because Hanna was in good hands. *God's* hands.

She'd never gone over the speed limit in her life. Not the few times she was late for work, not on the rare occasions when the school nurse called for Hanna to pick up one of her under-the-weather youngsters. Backing out of the drive, she flipped on the flashers and headlights, and drove as though a life depended on it.

Because maybe it did.

She'd been sitting in the hard chair beside Pete's bed in the emergency room for hours when the doctor suggested that Hanna take her mother and daughter home. "Pete's a tough little guy," Dr. Oken assured. "He's a bit banged up, but he's going to be fine. We just want to keep him overnight for observation. . .it's precautionary with head injuries."

He silenced her protests by adding, "There isn't a thing you can do for him. He's resting comfortably, so why not go home and let everybody get a good night's sleep?"

She peered through the opening in the pastel-striped curtain and saw Paige, feet on one orange plastic chair, head in her grandmother's lap, sound asleep. And Sarah's head bobbed as she struggled to stay awake. For an instant, Hanna was tempted to leave, at least for as long as it took to get them home.

Glancing at her watch, she realized it was nearly four in the morning. *They're going to release him soon, anyway.* There wasn't much point in going home now. . . .

If she'd been honest with herself, Hanna would have

admitted she *couldn't* leave Pete's side. Not for a few hours, not for sixty minutes, not for a moment. "I appreciate your consideration and your concern, doctor, but losing a few hours sleep isn't going to hurt any of us."

Dr. Oken nodded. "All right, then. I'll be back in a few hours. If things check out as I think they will, you'll all be home by noon."

She hadn't let go of Pete's hand since walking into his cubicle. Patting his hand, she nodded and sent him a feeble smile. Only when Dr. Oken was gone did Hanna allow herself the luxury of silent tears.

Strong, warm hands gently squeezed her shoulders. "How you holding up?"

She rested the fingertips of one hand atop his. "Fine."

Mitch knelt beside her and held out his arms. Without turning loose of Pete's hand, she melted against him. "I was so scared, Mitch. When I walked in here and saw him, hooked up to all those tubes and wires and machines." Burying her face in the folds of his shirt, she shook her head. "It was like whispers from the past. . . . I know Pete's accident wasn't nearly as serious as Paul's, but. . . ."

"Pete's okay," Mitch said, hugging her closer, "and I'm not going to leave you. No more whispers from the past, not now, not ever. I promise."

She met his eyes, read the look of genuine concern there. He loved her. It was as plain as that furrow in his brow.

Oh, Lord, she prayed, *he's exactly the kind of man I've wanted. But is he the man* You *want for me*?

If she hadn't learned anything else in her thirty

years on this planet, Hanna had learned this: Time was the greatest teacher of all, and patience the greatest *teller* of time.

She'd wait for God's answer. . .and hope it would match her own.

Just as he'd promised, Mitch stayed with her all through the night. In the morning, he left her just long enough to call Marge to ask her to reschedule his appointments. Fortunately, he didn't need to be in court today. Her mother had taken Paige down to the cafeteria for breakfast, and Dr. Oken had ordered one last precautionary x-ray of Pete's skull.

Hanna decided to take advantage of the time alone by heading for the chapel. She had much to be thankful for, and intended to list each item, one by one.

When she returned half an hour later, she heard voices coming from Pete's hospital room. . . .

"They should pass a law that says people over forty aren't allowed to drive!" was Paige's complaint.

"I'm sure that makes perfect sense to an eleven-year-old girl like yourself," Mitch said, chuckling, "but that means I'll have to hand in my license in five years."

Hanna stood just outside the door, smiling as she listened to the three-way conversation between Mitch and her children.

"All right then, the cut-off point should be sixty-five. . .since that's how old the policeman said the lady who ran over Pete was."

"You're awfully quiet, Pete m'boy," Mitch observed. "What do you think about all this?"

There was a lull in the conversation before the boy said, "I think everybody ought to take a test every year. If their eyes or their ears aren't working right, they shouldn't be allowed to drive. . .no matter *how* old they are!"

"Does that go for motorcycles and mopeds and trucks, too?"

"Anything with wheels!" Paige insisted.

This time, Mitch's voice ended the pause. "So, to be fair, the rule would include bicycles, too, then."

"Well, sure," came Pete's reply. "I guess. . . ."

Hanna could hear the confusion in her son's voice. Like her son, she wondered where Mitch was going with his line of questioning.

"You don't honestly think that lady *meant* to hit you with her car, do you?"

"Well, no. . . ."

"Then there's no reason to be angry with her, is there?"

". . .unless you count this big bump on my head. . . ."

" 'Put on compassion, kindness, meekness, and patience,' " Mitch quoted, " 'forbearing one another and, if one has a complaint against another, forgiving each other. . .for as the Lord has forgiven, so you must also forgive.' "

"Say. . .Mrs. Hanson made us memorize that in Sunday school a couple years ago, when the boys were fighting on the playground," Paige said.

"Yeah. I've heard it before, too," Pete agreed.

"Colossians, chapter three, verse twelve," Mitch stated.

"You know a Bible verse?"

"Don't sound so surprised, Pete. I know a couple of 'em."

"How come you know Bible verses if you don't go to church?"

"Who says I don't go to church?"

"Well," Paige began, "I've never seen you there. . . ."

"Sweetie," he said, chuckling, "there are hundreds of churches in Baltimore. . . ."

"So. . .you believe in God?"

"'Course I do!"

"But. . .but you're a. . . ."

"He's a Christian," Hanna finished, stepping into the room. Wrapping her arms around his waist, she added, grinning mischievously. "But you can hardly blame them for wondering, considering what you do for a living and all. . . ."

Laughing, Mitch pressed a light kiss to her temple. "You'd better watch out, pretty lady, or the nurses are going to get the idea you're flirting with me."

"They may as well get used to it, because I intend to flirt with you for a very, very long time."

He quirked a brow. "How long?"

She tilted her head and narrowed one eye. "Oh, I don't know. . .for the rest of my life, maybe?"

"The rest of your life!" Eyes wide, he looked at Paige, at Pete. "That's a lo-o-o-ong time!" Then, squinting, he focused on Hanna. "Hey. . .are you asking me what I think you're asking me?"

"What do you think I'm asking you?"

"To marry you."

Hanna gasped, and laughing, pressed a palm to her chest. “Me? Asking *you* to marry me? Don’t be—”

The trill of the telephone interrupted her denial. Wearing what Hanna could only describe as a smirk, Mitch answered it.

“Peter Marsh’s room. . . .”

Hanna, Pete, and Paige watched as Mitch nodded to whatever the person on the other end of the phone was saying. Then he covered the mouthpiece and leaned close to Pete’s ear. “My mother says to tell you to get better fast,” he whispered, “ ’cause she baked you something special this morning. . . .”

The boy’s eyes lit up. “Those great brownies she brought to Thanksgiving dinner, I hope!”

Nodding, Mitch turned his attention back to the phone. “Um-hmm,” he said. “Yes, Mom. Well, as a matter of fact,” he added, looking at Hanna, “she’s right here.”

Hanna took a step forward, thinking he meant for her to talk to his mother.

“She just asked me to marry her. What do you think of that?”

“Mitch Riley!” Hanna scolded. “I did no such thing!”

“Oh, yes, you did.” He looked to the kids for support. “Didn’t she?”

Paige and Pete, giggling, covered their mouths with their hands.

Frowning, he listened again to Marge. “But. . .but,” he sputtered. “I didn’t—” Mitch rolled his eyes, took a deep breath. “All right.” Nodding some more, he added, "Yes, I promise. . .I *said* I would, didn't I?"

He exhaled heavily and droned into the mouthpiece, "Mom says I have to ask you to marry me."

A considerable amount of squawking spilled from the telephone's earpiece.

"O-*kay*, Mom. . . ." On one knee now, Mitch took Hanna's hand. "Will you do me the honor of becoming Mrs. Mitchell Riley? Please?" And for good measure, he added, "Otherwise, my mom will be mad at me. . . ."

Hanna took the phone from him and, smiling, said to his mother, "Mrs. Riley, would you tell your son that I'd be honored to become his wife?" Laughing softly, she nodded at something her future mother-in-law said, then handed the phone back to Mitch.

" 'Bye, Mom. I love you, too," he said, and hung up.

Paige and Pete gave one another the "high" sign as Mitch gathered Hanna in his arms, and sealed their deal with a long, lingering kiss.

"Oh, isn't this the most *romantic* thing you've ever seen?" Paige gushed.

Pete clapped a hand to his bandaged forehead, and grinning, moaned, "Call the doctor; all this mush is makin' me sick."

epilogue

After a two-hour Christmas Eve service, Hanna and Mitch settled the children in for the night, then stacked the gifts under the tree.

Mitch built a roaring fire in the wood stove while Hanna stirred up a pot of creamy cocoa. "God Rest Ye Merry Gentlemen" wafted quietly from the stereo as they snuggled on the sofa, sharing a bowl of hot, buttered popcorn.

"Let's open just one present tonight. . . ."

"Mitch," Hanna scolded, grinning. "You're worse than the kids.

He jumped up and headed for the tree. "Here," he said, resting a merrily-wrapped package across her knees. "This one's for you."

She looked at the bright red bow, the red- and green-foiled paper, and the tag that said, "To the Woman of My Mother's Dreams." Laughing, Hanna pointed to a shiny silver box, topped off with a big blue bow. When he handed it to her, she patted the cushion beside her. "All right," she conceded once he sat down, "but just one." Then, folding both hands on top of her gift, Hanna said, "You first."

Mitch painstakingly removed the bow, the ribbon,

and the paper, and revealed a hand-knit sweater. He held it up. "You made this?" Meeting her eyes, he added, "But. . .when did you have time?"

"Here and there." She flashed him a loving smile. "When you love someone, you *make* the time."

Mitch held her tight, kissed her soundly. "It's terrific. Nobody has ever knitted me a sweater before. Not even my mother."

"Well," she said, trying to hide her blush, "I just hope it fits."

He shrugged into it. "Like a glove, m'love." Following a second, meaningful kiss, he nudged the box on her lap. "Okay. Your turn."

Hanna enthusiastically tore off the wrapper, uncovering the box top to a board game. "Monopoly?"

"Open it. . . ."

Glancing at the clock, she said, "It's nearly midnight. Don't you think it's a little late to play—"

"Humor me," he urged, grinning.

Hanna lifted the box top, saw a large white envelope inside. Brow furrowed, she picked it up and broke the seal. For a moment, she could only stare, gap-jawed, at its contents. And then she met his eyes. "*You're* the fat-cat developer Victor told me about? *This* is the deal you two have been—"

"Take a closer look at the deed, pretty lady," he instructed, eyes flashing with love.

Hanna did as she was told, and her eyes filled with tears.

"Well. . .read it!"

" 'This Deed, made the twenty-ninth day of

November. . . .' Oh, Mitch," she said, sniffing.

"Go on. . . ."

". . . 'between Victor Powers and Hanna Marie Riley'. . . ."

She gasped, met his eyes. "Hanna Marie *Riley*?"

Wearing a satisfied smile, he nodded.

Hanna wiped a tear away. "Say. . .how did you know my middle name was Marie?"

Mitch gathered her to him. "I have my ways," he said, snickering wickedly. "But there's more."

"More? How could there—"

"Have a closer look at the game. . .*Mrs. Riley*."

When she opened the board and smoothed it flat, her eyes were immediately drawn to the Luxury Tax square. There, taped to the huge cartoon diamond ring, was a bright-sparkling *real* diamond ring.

She held it between thumb and forefinger, watching as the stone reflected rainbow shards of firelight. "Oh, Mitch," she sighed, "it's. . .it's—"

The jangling phone interrupted her thank you.

Mitch answered it. "Hello?" After a moment of nodding and grinning, he said, "Mom says I have to put it on your finger."

Laughing and crying at the same time, Hanna fell into his arms. "Well, being a mom myself, I can hardly discourage a son from doing what his mother tells him to do. . . ."

" 'Bye, Mom," he muttered into the mouthpiece. "And thanks for playing along." Hanging up, he sat back, took Hanna's hand in his, and slid the ring into place. "There. Now it's official. I love you, Hanna."

"And I love *you*," she said, tilting her hand this way and that to catch the light, "and I'm sure you expect me to say this is the best Christmas gift I've ever received."

He looked hurt. Wounded, even. Hanna laid the bejeweled hand against his cheek. "It's a beautiful ring, and I'll wear it proudly, but *you* are the best gift I've ever gotten, bar none."

"Ugh," came a voice from behind them.

Mitch and Hanna, still locked in a warm embrace, looked toward the top step, where Paige and Pete sat, peering through the railing.

"Is it too late to call that doctor?" Pete asked, faking an upset stomach, " 'cause I think I'm gonna be sick."

"Be quiet," Paige chided. "That's the most romantic thing I've ever—"

"Help," Pete continued in a plaintive voice as he clutched his heart, "I'm surrounded by—"

But Hanna and Mitch never heard the rest of Pete's complaint, because Paige had clapped a hand over his mouth and wrestled him to the ground.

"You're serious?" Hanna asked, pointing toward the stairs. "You want more of those?"

"Serious as a one-eyed judge, ma'am," he declared, kissing the tip of her nose. He held her face in his hands and stared longingly into her eyes.

"You're kidding."

He shook his head. "Never been more serious in my life. How 'bout you?"

Her gaze slid toward the children, and she sent them a loving, maternal smile. Turning to Mitch again, she said, "I do. . .and that's no joke."

Loree Lough

A full-time writer for nearly thirteen years, Loree Lough has produced more than 2,000 published articles and dozens of short stories that have appeared in national newspapers and magazines. She has written two books in Barbour Publishing's *American Adventure* series for eight- to twelve-year olds, and twenty-two inspirational romances, including the award-winning *Pocketful of Love* and *Emma's Orphans* **(Heartsong Presents)**, and "Reluctant Valentine," part of the bestselling romantic collection *Only You* (Barbour Publishing). Loree lives in Maryland with her husband and a scared-of-her-own-shadow cat named Mouser.

Silent Nights

Tracie Peterson

Chapter 1

Wait a minute," Lynn Murphy said, hands on hips. "Do you mean to tell me that you're going to leave me on Christmas? That's just great; why am I not surprised?"

"Now don't take that tone with me," Frank countered his wife's angry retort. "This wasn't my idea. Mr. Bridgeton needs me to handle the case."

"And there isn't another lawyer at Bridgeton National Life, one preferably who isn't about to celebrate his tenth wedding anniversary, who can handle the case?"

"No," Frank said flatly, pulling a suitcase down from the bedroom closet. "There isn't."

Lynn felt an overwhelming urge to grab the suitcase and hurl it out the window, but instead she remained fixed in her spot. This kind of scene was happening more and more, and now only weeks away from Christmas, they were fighting again. Only this time, Lynn wasn't sure she even cared about the outcome. Frank was gone more than he was home, and when he was home, he kept himself wrapped up in a cocoon of work and business issues.

Dejected and totally discouraged, Lynn plopped

down on a chair as her husband swung the suitcase up onto the bed. He apparently noticed or sensed her mood, because his expression softened.

"Look, Lynn," he said, sitting down opposite her on the bed. "I know we have the plans for the trip, but we can just reschedule them."

"We can't reschedule our anniversary," Lynn replied. Deep within, her heart ached at memories of other special events rescheduled.

Frank sighed. "You know this job is important. It's our ticket to the future. I've worked hard to get where I am, and unfortunately that has often required my traveling on days when I'd rather be home."

"I don't believe you," Lynn answered flatly. "I don't believe you'd rather be home." She knew she sounded like a harpy, but she didn't care. "I married you for better or worse, but I'm beginning to think that I'm getting nothing but the negative end of that arrangement."

"It isn't always a bowl of cherries for me, either," Frank replied. "What about my desires for a family? You agreed once I finished law school and got myself established in a good job, you'd quit your job and start having children. I don't see you sticking with your promise."

The words stung Lynn. He had spoken the truth, but the circumstances and reasons were so complicated that she hesitated to even comment on his statement. "You wouldn't begin to understand my feelings on the matter, because you're never home long enough to find out what they are."

Frank frowned. "You'd made your feelings clear

when we were dating. I didn't realize they'd changed."

Lynn got up, hands raised in the air. "Look, why don't you just go back to packing. We're obviously not going to get anywhere this way. We never do."

She started to walk away, wishing he would call after her and apologize, but he didn't. So she turned at the door to their bedroom and looked back at him. Already in her mind, she'd decided to leave him. She'd given up on their marriage. *I don't even know you any-more,* she thought. It hurt so much to even think the words. She loved this man. Loved him more than she'd ever loved any other person. How could she just walk away?

In the living room, Lynn paced nervously as Frank finished his packing. Christmas was in little over two weeks, and she'd done nothing to prepare for it. She hadn't even bothered to go out and get a Christmas tree. She kept putting it off, hoping Frank might actually spend an entire weekend with her, and they'd make a day of searching for just the right tree. But Frank had only been home for three days since Thanksgiving, and his exhaustion and devotion to that stupid job kept him from being even decent company, much less creative or productive in thoughts of Christmas.

She went to the window and stared out on the Chicago skyline. They'd lived in Chicago for nearly four years, and in all that time, Lynn had never gotten used to the view. She had grown up in Kansas, Council Grove to be exact, and it wasn't until she went to college at the University of Kansas in Lawrence, that she began to explore anything else of the United States.

She'd met Frank in college. He was in his third year, and she was barely eighteen and into her first semester. He was everything Lynn respected in a man. He kept himself busy with serious ambitions toward his future, and he made and worked toward real goals—something Lynn never felt good at.

After a lifetime of parents who seemed to take nothing seriously, not even raising Lynn and her sister Monica, Frank was like a breath of spring air. Not only that, but Lynn had never seen any man who filled her thoughts the way Frank Murphy had. He was only of medium height and build, but he had a face that drew her immediate attention. He always wore a serious expression, but his eyes seemed to be alive with a depth of spirit that she found most attractive.

"I have to leave if I'm going to catch the early flight."

Lynn turned to see Frank setting his suitcase by the door. She stared at him and he returned her gaze, discomfort apparent in his expression.

"Look, you know I hate to leave while you're mad at me. When I get back, we'll talk this all out. I promise."

"You always promise," Lynn replied, her voice low.

Frank's expression contorted. "I suppose by that you mean that I promise, then fail to carry through. Is that it?"

"You said it, not me."

"You say it," Frank replied. "You may not use words, but you've made it very clear what you think of my word. I'd like you to reconsider what I said earlier, however. We made certain promises to each other when we married. I've fulfilled my end of the arrangement."

"Is that all our marriage is to you? An arrangement? Maybe I should arrange to become one of your clients. At least I'd see more of you."

"When you act like this, is it any wonder I dread coming home?" Frank threw out.

Lynn felt as though he'd dealt her a hard blow. "So you admit it." She bit her lip to keep from crying.

He shook his head. "Admit what?"

"That you dread coming home."

"I didn't mean it that way. You always twist what I say and use it against me."

Lynn felt ill. She knew their marriage was hopeless, but deep inside she didn't know what to do. She wanted to save it, but how? She didn't believe in divorce, the Bible made it clear that God hated the institution, and she certainly didn't want to participate in what God hated. Yet, how could she continue to live with a man who was obviously very unhappy with her whenever he was around?

"All we ever do is fight, Lynn," Frank said, his voice registering concern. "I don't want to fight with you. I don't want to leave with you angry at me. It's hard enough to go away, but knowing that you're mad at me is even worse."

Lynn shook her head. "It isn't hard for you to go away. You enjoy what you do, you've told me as much. You probably look forward to the next trip and plan it out in your mind, even when you have a few days to be at home. I just don't think I know you anymore, Frank. You used to be exactly what I wanted and needed in a man, but now I feel like we're strangers."

"Don't say that," he said, taking a step toward her. "You're just saying these things because I've ruined your anniversary plans. Look, it's just a date. What matters is that we fell in love and married. We can celebrate our marriage every day—in our hearts, in our actions, whatever."

He reached out to touch her and Lynn stiffened. "It's not just a date. It's important to me. December 29th is the date I gave myself over to the job of being your wife and partner. It's the day I re-evaluate the year and see what has gone before me, and what I might do to make the next year better. It's not just a date on the calendar to me."

"I was only implying that we shouldn't set it aside as the only time we can celebrate our relationship." He rubbed her arms gently, gazing steadily into her eyes. "I love you, Lynnie. Don't let me leave here without telling me that you love me, too."

She wanted to burst into tears, but instead she forced herself to lean up on tiptoes and kiss his lips. "I do love you, Frank. Whatever else happens. I'll always love you."

Frank smiled. "Good. Why don't you pick out a Christmas tree and have it delivered. I should be home by Thursday and we can decorate it together. Okay?"

"I'll see," Lynn replied. She already knew she wouldn't be here when he came back to Chicago. She didn't want to lie and tell him she'd be ready for some sort of homecoming celebration, when she knew she wouldn't be around to join in the festivities.

"That's my girl." He went to the hall closet and

pulled out his coat. "I'll be back before you know it," he called out, then grabbed up his suitcase and was gone.

Lynn went to the sofa and sat down in an almost stunned silence. Switching on the radio she heard violins playing a haunting rendition of "Silent Night."

In her typical fashion, Lynn began to play at the words. She usually did this with pop songs on the radio, making up her own lyrics to the tunes. Even as a child, she had played at this, personalizing every song she heard.

"Silent night, lonely night," she sang in time with the music. "You're gone again and nothing's right."

Tears came to her eyes and she began to cry in earnest. Her marriage was over. There seemed no hope of reviving the dying embers of Frank's love for her. Her own love for Frank still burned hot, which was why she found it so hard to see him go off every week—to give his life to a job, rather than to her.

"Oh, God," she prayed aloud, "nothing is the way I'd hoped it would be. I had such high expectations for our marriage. I just knew that everything would be wonderful, but so far, it's been so very hard. I don't know where to go or what to do, but I know I can't stay here. I can't live like this anymore." She pulled a pillow into her arms and cradled it while she cried. "I've become a shrew and a nag, and please forgive me God, but I think I hate myself."

A jazzy version of "Jingle Bells" came on the radio and soon an announcer was telling her how she could get her horseless sleigh cleaned for the holiday season. Snapping the radio off, Lynn tossed the pillow aside.

"I'm not accomplishing anything by sitting here feeling sorry for myself. God expects us to be people of action, not of reaction," she reminded herself. This morning's sermon had touched on this matter and it had made a deep impression on her.

"There isn't a whole lot that's useful about reactions," her minister had said. "We react to things every day. We react to the red light, when we wanted a green one. We react to our favorite shoes going on sale. We react to our car not starting. We react to the news that someone we love is going to die. Reactions can be bad or good, productive or destructive, but reactions in and of themselves will never accomplish the fullness of God's plan for us. Actions truly speak louder than words or reactions."

Lynn almost smiled at the memory. She seriously doubted Pastor Gates would have figured his words would lead her to separate from her husband. But they were useful in figuring that something needed to be done. She needed action in her life. She needed to do something that would result in something else. And, at this point, anything else was preferable to the pain she was enduring within her marriage.

Picking up the telephone, Lynn dialed the number for her boss.

"Dr. Madison," the female voice announced on the other end of the line.

"Hi, Cindy, it's Lynn."

"Well this is a surprise."

"More than you realize," Lynn countered. "Look, Cindy, I have some personal problems, and I want to take an emergency leave of absence."

There was a pause. "No problem. I hope this won't interfere with your anniversary trip."

"There is no anniversary trip. Frank canceled on me. I just found out about it."

"Oh, Lynn, I'm so sorry. I know how disappointed you must be."

Lynn frowned at the telephone. "No, I don't think you do. Look, I've decided to separate from Frank for a time. That's why I need the leave. I want to take at least a month and isolate myself somewhere and decide what's to be done. I just needed to know that I could take the time. I want it to start as of tomorrow."

"That's fine, Lynn. I'm really sorry about you and Frank though. Do you want to talk about it? I mean, I might be a health clinic MD, but I'm also a married woman who's trying to juggle career and family."

"No, I don't really want to talk about it. . .at least not just now," Lynn replied, hoping Cindy's feelings wouldn't be hurt. "Are you sure you can spare me from the clinic?"

"I'm absolutely positive. It won't be easy, you're the best office manager I've ever had. But we'll manage. I want you to go and work through this. I'd hate to see you and Frank call it quits."

"Me, too, Cindy. Me too."

Lynn hung up the telephone without any idea of what to do next. She wondered where she should go. Her parents were in Europe and her sister Monica's busy life and family in San Francisco would never allow Lynn a moment's peace. Then, like a phoenix rising from her past, a thought came to Lynn. There was only one place to go.

Picking up the telephone once again, she dialed the Council Grove telephone number.

"Hello?" came a gravelly male voice.

"Gramps, it's Lynn."

"Well, Lynnie, what do I owe this pleasure to? It ain't my birthday and Christmas is a few weeks away."

Lynn couldn't keep the tears from coming anew. "Oh, Gramps, my life is a mess. Can I come for a visit? For a very long visit?"

"You know you're always welcome. Frank coming too?"

"No, you might say I'm running away from home."

Gramps laughed. "You're a little old for that aren't you, darling?"

"Maybe," Lynn admitted, "but I'm coming nevertheless."

"When?"

She breathed a sigh of relief. He'd just accepted things as they were without asking a bunch of prying questions. "I'm going to pack and leave tonight. I'll drive until I get sleepy, then stay the night somewhere. I should be able to get in by late tomorrow."

"Just don't take any chances," the old man replied. "I'm not going anywhere."

Lynn gave her word to be careful, then hung up the phone. She glanced around the apartment as if seeing it for the last time. "This is the only way," she whispered to the air.

Chapter 2

Lynn pulled her car onto the long dirt and gravel drive to the Lewiston farm and uttered a sigh of relief. She was a bit more road-weary than she'd thought she'd be. The long, lonely drive had lent itself to nothing but stark, barren fields and boring interstates. Coming into Kansas was rather like taking a step back in time from Chicago. Where things moved at a nonstop pace in the big city, Lynn knew Kansas life moved much slower. People were inclined to chitchat with each other, as was evidenced when she'd stopped for gasoline in Junction City. She'd thought herself to be safe at one of the self-service pumps, but she'd no sooner stepped up to the pump than an older woman smiled from the opposite side and bid her good day. People in Chicago learned to keep their thoughts to themselves and not even make eye contact. It was amazing what could be taken the wrong way.

The two-story, white farmhouse came into view as Lynn cleared a small grove of leafless trees. She had found this place a haven for as long as she had memory. Of course, Grammie Ketta wouldn't be there. She had died three years ago and it had nearly broken Lynn's heart. Grammie had always given Lynn a listening ear and a sympathetic nod whenever there were problems to be discussed. Grammie never pretended to have the answers, she simply offered the kindness of truly caring about what Lynn might have to say.

Lynn had just pulled the car into the space beside Gramps' ancient Chevy pickup, when she spied the old man coming around the house. He hadn't changed much in the three years since Grammie's funeral. He stooped a bit more from his eighty-one years, and his gait seemed a bit slower, but he was the same old Gramps.

Jumping out of the car, Lynn raced to the old man. He embraced her with a bear hug that suggested his strength was as great as ever. Tears came to Lynn's eyes as she held onto the old man.

"You're liken to squeeze the tar out of me girl," Omar Lewiston said with a chuckle. "What's that Frank feeding you these days?"

Lynn pulled away and tried to smile. "I'm just so happy to be here."

"Happy, eh?" He seemed slightly embarrassed by her tears. "Then what's all this about?"

Lynn sniffed and wiped at her eyes. "I'll tell you after supper. How about I take you out?"

"No need for that. I figured you'd be coming in about suppertime and fixed us a bite. How's the car running?"

He was referring to the cause of her extra day on the road. She'd had car trouble near Columbia, Missouri and ended up spending an extra night and part of the next day getting it fixed.

"It was the water pump," she told him. "Never

knew they could make that much noise going out."

Omar nodded. "Let's get your stuff in the house, then we can eat. It's supposed to blow up a snow tonight."

"I know. I heard them mention that this same storm system dumped a foot of snow on Denver. Sure hope we don't get that much."

They chatted amicably about the weather and the look of the sky while Lynn unlocked the trunk of her car. Inside were three large suitcases.

"Planning to move in?" Gramps asked with a grin.

"I just might need to do that," Lynn replied soberly. "But for now, I was hoping you'd tolerate an extended visit."

Gramps nodded. "Sure. Sure. Whatever you need. You know that."

Lynn smiled. "Thanks Gramps."

Later they sat at the kitchen table, white ceramic bowls filled to the brim with homemade potato soup. The women of Gramps' church tried to look after him and kept his freezer stocked so that all he had to do was heat up a meal from time to time.

"This is very good," Lynn said, warming up from the inside out.

"Isadora Blackman makes the best soup in the county, but Lizzy Jenkins runs a short second."

"Is this Isadora's or Lizzy's?" Lynn asked with a smile.

"Neither one. It's your Grammie's recipe and my handiwork."

"It's wonderful. Tomorrow, I'll cook for you," Lynn told him. "After all, I'd hate two years of gourmet cooking classes to go to waste."

With Frank continuing to put in longer and longer hours, Lynn had taken up a number of hobbies to keep herself busy. Cooking classes were only one of a variety of classes that had taken her time and energy. There had also been piano lessons, quilting, sewing, aerobics, and even bowling. The lessons and subjects had been too numerous to remember.

"So, you gonna get around to telling me what's going on with you and Frank?" Omar asked, not even trying to disguise his interest in the matter.

Lynn shrugged. "What's to tell? He's never around. He's always breaking promises and he works outrageously long hours. I don't even feel like I know him anymore. Maybe I've never known him. We got married so young, and after such a short time of dating. Frank was already consumed with college and then law school and I kept telling myself he would change as soon as he graduated and got a job. But he didn't."

"Nothing wrong with working hard, Lynnie."

"Don't you dare take his side," Lynn said half mocking, half serious. "Frank's a bona fide workaholic. He never takes time off and he never keeps his promises. We were supposed to go on a trip to Mexico. Just Frank and me and the sun and the sand. We were going to celebrate our tenth wedding anniversary, but he canceled on me."

"And that's worth leaving the man over?" Gramps asked seriously.

Lynn shook her head. "No, and if it were just that simple, I wouldn't be here. There's so much going on and so many reasons for why I'm here. All I ask is that you give me a few days to sort it all out in my head. I just need time."

"I sure like Frank. I think you two are good together."

"Whenever we're actually together," Lynn muttered between spoonfuls of soup.

They ate in silence for several minutes, then as if she'd never made the request for time, Omar asked, "Why do you suppose it's so all-fired important to the boy to spend all his time working?"

Lynn knew he didn't mean to torment her with the question. "I guess because he wants to be rich. Money has always been important to him. I don't know why, but it is."

"You've been married ten years to the man and you don't know why he works as hard as he does? You two ever think of talking your problems through? Maybe ask him why he has to work like that?"

Lynn sighed. *If only it were that simple.* "I've asked him to slow down, but he insists on being practical. He says it's important to plan for the future. We have a nice nest egg, a beautiful home, and everything we could ever want, but it's still not enough for Frank."

"What about a family?" Gramps asked innocently.

Lynn swallowed hard. "We both want one, but—"

"But what?"

She got up from the table. "Please, Gramps, just give me some time to think. I'm going to go for a short walk, if you don't mind."

"Go ahead, but it's already starting to snow. I wouldn't stay out there too long. Sun's going down and it won't be light for long."

"I promise not to stay past sunset."

Donning her coat and gloves, Lynn stepped back out onto the porch and exhaled loudly. She had hoped Gramps would understand her need to remain silent. How could she explain the situation to him when she was so confused herself that there didn't seem to be any answers?

Fat, wet flakes of snow covered her head and shoulders as she walked down the porch steps and headed toward the machinery sheds. Uncle Kent used to farm this land when it had become too much for his father, but Gramps had told her that her cousin Gary, Kent's oldest son, had long ago taken over. Kent and his wife had wanted to do a bit of traveling before old age set in and so they now spent their winters in Texas and their summers wherever the urge took them.

She pushed at one of the shed doors and found it locked. This was something new. Gramps never used to lock up anything. She supposed, however, that crime was possible everywhere and that small town Kansas was just as vulnerable to theft as Chicago.

Deciding to go to a favorite spot, Lynn retraced the path that she'd so often taken as a child. The only time she'd been truly happy was here on the Lewiston farm. Her mother and father were so seldom around, always traveling with one symphony or another. They were musicians and their lives were spent in whirlwinds that seldom slowed enough to take notice of the two daughters they'd brought into the world.

Lynn and her sister had grown up with nannies and baby-sitters during the school year and Grammie and Gramps in the summer. Summers were always better. Nannies and sitters changed with the years, but Grammie and Gramps were always the same. They filled the need for security and consistency that Lynn could not otherwise find.

Coming to the end of the path, Lynn picked her way up a rock pile that had been there as long as she could remember. Gramps planned to use the rocks to build a smokehouse but had never gotten around to it. Now they sat, much the same as they had for thirty years. At the top, Lynn had a view of the snowy valley. Winter had painted the sky a dull, gunmetal gray. It seemed to match her spirit.

"What do I do, Lord?" Both she and Frank were Christians. They believed in honoring God and living their lives in accordance with the Bible. And because of that, Lynn was uncomfortable with her contemplation of leaving her marriage. Divorce was out of the question. Frank hadn't cheated on her or beat her or done anything but work himself half to death. He wanted children and pressured her on a regular basis to give him some as she had promised she would, but memories of her own disappointing childhood left Lynn reluctant. Her parents were never there for her. How would it be with Frank? Would their child or children suffer because of his long absences? Would they sit at the window and wait for a father who had to delay one more day in Pittsburgh in order to satisfy his client? Or would they grow resentful and bitter as she had?

The cold evening air chilled Lynn to the bone. Hugging her arms to her body, she wondered how she could ever sort through the mess of her marriage.

Hours later, Lynn prepared for bed in the same room she'd shared with Monica when they were children. This was their summer room, their dream room. Here they had helped Grammie hang new curtains every summer. Here, Lynn and Monica had shared their innermost secrets about what life would be like if Mom and Dad would give up the symphony and come home for good.

Lynn smiled at the books on the bookcase shelves. *Little Women, Eight Cousins, Pride and Prejudice,* among others, greeted her like old, dear friends. These were the books she'd dreamed her dreams upon. Books of good families and wonderful homes where people were more important than things.

With a sigh, she sat down on the iron-framed bed and smiled at the same old squeaky springs. She bounced up and down just a bit, to remind herself of the times when she and Monica had bouncing competitions. Tears came to her eyes. She almost wished she could be ten years old again. Wished she could go back in time and plead with her parents to change their lives before they grew up and apart.

What would she say to them, if she could go back and make things different? What would she say to Frank? How could she explain to him that her own haunted memories of childhood kept her from wanting to have children of her own?

She bristled at this thought. She'd never so much as allowed the idea to be spoken into words. Even thinking of it caused her to look around the room in a panic. She had never told Frank how she felt. He had first met her when he found her working in a rescue shelter's day-care center. She had been knee-deep in toddlers, loving every minute of it. She adored kids and they seemed drawn to her, but how could she bring a child into the world only to allow him or her to suffer the things Lynn herself had suffered?

She thought back to the missed birthdays and of holidays spent waiting for parents who never showed up until well after the celebration had passed. She thought of waiting all week to tell her mother about the scores on her sixth-grade mastery test, only to have that year's nanny extend the message that her parents were off to perform for a last minute charity benefit.

The pain still gnawed at her like a sore that refused to heal. She had spent so many disappointing hours watching, waiting, and wondering when her parents would arrive home—hoping against all of the odds that they'd surprise her and pop in unexpectedly. But they never came home early or unexpectedly. Instead, they were often absent and predictably late.

Crawling into bed, Lynn allowed herself to cry freely. She thought of the loneliness she endured in her marriage. She knew Frank loved working for Bridgeton National Life, but couldn't he see that his constant traveling was tearing their marriage apart? Didn't he ever wonder how she felt about the situation? How hard it was to go to bed alone, wondering where he was and if he missed her.

"How can I bring children into this world if this is all I have to offer them? How do I dry their tears when their father never comes home except to get caught up on laundry?"

Would it be worth trying to explain the situation to Frank?

"It won't change anything," she muttered. Frank would never understand her anxiety over the matter. She just knew he'd laugh it off. *He'd call me silly and tell me I was borrowing trouble. Well, maybe he won't see my leaving as silly, although I've probably borrowed myself plenty of trouble by coming here without leaving him so much as a note.*

For a moment she felt a guilty twinge. She'd left in such a hurry that she'd actually forgotten to leave Frank a note as to her whereabouts. But after she'd driven as far as Bloomington, her first stop for the night, Lynn was actually glad she'd forgotten.

"Let him see how it is to worry," she told herself.

But now she felt even worse. No one deserved to fret and worry in that manner. In this day and age of people disappearing due to serial killers or simply being in the wrong place at the right time, Lynn knew it would be horribly unfeeling to leave Frank without any word at all.

But would he even care? Maybe he'd come home and find her gone and celebrate. At least she wouldn't be there to nag or condemn him. He'd not have to dread being there. Tears streamed down her cheeks. He actually dreaded coming home to her. It was just too much to bear.

Chapter 3

"You've reached the Murphy residence," came Lynn's voice over the telephone. "We're unable to come to the phone right now, but if you'll leave a number and a brief message, we'll get back to you as soon as possible." Beep.

Frank scowled. "Lynn, if you're there, pick up the phone. This is the third time I've called and you haven't bothered to answer any of my messages."

He waited for several seconds, hoping she'd pick up the phone, but she never did.

Slamming the receiver down, Frank wondered what to do next. He'd hoped to catch her at home in order to properly apologize for the callous way he'd treated her dreams of a proper anniversary celebration.

She deserved to have her special day, and he'd made the mistake of implying that it was the same as any other date. That they could celebrate anytime. Well, obviously she didn't feel that way and he should have respected her feelings.

Glancing at his watch, Frank figured the only thing he could do was try Lynn at work. She wasn't supposed to be there for another hour, but it was always possible she'd gone in early.

Dialing the number, Frank waited expectantly for Lynn to answer.

"Dr. Madison's office," a female voice, clearly not belonging to his wife, answered.

"Ah, I'm calling for Lynn Murphy."

"I'm sorry she won't be in the office today."

"Did she call in sick?"

"I'm sorry sir, I'm not allowed to give out that information."

"Look, this is her husband and I'm out of town. I've been trying to reach her for three days. Let me talk to Dr. Madison."

"Just a minute," the woman replied.

"Frank?" Cindy Madison's voice reassured him.

"Cindy, where's Lynn?"

"You mean she didn't tell you?"

"What are you talking about?" Frank questioned, a sickening feeling twisting his stomach in knots. "Tell me what?"

"Frank, she's taken a month off. She called me Sunday at home and asked for an emergency leave."

"Lynn never takes time off unless it's important. Did something happen with her grandfather?"

"No, Frank," Cindy replied flatly. "She left because of you."

"What!" he replied, more loudly than he'd intended.

"Look, I can't hang on here. I'm not sure where she went, but she asked for the time off. She was pretty upset, Frank, and I think she's trying to figure out what to do about it."

Long after Frank had ended his conversation with

Cindy Madison, her final words rang in his ears. "She's trying to figure out what to do about it."

Frank caught a cab at O'Hare International Airport and headed for his apartment. He still found it hard to believe that Lynn had actually left him. He knew there were problems with their marriage, but to suggest their problems were insurmountable was ridiculous. He paid the cab driver and greeted the doorman.

"Good evening, Mr. Murphy."

"Evening," Frank murmured, inserting a key into his mailbox.

"Hope the missus is having a pleasant trip."

"What?" Frank questioned, now giving the man his full attention.

"I helped Mrs. Murphy bring her suitcases downstairs. Is she having a good trip?"

"I hope so," Frank replied, not liking this confirmation one bit. "I've been out of town, so I haven't had much of a chance to talk to her." He added the latter to keep the building staff from speculating on the status of his marriage.

He caught the elevator and while thumbing through his mail, waited for the floors to click by. She couldn't be gone. She just couldn't be gone.

Yet, by the time he'd opened the door to their apartment, he knew she was very clearly absent. Silence greeted him as it had on several other occasions when Lynn had been off to one class or another, but this was different. This silence seemed very final.

Setting his flight bag aside, Frank tossed the mail

on the coffee table and went to search the bedroom. Flipping on the light, he found a perfectly ordered room. The bed was made, the clothes were all put away. There wasn't a single sign to suggest anyone had been around for days.

Going to the closet, Frank's suspicions and fears were confirmed again. Most of Lynn's clothes were gone. Empty hangers seemed to taunt him. Going to the bed, he checked underneath and then sat down in a dejected manner. Her suitcases were gone.

"What did you expect?" he asked himself. "Cindy told you she'd taken time off. She never takes time off unless it's an emergency."

A feeling of hopelessness washed over him. Reaching for the telephone he dialed the one person who could offer him comfort at a time like this. Perhaps, too, she would have insight into Lynn's actions and have suggestions for her son.

"Mom?"

"Frank, is that you?" Cissy Murphy questioned.

"Yes, it's me. Look something's going on here and I need some advice."

"Are you okay?"

He heard the concern in her voice and desired only to put her mind at ease. "Yes and no. I mean, physically, I'm fine. Mentally and emotionally, I'm a mess. Lynn's left me."

"What? Is this a joke, Frank?" Cissy questioned in disbelief.

"I wish it were that simple. But it's not. Lynn left while I was away on business."

"Why?"

"I wish I knew," Frank replied. Then stopped. "No, that's not true. I have my ideas."

"Did you fight?"

"Yes. We argued before I left, because I canceled our anniversary trip to Mexico."

"Why did you do that?"

"Bridgeton needs me to oversee a meeting with one of our clients. I've been on the case all along and I figured I'd better be the one to handle the job."

"You let work take precedence over celebrating your anniversary with Lynn?"

"I wouldn't have considered it if it had been another case," Frank said, but even as he spoke he knew it was a lie. "Well, maybe that's not exactly true."

"Frank, I've talked to Lynn many times on the telephone. Usually when I call, you're off on one business trip or another. Don't you realize how lonely she gets? She tells me about all the different classes she's taking, and she's only doing it to fill the emptiness in her life. An emptiness that you've helped to create."

"My job is important. I've worked hard to get where I am, and I don't want to do anything that might jeopardize it. I saw how you and Pop struggled, and I don't want that for my family."

"Frank, you won't have any family if you can't find a way to have time for both your job and your wife."

"I know. That's part of the problem. I want to start our family now, but Lynn is against it. We both agreed that once I finished college and found a good job she'd quit her job and start having kids. But every time I bring up the idea, she refuses."

"On what grounds?" Cissy questioned softly.

"She never says much. She always brings up my job and how much I'm gone and how hard I work."

"I don't blame her."

"But can't you see, Mom? I know what it is to be poor. I saw the way you had to make do with so little. I saw Pop go off to a job he hated, and he still never made enough money to do much more than put a roof over our heads."

"Is that why you drive yourself so hard?"

Frank could hear the disbelief in his mother's tone. "Well, it certainly plays a part. I want a better life for my family."

"A better life? But Frank, I thought you had a happy childhood."

"I did. That's why I want a family of my own."

"But you make it sound as though we lived in poverty."

"Well, we did. We didn't have much in the way of material possessions and there were never any extras. I remember how hard you worked to get material to make a dress for Irene's prom," he replied, remembering his older sister's desire for a full-length gown of green velvet.

"Frank, we certainly weren't rich in possessions, but we had a great deal that kept us happy. When you think about your childhood, what are the memories that make you feel good? What are the things that made you say, 'Yes, I had a wonderful childhood'? Think on those things and tell me what you see."

"That's easy. I remember the security in knowing that you and Pop loved me. I remember your encouragement and counsel. I remember that you always took time out for me."

"None of those things have anything to do with money, Frank."

"Yes, I know, but I also remember worrying about you and Pop. I would overhear you talking about the finances. Wondering how we were going to get through from one month to the next. It worried me. I knew then that I would find a job that paid a lot of money, and I would never put my family through that same concern."

"I'm sorry you worried. Your father and I never intended for you kids to ever concern yourself with such matters. I know you didn't have every material possession you ever desired, but you had our love and trust."

"I know that, and it means the world to me."

"So why do you imagine that your family would want anything less? Lynn probably doesn't even know you feel this way. If your attitude towards work is as much a mystery to her as it always has been to me, then I can't say as I blame her for leaving. As the saying goes, money can't buy happiness."

"Yes, but it buys all the things that help to make life better. Money provides the extras in life. Money sees to it that you have what you need, when you need it."

"And here all this time, I thought God did that," Cissy replied sarcastically.

"Mom, you know what I mean."

"No, Frank, I don't think I do. Look, you were raised to put your trust in God. I was there when you made a public acceptance of Jesus as your Savior. You can't serve both God and money. The Bible makes that real clear. You'll only come to hate one or the other."

"I'm not serving money," Frank protested.

"No? You told me a few minutes ago that 'Money provides. . .' that 'Money sees to it. . .' Sounds to me like money has taken the place of God. You trust money to get you through. You trust money to make your way easy and clear. You give yourself over to a job that consumes all your time and energy, and then wonder why your wife would walk out on you."

"You aren't much help here, Mom. I suppose you're saying this is all my fault?"

Cissy laughed softly. "I'm sorry for laughing, but you sound so much like a little boy again. Remember the time you accidentally broke the back window? You were playing baseball with your brothers and some of the neighborhood kids."

"I remember."

"You said much the same thing then. 'I suppose you're saying this is all my fault,' you told me. Then you reminded me that Brian had pitched the ball and Terry hadn't been able to catch your pop fly. You said it was as much their fault that the window was broken."

"I remember," Frank replied, easily seeing what his mother was suggesting.

"Frank, it doesn't matter who broke what. Placing blame isn't going to fix the problem. You need to make some tough choices here. Either you serve God or you serve money. Either you want a life with Lynn, or you don't. It sounds overly simplified, I know, but that's about as clear as it gets."

"I have to work for a living," Frank protested.

"Yes, but you also need to take some time out to live," Cissy countered. "You need to work to pay the rent and buy the groceries. That much is true. But hoarding money in case something happens, losing sleep over all the 'what ifs,' and losing a wife because you're never home is hardly worth working toward. You're going to have to decide on your priorities, Frank. Either you give yourself completely to your job, or you find a way to compromise and be there for Lynn as well."

"I thought I was here for her."

"Not when you consider that since Thanksgiving you've only been home three days, and none of those were consecutive days. And now you've canceled the one thing she was most looking forward to?"

"I suppose you're right, but it doesn't make it any easier. I don't know where she's gone. I don't even know where to start."

"Search your heart, Frank. Think of all that Lynn needs right now. She's lonely. She's going to search for that place that makes her feel secure and whole. She's going to look for where she can find love."

"I thought she found that here."

"I know, honey, but you're going to have to look beyond what you thought to be true. Pray about it. I will too. I know God will show you the answer."

Frank ended the conservation and sat staring at the

wall for several minutes before actually hanging up the telephone receiver. What his mother said had hurt him deeply, but not because she had dared to say the words. No, it hurt because they were true, and Frank didn't know what to do about it.

Taking up his Bible, Frank searched for the verses his mother had spoken of. The sixth chapter of First Timothy loomed up to accuse him.

"People who want to get rich fall into temptation and a trap and into many foolish and harmful desires that plunge men into ruin and destruction. For the love of money is a root of all kinds of evil. Some people, eager for money, have wandered from the faith and pierced themselves with many griefs," Frank read aloud.

"But I don't love money. I simply see it as a necessity and to keep my family comfortable and happy—" He fell silent remembering his mother's words. He had grown up happy and yet their father's wages had never come near a fourth of what Frank made. They were happy because of their commitment to one another. They were happy because of the love they shared, not because of the security they had in their financial status.

Leaning back on the bed, Frank closed his eyes in complete exhaustion. "God, have I been serving money? Is that what this is all about?" He knew the answer, but still found it impossible to admit to himself. Just as he found it impossible to believe that Lynn wouldn't suddenly appear in the bedroom to welcome him home once again.

Chapter 4

Frank awoke the next morning feeling strangely refreshed. He had an energy about him that gave him the strength to go forward. His first task was to figure out where Lynn had gone. His mother said he should think about a place where Lynn felt safe and secure—here she knew happiness and love. The only thought that came to mind was the farm her grandfather owned near Council Grove, Kansas.

Frank remembered when he'd first met Lynn. She had spoken with fondness of summers spent with her grandparents and of the happiness she had known with them. He thought back to the funeral of her beloved grandmother. A funeral he'd had to send her to alone. She'd come home saddened by the loss of her grandmother, but strangely at peace from the time she'd spent with her grandfather.

Reaching for the telephone, Frank called directory assistance and asked to place a call to Omar Lewiston.

"Hello?" It was clearly the voice of an old man.

"Omar? This is Frank Murphy."

"Kind of figured I might be hearing from you sometime soon."

"Does that mean Lynn is with you?"

"She's here all right. Not too happy and not at all her talkative self, but she's here."

"Do you think she'd be willing to talk to me on the phone?"

"I don't know," Omar admitted. "She didn't say that she wouldn't. Let me go get her."

Frank waited in silence while Omar went in search of Lynn. He prayed that she'd come to the phone and at least let him explain how important she was to him. Maybe he could offer to rearrange the trip plans. Maybe they could go to Mexico after New Year's.

"Hello, Frank." Her words were clipped, her tone devoid of emotion.

"I'm so glad you're safe. I was so worried," Frank began. "Why didn't you at least leave me a note telling me where you'd gone?"

"I didn't think you'd even notice I was gone," Lynn said flatly.

"Lynnie, that's not fair. You know I love you. I was frantic when I couldn't reach you and then I called Cindy and found out you'd taken a leave of absence. Why didn't you wait to talk this over with me when I got home?"

"Who could ever say when that might be?" Lynn countered angrily. "I've sat at home many a night waiting for you, and you might say, I'm done waiting around."

"What do you mean by that?" Frank asked, fearing he already knew her meaning.

"I mean that I'm here with Gramps and I'm thinking hard about what's to become of our marriage."

"I see."

"No, Frank, I don't think you do." She paused and Frank wondered if she was working to control her temper or her emotions. "I'm considering a divorce, or at the very least a permanent separation."

"No!" Frank couldn't stand to even hear the words. Running a hand through his sandy brown hair, he shook his head. "You can't mean that."

"Oh, but I do. I've tried to make it work, but you know Frank, it's hard to make a marriage of two people when one is never around."

"I know and I'm sorry. That's one of the things I want to talk to you about. I know my schedule caused all this, and I'm going to do what I can to put things into proper order."

"It's too late for that."

"No, it's not. Don't say that."

"Look, I know we see things differently. Probably so much so that it's impossible to make a marriage together. I don't believe in divorce, and I know God hates it, but I can hardly ask you to stay in a marriage when I don't plan to be around to be a wife to you. I'm here to think things through and figure out what's to be done."

"Don't you suppose that's something we ought to work on together?"

"There were a lot of things I figured we were supposed to do together," Lynn replied. "You apparently had other thoughts."

Frank didn't know what to say. They were getting nowhere at this rate and he hated trying to resolve anything over the telephone.

"Please just come home and work on this with me. I'll take a few days off from work and—"

"That'll be the day!" Lynn retorted angrily. "You couldn't take a few days off to go on a long-planned anniversary vacation, why would you take time off for this? After all, money's not involved."

Frank felt his own anger stirred at this. The problem was her words hit too close to the truth of the matter. "Look, I want to save this marriage."

"Well, I'm not sure I do," Lynn countered.

"I don't believe you. I know you love me."

"Yes," she replied, her voice softening. "That much is true. I can't deny my love for you. It's the only thing that's kept me there this long." She said nothing for several seconds, then added, "I think you've made a choice in your life that doesn't include me."

"That isn't true and if you'd get off your high horse and come home, you'd see it for yourself. I love you, Lynnie. You have to know that."

"Well, I don't think I do," Lynn replied, her voice once again taking on a tone of defensiveness. "You're seldom home and when you are there your mind is clearly given over to your job. You badger me about having a family, yet you cannot begin to imagine what it is to grow up without a father. Now why don't you just leave me alone and give me the space I need? I'm happy here, which is something I can't say for our place in Chicago." With that she slammed down the phone, never giving Frank a chance to reply.

Rage coursed through him like a wildfire, but even as Frank slammed down his own receiver, he knew

Lynn had some very valid points. Her feelings were completely justifiable, but he couldn't bear that she was happier away from him than with him.

Remembering that his boss George Bridgeton had no idea he was back in town, Frank showered and dressed and made his way over to the office. He'd already decided that if it took taking time off of work to prove his devotion to Lynn, then he'd simply have to make it happen. No doubt Ray Wagner, his newest protegee, could handle his caseload until he was able to return.

"Frank!" George exclaimed in greeting. "I didn't expect you back until tomorrow."

"I know, but something has happened," Frank explained, unfastening the bottom button of his suitcoat.

"With the case?"

Frank shook his head and took a seat. He watched as the older man's expression changed from worry to curiosity.

"Then what?"

"I'm having some problems at home. I need some time off."

George nodded. "Well I know you had planned to take those two weeks off over the holidays, but the Greigs' case came up and—"

"I know, but I want Ray to handle it," Frank replied, still unable to believe he was actually saying the words. It had come to dawn on him as he'd made the drive to the office that he was actually fearful of anyone else stealing his thunder. His mother's words had caused him to do some heavy-duty soul-searching and Frank didn't like the things that kept coming into view.

"May I ask why?"

Frank took pity on the man. George had been a good friend as well as a boss. They were going on four years of working together and Frank knew George respected him. "There are some personal problems that need my attention. I'd rather not say anything more about it just now. Suffice it to say, I need to leave today and I'm not sure how much time I'll need."

"I see," George said, shuffling the papers in his hands. "Will we be able to reach you for troubleshooting?"

Frank sighed. "I suppose if matters were critical, but otherwise, I'd prefer to be completely out of the loop. I don't want to have the conflict of my attention being divided between two issues."

Frank watched as George seemed to consider the matter for a moment. "All right, Frank. You've been a valuable asset to this company, and I know you wouldn't leave if it weren't of the utmost importance. Call me periodically to touch base, but otherwise, we'll try to leave you alone."

"Thank you," Frank said extending a piece of paper. "Here's where you can reach me, but only if it's critical."

George took the paper and studied for a moment. "Are you sure there's nothing else I can do?"

Frank smiled. "You could pray. I've known that to work miracles and right now I need one of major proportions."

George nodded. "I'll do that, Frank."

Two hours later Frank was packed and headed down the interstate. His thoughts were consumed with images of Lynn. Lynn, when he'd first met her. Lynn, when she'd walked down the aisle to marry him. Lynn.

He could see her soft, blond hair feathered around her face and cut to the shoulder. He imagined her blue eyes gazing with longing into his own. He remembered her laugh and the way she always made him take things less seriously. But this time he couldn't take things less seriously. This time his entire future was on the line.

He picked up speed as he cleared the downtown traffic and headed out of town. He almost reconsidered driving to Kansas in favor of flying. A flight could have him to Kansas City in a few hours and from there he could take a commuter flight to Topeka and rent a car to drive down to Council Grove. He could be there in time for supper. It sounded very appealing.

But in his heart, Frank knew he needed to take the time to reconsider his life and what he'd done. He needed to think through the way he'd allowed memories of poverty to direct his course. His mother was right. He'd allowed money to run the show—to rule him, in a way.

Lynn must have picked up on that fact long ago, so why hadn't she said something?

But hadn't she?

Frank was reminded of conversations they'd shared in the past. Conversations where Lynn had begged him to take time off to be home more. He remembered not only the canceled anniversary trip, but other trips they had canceled because of Frank's schedule.

He remembered, too, that Lynn had taken up a variety of activities, which at first Frank had seen as a blessing. But now he realized she was only trying to fill the void he'd created. She was a married woman with an absentee husband. Who could blame her for her discontentment?

He pounded the steering wheel. "What a fool I've been," he declared. "I thought I could build her contentment out of financial security and material possessions, and instead, I drove her away."

But is it too late? he wondered. Could he find a way to win her back?

"Please God, tell me it's not too late."

Chapter 5

"I can't believe he expects me to just drop everything and come running back home," Lynn told her grandfather.

Omar smiled and rubbed his balding head. "Could be he expected you to take your marriage vows seriously. You know, 'til death do us part'?"

Lynn turned back to give her attention to the frying pan where chicken sizzled and popped. "You would say that. You and Grammie had sixty good years of marriage. It would be easy to stay until death if you were married to the right person."

"I never said it was easy," Omar replied.

Lynn looked over her shoulder to see the grin on the old man's wrinkled face. "What do you mean?"

"You think your Grammie and I didn't have our problems? I'm telling you, girl, life with that woman was like being on one of those amusement park roller coasters. We were up one minute and down the next. Life's like that, don't you know."

Lynn turned the heat down on the chicken and came to take a seat opposite her grandfather. "But you two never fought, right?"

Omar laughed heartily at this. "We had some horrible

fights. Grammie made me sleep on the couch more than once."

Lynn knew her expression registered shock. She couldn't help the fact that her mouth had dropped open, and this only made Omar laugh all the harder. "I can't believe you and Grammie ever had problems."

"Oh, Lynnie, everybody has problems. Marriage is hard work. People are individuals and you can't put two individuals together and not expect to have two different opinions and two different solutions for everything. Your Grammie and I had to learn to work through our differences, just as you and Frank will have to do. That is unless you plan to divorce him."

Lynn shuddered. "No, I know that's wrong. But at the same time, I just can't imagine waltzing back into the same situation without resolving some of the problems. Frank just doesn't understand my feelings."

"Have you ever tried to explain them to him?" Omar asked.

Lynn opened her mouth to readily admit she had, but she knew it wasn't true and instantly shut it again.

"I thought not. Why is that, Lynnie?"

Lynn shrugged. "I suppose it's because I've always figured if he cared about me, he'd try to find out these things on his own. Besides, he's never around to talk to for more than a few minutes."

"So your main problem is that Frank is gone all the time?" Omar questioned. "Is that how you see it?"

"Well, it certainly hasn't helped things. Frank talks constantly about having a family and yet he's never there to see how things are. First of all, we certainly couldn't raise a family in that apartment. So what does Frank expect me to do? Am I supposed to go out and find a house or a bigger apartment while he's off on yet another of his business trips?" She barely paused for breath before continuing. "And if we did have children, who would end up raising them? I would. I would be alone most of the time. Frank would be an absentee father and I know how it feels to be on the receiving end of one of those."

Omar nodded. "And it scares you to death to think you might have to relive those memories."

Lynn felt her defenses rise. "Of course I find it frightening. Those were horrible times, Gramps. Mom and Dad were always gone, always playing one concert or another, always sending sweet little cards with lovely messages and balloons and flowers, but never themselves."

They both fell silent for a moment and then Omar reached out and patted her arm. "But it's in the past."

"But it will be the future if I go back to Frank and start having babies!" Lynn exclaimed. "Don't you see? Frank is going to have to change his ways. This whole situation is his fault."

Omar shook his head. "Takes two to make a marriage and it takes two to break one up. What's your fault in all of this?"

"My fault?" Lynn questioned indignantly. "I'm sure I don't understand what you mean. I'm not the one on the road all the time. I'm there at the apartment, faithfully waiting for Frank to return from conquering the dragons of the insurance world."

"Think about it a minute, Lynnie. You must have

played some part in this."

Lynn settled back against the dinette chair. "If you call it a fault that I refuse to have children until I'm sure about becoming a parent, then I guess that's my fault in all of this."

Omar chuckled. "Maybe you could also point to a bit of pride and stubbornness, as well."

Lynn let out a sigh. "I thought you would be on my side."

"I am on your side. But I'm also on Frank's side. You two are one, now. Don't you see that? What affects the one, equally affects the other. You can't just walk away from your marriage and say, 'Well, that didn't work so I'm off to live with Gramps.' Lynnie, it doesn't work that way."

Her shoulders sagged dejectedly. "I just don't have the energy to try and make it work anymore. I'm lonely, Gramps. I'm lonely and sad so much of the time that I don't even like myself anymore."

"That could certainly be a big part of the problem," Omar suggested. "How can Frank like you if you don't even like yourself? I went through a spell like that with my Ketta. She gained a whole bunch of weight after having your mother and she wasn't very happy about it. Said she looked horrible and that she'd just as soon hide in a cave. At first it wasn't that big of a deal. I'd tease her a little, console her a little, do whatever I could to make her feel better. But things just got worse and worse. Pretty soon she didn't want to go anywhere with me, so I had to go to functions by myself. Then I'd get home and she'd rant and rave because I left her alone. I didn't know what to do. I tried to reason with her that some things just had to be done and some events couldn't be avoided, but when she even stopped going to church on Sunday, I knew we'd come as far as we could."

"What did you do?" Lynn questioned, absolutely fascinated that her Grammie had ever worried about things like weight and appearance.

"For a time I didn't do anything. We didn't talk about it, and I stopped trying to help her see reason. The weight stayed on, and she might have even added to it, but it didn't matter to me. I loved her and she looked just fine to me. Then one day, Ketta's good friend Mary came to call. Mary wasn't at all sympathetic like I had been. Mary told Ketta that she was a vain and prideful woman and that both were sinful traits for a woman of God. I was just outside the house, painting the windowsill, but I could see your grandma's face through the window. She looked like Mary had punched her in the nose. Here she had expected a sympathetic and compassionate ear, but Mary told her to stop feeling sorry for herself and either do something about the weight or accept that she was who she was."

"What did Grammie say?"

"For a time, she said nothing. Then she started to cry. She told Mary she couldn't stand the way she'd been acting, but that she seemed hard-pressed to figure out how to change things around. She apologized and promised Mary to do better, but Mary stood her ground. She told Ketta apologies and guilt and promises and so forth were all well and fine, but she wouldn't feel better until she accepted things for what they were. She took your Grandma to the mirror in the hall. I had to move to painting the front door jamb, which I hadn't planned to paint, in order to hear what she had to say."

Lynn grinned. "I can just see you there with your ear straining to catch every sound."

"Yes sir, I was pretty good at eavesdropping. Anyway, Mary told your grandma to take a good look at herself and tell her what she saw. Ketta said, 'I see a fat woman.' Mary just nodded and said, 'What else?' Well Ketta was kind of stumped for a minute so Mary started talking for her. 'You're also a tall woman. You're an attractive woman with beautiful blond hair that doesn't bear a hint of gray. You're a wife and mother and a Sunday school teacher. You're a godly woman who loves her family and has shown great acts of kindness to those around her. At least you were that woman—are you still?'

"Well, by this time, Ketta started crying and she could see what Mary was trying to say. The weight was just one aspect of her physical make up, but it had very little to do with why people loved and needed her. That was an important turning point for her. You'll have to find that important turning point for yourself. You'll have to see beyond the physical and the things that seem so apparent. You need to dig down deep inside and see what's truly motivating your heart. Ketta felt her weight made her unworthy and she focused so much on that one thing, that the things that had made her worthy to so many people were forfeited. Well, at least for the time being. She found her way back.

Learned to be content with herself and pretty soon, the weight wasn't an issue anymore. She started getting involved again and doing all the things she'd done before and pretty soon she realized the weight had dropped off on its own accord."

"But how does that help me?" Lynn asked.

Omar patted her arm again. "You're afraid of a great many things right now. You feel unloved and unworthy for whatever reasons you want to choose. You need to look into your heart and figure out what the real problem is, Lynnie. I seriously doubt that either you or Frank are truly dealing with the real problem. Frank obviously is worried about having enough money for his family. Has he ever told you why? Did he grow up without a great many of the things he needed?"

"I don't know," Lynn said, shaking her head. "He's never really talked about it. All I do know is that he had a happy childhood and that's why he wants lots of kids. He wants to relive those moments, I guess."

"I'd talk to him," Omar told her seriously. "I'd tell him why you're so afraid. How painful your own memories are, and how you fear your children will grow up under someone else's care like you did."

Lynn got up to turn the chicken, all the time thinking about what Gramps had said. Maybe there was something to it. Maybe she was only seeing the surface problem as the issue, instead of the real, underlying cause.

"Mom and Dad were never there for me," she said all of the sudden. "They missed my high school graduation and very nearly missed my wedding. They were gone when I had school programs." She paused for a moment remembering a particularly painful memory. "Even when I had the lead in the school play when I was a freshman in high school, they were on the road somewhere performing."

"And your point is?" Gramps coaxed.

Lynn put the turning fork down and rejoined Omar at the table. She didn't sit, however, but stood staring down at him. "My point is, they were gone more than they were there. They missed most every important moment in my life. They were never there, Gramps and I really resent that."

"So, you going to keep carrying the bitterness around with you all of your life?" he asked softly.

Lynn studied the balding head and wrinkled face for a moment. His glasses and bulbous nose made him look even older than his eighty-one years, but Lynn didn't care. She loved this man more than anyone in the world and he was the only one who could ask such a question of her and not have Lynn retaliate in anger.

"I suppose you have a point, Gramps."

"Doesn't solve the problem, but it sure sheds some light on things, don't you think?"

Lynn nodded. "Yes, I guess it does. I suppose I have a great deal to think about."

"You can't ever help the future by carrying the mistakes of the past into it. We need to learn from our mistakes, and the mistakes of others. Your mom and dad were wrong to leave you so much. They probably should have never had children, just as you feel you shouldn't have them. But I know I would have regretted that choice. I loved having you around. I loved, maybe selfishly so, having you girls spend the summer with us. I'm sorry it wasn't enough."

Lynn instantly felt remorse for her words. She'd never meant to make Gramps feel bad. "You and Grammie were my life. You were the only ones who got me through the bad times. Don't ever think you weren't enough," she said, hugging the man around the neck. She kissed his bald head and added, "You were, and still are, everything a girl could want in a grandfather. I wouldn't change anything about you."

Omar laughed. "If your Grammie were here she'd give you a long list of things she'd like to have seen me change."

"Then I would certainly have to question her sanity," Lynn replied. "Because I think you're perfect."

Chapter 6

Frank wasn't sure what kind of greeting he'd get when he reached the Lewiston farm, but he held onto his determination to force Lynn's hand. If she wanted to play a game of bluff or otherwise, he was going to stand his ground and see the thing through. There was no way he could allow his marriage to just fall apart, and whatever he needed to do, he would do.

At least this was his resolve as he parked his car in the Lewiston driveway. Without worrying about his things, Frank made his way to the house and drew a deep breath. "Help me through this, Lord," he whispered, then knocked loudly on the screen door.

The cold air chilled him as he waited for someone to answer. He'd passed through snow and sleet on his way from Chicago to Council Grove, but his desire to see Lynn and figure a way to make things work had been all the encouragement he'd needed. Even when the road advisory on the radio had suggested all nonessential vehicles stay off the roads, Frank had pushed on. Now, as the snow came down in earnest and the lead gray skies seemed darker than ever, he wondered if he'd be allowed to stay.

The door finally opened, and Frank came face to

face with Lynn. He smiled kind of sheepishly, hoping she would see it as a gesture of his willingness to work on their problem.

"Hi," he said softly.

"What are you doing here?" Lynn questioned. Then looking beyond him at the snow, she added, "We're due for at least six inches of snow. Didn't you think about that before heading down here?"

"I thought maybe you'd be at least a little glad to see me. I thought maybe we could talk through our problems."

Lynn seemed to consider this before stepping aside for Frank to come into the house. "I suppose since you're here and since the weather is turning bad, I have no other choice but to let you stay."

Frank laughed. "At least you still care enough to take pity on me."

Lynn had turned to precede him down the hall, but at this she stopped and her expression looked so pained that Frank immediately wanted to comfort her. "I never said I didn't care, Frank. It wouldn't hurt this much if I didn't care."

He immediately felt sorry that he'd laughed and made a joke of the situation. "I didn't mean it that way. I was just hoping to lighten up the situation."

Lynn said nothing more but led him into the kitchen. "Do you want some coffee?"

"Sure, that sounds great," Frank replied, wondering how to get her to open up and discuss the issues at hand. "Will you have some, too?"

Lynn looked at him blankly for a moment, then

nodded. "All right." She brought two cups of black coffee, then sat down at the small dinette set.

Frank looked at the set and smiled. "You know reproductions of these are selling like hotcakes up in Chicago. That 1950s chrome and Formica seems to appeal to a lot of folks."

"Probably reminds them of what they used to know," Lynn replied softly.

Frank took the seat opposite her and nodded. "Probably. Say, where's Omar?"

"He's gone out to take care of some things around the yard. He says when the weather folks say six inches it's more likely to be twelve. Snow is very hard to predict."

"I see." He sipped the coffee, then decided to get right to the point. "Look, I know you're hurting, but I'm hurting too. We can't just let this thing come between us. I've always known that we'd have our ups and downs, I just never expected you to run away at the first threat of trouble."

"It wasn't the first threat of trouble that sent me running," Lynn replied, her eyes never quite meeting his.

"All right, then why don't you tell me what this is all about?"

Lynn drew a deep breath and nodded. "I suppose I should. Gramps would say it was only right." She looked down at her cup and sighed. "I love you, Frank. There's no doubt about that. I've loved you since I was eighteen years old. I wouldn't have married you otherwise. I loved you for your serious, take-charge attitude and for the drive and motivation that I knew would see us through the problems to come."

"But?" Frank interjected, knowing beyond a doubt that there was more to come.

"But I can't go on like we've been living. You're never home. You care more about your job, than you do about me." She held up her hand as Frank started to protest. "No, hear me out. You drove all this way, now the least you can do is listen."

"All right."

"It isn't just the trip being canceled or the fact that you're seldom around to go places with me. It's that even when you are home, you aren't there. Your mind is on your clients and the problems you have to resolve in order to remain top dog at Bridgeton National Life. You know more about your client's needs and concerns than you do mine.

"I've tried to make it work. I've tried to fill the void, but it just isn't any good any more. I feel like I'm tap dancing on top of a moving train and sooner or later I'm going to fall off or crash up against a tunnel or something else. I'm tired, and I'm not sure I have the energy to go on trying."

"I didn't know you felt this way," Frank said softly. He felt confused by her words, wondering how things could have gotten to this point without him realizing that something was amiss.

"I suppose my fall or my tunnel came in the form of your desire to have a baby," Lynn said. This time she raised her face to meet Frank's gaze.

He could see the pain. Her anguish and sorrow cut

him like a knife. She wasn't just being testy or selfish. Lynn appeared completely consumed by her misery.

"It isn't that I don't want to have children, Frank. I think you know that full well. I've always wanted kids. I even wanted the big family you dreamed of. But what I don't want is to raise those children alone. My mother and father were never around when I was growing up. The symphony consumed all their time and took them on the road nearly as much as Bridgeton Life takes you.

"I had nannies and baby-sitters and in the summer I had Grammie and Gramps, but it wasn't enough. I needed my mother and father. I needed them both and they were always gone or too busy. I remember once when I tried to tell my father about a difficult test I had managed to ace. He was busy going through sheet music at the time and I figured I only had half of his attention. But in truth, I didn't have any of it. When I told him about the test he said, 'Well, try harder next time.' If he'd slapped me in the face it would have hurt less."

"Lynn, I'm so sorry," Frank told her. He'd had no idea that she was harboring this hurt from the past. "Why didn't you ever tell me about your childhood?"

Lynn shrugged. "I didn't want anyone to know how painful it had been. I thought I could leave it in the past, but when I saw you becoming the same man my father had been, I knew it had followed me right into the future."

"I'm not like that," Frank replied.

"Yes, you are," Lynn said indignantly.

"How can you say that?" Now Frank was starting to get mad. This accusation was far from the truth. He was like his own father, gentle and caring. He would be the same kind of father to his children. He certainly wouldn't resemble the kind of man Lynn had just described.

Lynn looked at him sadly. "I can say it because I've seen it in play. Do you remember when we had Chinese food when you got back from that post-Thanksgiving trip?"

"Sure. It was great."

"You asked me then if it came from the Red Dragon Restaurant," Lynn continued. "I told you no, that I had made it. It was a recipe I learned in cooking class. Do you remember what you said?"

Frank scanned his memory, but it was blank. He didn't remember Lynn saying she had made the meal. "No," he finally replied.

"You went on with your conversation as though I'd said, 'Yes.' You said, 'I've never had a bad meal from the Red Dragon and this one is no exception.' Then you proceeded to compliment their seasonings and the tenderness of the pork."

"I can't believe that I did that," Frank said defensively. He couldn't remember any of it and this alone bothered him as much as her words. "I'll bet you just misunderstood what I meant."

"Like I've misunderstood spending 360 days of the year by myself?" she retorted angrily.

"That's not fair. I haven't been gone that much. Look, I know I travel a lot, but that's what my job required."

"And the job of parenting requires a mother and a

father. And while I realize a great many children grow up without one or the other, and sometimes without both, I will not raise a child by myself."

"Who said you'd have to?" Frank countered, stunned by her supposition.

Lynn slammed her hands down on the table. "Who did you plan to have help me? You're never there. We're you going to hire a man to play your part?"

"That's hardly fair, Lynnie."

"Maybe not, but it is accurate."

"No, it's not."

"Then tell me," Lynn began, her voice much calmer, "what did you plan to do? Were you going to quit your job? Were you going to cut back your hours? How were you going to ensure that I didn't raise our baby alone?"

Frank ran his hand back through his sandy brown hair. It was a nervous habit he'd picked up whenever tough issues gave him cause to stop and rethink his strategy. He realized he would have to come clean with Lynn about his own past. He would have to explain his fear of poverty and the fear he had for his family.

"I have to. . .tell you something," Frank said hesitantly. "Just as you have fears from your childhood, I have my own." Lynn looked at him oddly, but said nothing, so Frank continued. "I grew up in a big family, which you knew. There were a total of seven people living in one house, my four brothers and sisters and my mom and dad and me. My dad had a low paying factory job, and while he did his best to see that we had what we needed, sometimes that just wasn't possible.

"I can still remember my mom and dad praying about the finances—giving their worries over to God, because they had no idea where the next meal was going to come from. Once, my mom told us kids we were having a contest and that the person who came up with the most creative way to use her homemade catsup and bread for a meal would win a prize. We kids thought it great fun. We made catsup sandwiches and soup from catsup and water. My sister even tore up chunks of bread and blended them in catsup and sugar and baked it in the oven. We ate and laughed and joked about what was best. My sister won the prize, a much coveted candy bar, which she promptly allowed my mother to cut into five equal pieces. I never knew until I was older that the game had come because there was nothing else to eat. Mom had nothing but bread and homemade catsup to feed her five children. The candy bar had been gift from the lady next door who thought my mom was starting to look a bit on the thin side. Of course, Mom never had any of it and we kids were too excited to worry or wonder where it came from."

Lynn's expression seemed to soften. "I can't even imagine. We never worried about our food."

Frank nodded. "That's why money concerns me so much. My mother admonished me that I was making money my god. And I think she just might be right. I figured if we had a good nest egg and all the material things my folks lacked, then I could relax and bring children into the world and they would never have to suffer like I did."

"But I thought you said you were happy."

"I was," Frank answered.

"Then this attitude is foolish."

"No more so than yours. You figure because your parents were always gone, that I would be that way with my children."

"Well, isn't that how it will have to be? If you're going to worry about whether or not we have enough to eat, you'll just keep on working at that ridiculous pace you've set and the kids and I will be left to fend for ourselves."

"That's not true!" Frank declared, his anger getting the better of him.

"It is true!"

"No more so than—"

"You know," Omar said, coming in through the back door and shaking off snow, "I could hear you arguing as I came up the walk. I don't think I've ever known two bigger ninnies."

"Don't you dare take his side," Lynn said, getting to her feet. "I won't have you both ganging up on me." With that she stormed from the room, leaving Frank and Omar to stare at each other.

"What was that all about?" Frank questioned.

"Oh, we've been discussing this situation," Omar said, going to the coffee maker to pour himself a cup of coffee.

"And did you come to any conclusions?"

Omar smiled. "I'll tell you the same thing I told her."

"Which is?"

"You've shared ten years together and it's downright foolish to throw that away. You both need to decide what's important and what isn't and you'd better do so in a hurry."

"Family is important to me," Frank replied flatly. "I want children and Lynn's afraid I'll never be around long enough to help raise them and be a real father to them."

"You suppose your long hours and traveling has anything to do with her fears?" Omar questioned, taking the chair Lynn had vacated.

"I suppose it does, but a man has to work. I can't just up and quit a good job in order to be home all the time. I don't know what Lynn expects from me, but when we married, we both agreed that I would work and she would stay home and take care of our children. She used to like the idea."

"Maybe she liked the idea of family. You know her own was kind of taken from her at an early age."

"She told me about her parents. She said that's why she was afraid of having kids. I think she's way off base here. I see nothing wrong with having children and still maintaining my job. I probably wouldn't travel as much, but—"

"You'd better get you a mighty fine picture album," Omar interjected.

"Huh?" Frank was taken totally aback by this.

"You'd better get a picture album. One with lots of pages," Omar answered. "You'll need it if you plan to keep up with your traveling and long hours and still want to see those kids. Course, it won't be the same as being there with them, seeing them do things for the first time, speak their first words. Photographs aren't the same as making your own memories."

The old man finished his coffee and got up. "You can have the room at the top of the stairs. I'd suggest with the way that snow is coming down, you'd best be bringing your things in right away."

Frank could only stare and nod. His mind was still on Omar's words. Reluctantly, he got to his feet and made his way out to the car. He had no reason to doubt Omar knew what he was talking about, but the truth bothered Frank in a major way. A lot of men raise good families and don't necessarily work an eight to five job, he told himself. He thought of his friend Mike and how happy Mike seemed with his family, in spite of his traveling position. Then just as quickly, Frank remembered a conversation he'd had with Mike. Mike had spoken of missing his oldest son's birthday. It was a meeting that couldn't be avoided, and Mike had bought the child an outrageously expensive gift to make up for it, but his son wanted nothing to do with it or him.

Would my kids feel that way? Frank wondered as he pulled his suitcases from the trunk. The ordeal had really hurt Mike. Glancing back at the house, Frank realized he hadn't begun to think this thing completely through. Lynn was angry and hurt, and Omar was stuck in the middle. With a sigh, he headed back to the house. He had a tough road ahead of him, if he was going to figure out a way to save his marriage.

Chapter 7

By the time Lynn came down to breakfast the next morning, both Omar and Frank were wrestling a Christmas tree into the house through the back door.

"Good morning," Frank called enthusiastically.

"Morning," Lynn answered, trying hard not to look directly at him. She'd cried most of the night and now her eyes were red and swollen. There was no hope Frank wouldn't realize what had taken place, but nevertheless, she tried to conceal her face.

"Omar suggested we get us a Christmas tree. I thought it sounded like a smart idea."

"Figured you two could decorate it while I go to town," Omar added.

Lynn poured herself a cup of coffee. "What about the snow, Gramps? Do you think it's wise to drive by yourself? I could take you wherever you needed to go."

"I wouldn't hear of it. Don't go figuring me for an old man who can't take care of himself," Omar told her. He and Frank maneuvered the tree past Lynn and into the living room.

Lynn followed at a conservative pace. She had no heart to tell her beloved Gramps that her heart wasn't into celebrating Christmas. She was confused by her feelings and this just wasn't helping matters at all.

She watched silently as the men arranged the tree and stood back to admire their handiwork. Frank looked so good to her and all she really wanted to do was run and throw her arms around him. He looked much like he had the first time she'd laid eyes on him. He had come down to do community service at the local homeless shelter. Lynn was working in the day-care center and playing with about half a dozen toddlers when he'd popped into the room. He'd worn blue jeans, just as he did now, and a sweatshirt that very nearly resembled the one he wore today. His hair was tousled and windblown and his blue eyes studied her with such intensity that he had made her blush.

Pulling her thoughts back into the present, she realized Frank was studying her now, just as he had studied her then. Only this time he didn't smile.

"You kids have a good time with this. You'll find the box of decorations over there on the piano bench," Omar said, pointing. "I'll be gone for a couple of hours, so don't look for me until after lunch."

Lynn wanted to say something, but her throat constricted the words. Frank walked with Omar to the door, said something that she couldn't hear, then laughed and patted the old man on the back. They seemed conspiratorially chummy. Too chummy as far as Lynn was concerned. This was her haven and sanctuary and Frank had invaded it.

Frank closed the door and turned to give her a sympathetic nod. "I see by your face, you've spent most of the night crying. I won't say I did the same, but

I sure didn't sleep."

Lynn hadn't expected him to admit to being just as troubled over the situation as she was. "I don't suppose either of us will sleep much until we get past this."

Frank shook his head. "I don't want to get past it if it means losing you. Lynn, I don't want to give up on our marriage. It's that simple. I'll do whatever I can to make it work."

"I wish I could believe that," Lynn replied, walking absentmindedly over to the box of Christmas decorations.

"You can," Frank assured her, coming to stand beside her. "Look, we've got some issues to sort through. Just tell me what you want me to do, and I'll do my best to see it through."

Lynn shook her head. "I don't want to run your life. As much as you might think that's the case, it isn't."

"What do you want, Lynn?"

"I don't know." She pulled out a string of lights and let Frank take them from her. "It just doesn't seem like we're cut out to be married to each other."

Frank had just started to wrap the lights around the spindly spruce. At Lynn's words he stopped. "Do you really believe that? After ten years of marriage?"

Lynn picked up a crocheted snowflake ornament and shrugged. "I don't know what I believe anymore. I thought I knew. I thought I understood it very clearly. But last night I prayed and prayed and nothing seems very clear."

"What about our love? Isn't that clear?"

Lynn looked up and allowed her gaze to lock with his. "My love is."

"But mine isn't? Is that it?"

"I don't feel very loved," she barely whispered.

Just then the telephone rang, and Lynn moved to picked it up. "Lewiston residence." She glanced to where Frank stood trying to adjust the string of lights. "Yes, he's here."

Frank looked up as if surprised. "It's for me?"

Lynn nodded and put down the receiver. "Why am I not surprised?"

Frank went to the phone, while Lynn forced herself to focus on decorating the tree. George Bridgeton, himself, was calling for her husband. It would be important and it would no doubt require Frank's utmost attention. It might even necessitate his return to Chicago.

Her heart ached at the thought. Surely he wouldn't just up and leave. Not when so much was at stake. Lynn tried not to listen to Frank's animated conversation, but she couldn't help it.

"If there's another way to do this, I'd rather not," Frank said firmly.

He glanced at her, but Lynn looked quickly away. She didn't want him to feel pressured by her stares. If he stayed, she wanted him to do so because he wanted to. Because he knew how much it would mean to her if just once he told Bridgeton National Life, "No."

"All right, where?" Frank asked, running a hand through his hair.

Lynn could always tell his degree of frustration by this move. Things weren't going well, and suddenly she knew she'd lost another round.

"Yes. I understand," Frank replied. "But you owe me." He hung up the phone and looked at Lynn with such a pained expression that she almost forgot to be hurt. Almost.

"I have to fly up to Chicago."

"I figured as much."

"I tried to get out of it. You must have heard me," Frank said, coming toward her.

"I tried not to listen," Lynn replied, turning away from him on the pretense of hanging another ornament.

"George said the case is falling apart. It could cost Bridgeton millions."

"Sorry to hear that." She knew her tone left him little doubt as to her mood over this latest development.

"I have to drive to Topeka. I'm supposed to catch a hop to Kansas City and then to Chicago. I'll be back as soon as possible."

"Whatever," Lynn replied, trying hard not to cry. He was leaving her again. Leaving her for his job and making it very clear that she could never hope to count on him being there solely for her.

"Lynn," he said, barely whispering her name. He'd come to stand directly behind her and put his hands on her shoulders. "We can get through this, but we have to be willing to work together. We'll have to compromise a few places, but I know we can work this out."

Lynn refused to turn and let him see the tears that had come to her eyes. "I'm glad you're so certain."

Frank turned her very gently and lifted her face to meet his. "Please don't cry. I love you, Lynnie. I love you more than you will ever know." He traced a tear with his finger. "I promise to make this as short as possible."

"Just go," Lynn told him, trying to pull away.

He wouldn't let her go and instead, encircled her with his arms and held her tightly against him. "I don't want to go," he whispered.

"But you will," she countered, growing completely still in his arms. "You will."

And a half an hour later, he did just that. Lynn listened to the echo of the door latching and forced herself to keep from running after him. *I have to be strong,* she told herself. *I can't fall apart.*

She heard his car start up and felt her resolve waver. Almost running to the radio, she switched it on and turned up the volume. A rich baritone voice was just concluding "O Holy Night," and the DJ was segueing right into a choral version of, "O Christmas Tree."

"O Christmas tree," Lynn joined in rather bitterly. "O Christmas tree, guess once again it's just you and me."

Frank sat opposite George Bridgeton and handed him a stack of signed papers. "It's finalized and both parties have agreed to the settlement."

George smiled broadly. "A job well done. I can't thank you enough."

"I'm glad I could help, but I'm sorry to say, it will probably be the last time."

George's smile faded. "What are you saying, Frank?"

Frank had given the matter much consideration. For as long as the negotiations had taken between the two parties, he could hardly think of anything but Lynn's sorrowful expression upon the news that he was leaving.

"I suppose I'm resigning my position," he replied. "I know it sounds crazy, but this job has taken a huge toll on my marriage, and I can't go on without making significant changes."

"Such as?" George asked softly.

"Such as an eight to five schedule where I can be fairly certain of going home each night at a regular time."

"What else?"

Frank sighed. "That's pretty much it. I need to stop traveling so much. In fact, for a time, I probably need to stop traveling altogether."

"And if I told you I had a position that would allow all of this and result in an increase in salary, would you stay?"

Frank looked at George for a moment before answering. "Are you saying such a position exists?"

George grinned. "I am."

Frank swallowed hard. He hadn't dared to allow himself to even believe such a thing was possible. He'd prayed for practically the entire flight home, begging God to give him the strength to forget his worries over money. He wanted to prove once and for all to Lynn that she meant more to him than the job. Now it appeared, God had honored his faith—faith that hadn't come easy given the details of his past.

"I can't begin to explain what I've been through," Frank replied. "I've been praying constantly about the situation and it seemed my only hope was to quit my job. Lynn feels I've put my career ahead of her, and I can't say as I blame her. I'm gone more than I'm home and lately I've been bugging her about having a family. She put her foot down and told me she wasn't about to start having kids if there wasn't going to be a father around to help raise them."

"Smart woman," George said, quite seriously. "And just so you know it, Frank, I've been praying, too. Ray told me what happened and how you found out that Lynn had gone without a word. I just started adding everything up and figured a change of pace was probably in order for you. However, I didn't want to force it on you."

"So what did you have in mind?" Frank asked, almost afraid to know.

"I'd like you to be my vice president. My wife would kind of like to see me take more time off, too." He laughed. "Sounds like our wives could probably become good friends. We'll have to get them together sometime."

Frank laughed for the first time in days. It felt as though a tremendous weight had been lifted from his shoulders. "This is almost too good to be true."

"It's answered prayer for both of us. We can discuss the details of the position later, but I have a feeling that like Dorothy in *The Wizard of Oz*, you're just itching to get back to Kansas."

"Yes, sir," Frank admitted, "I am."

"Then go. There's a ticket waiting for you at O'Hare and a commuter will take you from Kansas City to Topeka. The rest is up to you," George said with a smile.

"You can't imagine what this means to me," Frank replied, getting to his feet.

"I was once young like you. I missed out on a great deal that related to my family and I've always regretted it. I hope to keep you from doing the same thing."

"Me, too."

"Now aren't you glad I talked you into Christmas

shopping?" Omar asked Lynn.

Lynn smiled up at him. "Yes, it was a good idea." She continued glancing into the shop windows of Main Street Council Grove. "I still haven't figured out something for Frank. Not that he probably wants anything from me."

"A photo album," Omar said without any explanation.

"What?"

"Trust me. Get the man a photo album. They've got some real pretty ones in here," Omar said, pulling Lynn into one of the stores.

She shrugged and let Omar lead her to where the photograph supplies were stashed rather sloppily on a shelf near the back of the store. Omar looked through the meager supply, then waved over a store clerk.

"Where's that real nice album you had here last week? The one with the silver plating on the front—makes it look like a picture frame."

The girl smiled. "Oh, I know the one you mean. I think we still have one of those in the back. Hold on a minute." She took off down the aisle and Omar smiled.

Lynn had no idea what the big deal was with a photograph album, but at least it was something to give Frank—just in case he came back in time for Christmas. She felt completely empty inside. Frank meant the world to her. She'd spent most of the time since he'd gone praying and thinking, and the conclusion she'd come to was to go home.

She walked a few steps away and toyed with a selection of wallets while Omar conducted business with the salesgirl. *Home.* That's all she really wanted.

Staying with Gramps had been a blessing, but when Frank had come to her there, she realized how empty even this haven had been. She belonged with Frank. She loved Frank. And somewhere in her silent nights she had decided that even if she couldn't have him on a full-time basis, she would take whatever she could get. She would go home to her husband and raise the family they both wanted, and whether or not he ever understood her need, well, she'd live with the consequences.

"You going to stand there staring off into space all day?" Omar questioned.

Lynn looked up and realized he'd finished with the selection of the album and now stood at her side. "Sorry," she said, smiling sheepishly.

"Come on," he said, acting as though it weren't important. "I have the album. You'd better pick out some wrapping paper."

Lynn nodded and followed, but her thoughts were of her marriage and of all the complications she had created by running away from her problems. God had come to her in a very real fashion in His Word—encouraging her to let loose of her worries about the future.

Overhead the store intercom played Christmas carols. Lynn smiled as the singers joyfully exclaimed, "Let it snow, let it snow, let it snow."

"Let it go, let it go, let it go," she murmured to the tune.

"What was that?" Omar questioned, looking at her curiously.

"Oh, nothing," Lynn countered. "I was just singing."

Chapter 8

Lynn and Omar returned from the Christmas Eve services, neither one saying much about Frank's obvious absence. Lynn could tell Gramps wanted to comfort her, but he said nothing, choosing instead to concentrate on the snowy road.

"I'm going home," Lynn finally said.

Gramps nodded. "Thought it through, did you?"

"Yes. I've decided that having Frank part of the time is better than not having him at all. I love him, Gramps."

"I know you do, and you know what else?"

"No, what?"

"He loves you, too. I had a nice long talk with that boy when we were scouting out a Christmas tree. He's going through a hard time, but he knows what's right and wrong and he knows what he needs to do. I think if you give him half a chance, he'll make this work out for the both of you."

Just then, as they rounded the bend to the Lewiston farm, the truck's headlights beamed out across Frank's car.

"I hope you're right, Gramps," Lynn said softly. "I pray, you're right."

Omar parked his truck beside the cars, the tires

sliding ever so slightly in the packed snow. Omar handled it without any noticeable concern. "Not bad for an old man, eh?"

"No," Lynn replied, leaning over to give him a kiss on the cheek. "Not bad at all. In fact, I'd say you're something pretty special, Gramps."

Just then, Frank switched on the porch light and emerged from the house. He pushed his hands deep into his pockets. "I let myself in," he called out as Omar and Lynn got out of the truck. "Hope you don't mind."

"You're family," Omar replied. "I would hope you'd have sense enough to let yourself in out of the cold."

"We went to church," Lynn offered as explanation.

Frank looked at her and smiled. It warmed her through to the bone. How she loved this man. When he looked at her the way he was just now, Lynn could very easily forget there was ever any problem. She missed him. Missed his touch and his kiss. Missed his teasing and his long speeches on the injustices of the court system. She just missed him.

"I thought you might have. I tried to get here earlier, but the commuter flight was delayed in Kansas City."

"Lynnie, I'm going up to my room. I kind of figure on getting to bed early tonight," Gramps told her as they climbed the porch steps. He gave her a wink, then kissed her lightly on the head. "If you need me, you'll know where I am."

He walked into the house, letting the screen door bang against the jamb. Lynn stared after him for a moment, then turned her attention to Frank. *Please God,* she prayed, *let us work this out so that we both feel good about going home together.*

"I'm glad you're here," she finally said.

"You are?" Frank asked hopefully.

Lynn nodded. "Yes. Come on inside. I think we should talk."

They settled themselves on Omar's well-worn couch. Everything in the house looked like it had been purchased in the 1950s and the couch was certainly no exception with its rectangular straight-backed style and orange-rust upholstery.

Lynn turned slightly so she could see Frank's face. She drew a deep breath and nervously smoothed down the edges of her pink angora sweater. "I've been thinking."

"Me, too."

"Things aren't perfect, but they're even worse now that we're completely apart."

"Yes," Frank agreed, his blue-eyed gaze piercing her heart.

"Oh, Frank," she murmured his name. "I've been so lonely. I thought it was bad at home, but it's worse here. I came to Gramps' house, remembering how I always felt secure and happy here, but that was before I met you and fell in love."

"I'm sorry you were lonely at home." His voice was soft and warm, the sincerity of his heart quite evident. "I never meant it to be that way."

"I know."

Silence filled the room for several seconds before she continued. "I know you have to work, and now I guess I can better understand why your job is so important to you."

"I quit my job."

"What!" Lynn nearly jumped up from the couch. "You what?"

Frank grinned mischievously at her. "That's what you wanted, isn't it?"

"Well. . .no. . .I mean. . .maybe," she sputtered. "What are we going to do? Did you really quit?"

Frank laughed and rubbed the palm of his hands against his jean-clad thighs. "In a sense. I went to George as soon as the case was settled. I told him I couldn't continue to travel and work all the crazy hours I was giving him. I told him it was destroying the only really important thing in my life. You."

Lynn felt tears come to her eyes. "Oh, Frank. I can't believe it."

"Well, it's true," he said. "George was very understanding. Said, he'd been praying about it and he knew I needed a change. He accepted my resignation and offered me another position."

"Another position?"

"Yes. You're now looking at Bridgeton National's newest vice president."

"And you won't be gone so much of the time?"

"Nope," Frank said, smiling. "I'm going to be an eight-to-fiver and I'll leave traveling to Ray. There might come the need for an occasional trip or a few overtime hours, but George assured me it would be minimal. He even gave us a Christmas present."

"This was gift enough," Lynn said, barely able to speak.

Frank held up two airline tickets. "Our trip to Mexico."

"What?" Lynn could hardly believe what she was seeing or hearing. "Our anniversary trip?"

"Yes, ma'am." Frank held them out to her, but Lynn pushed them aside and slowly came across the couch to put herself in Frank's arms.

"Last night, I told God that if I could only have you part of the time, even a few days out of the year, it was better than never having you at all." She inhaled deeply and smiled at the scent of his cologne. There was a great deal of happiness in familiar things, she decided.

"I told God that even if most of my nights were silent nights I'd be all right, so long as you came back to me once in a while. I told Him I'd go home and live with whatever time you could give me."

"Oh, honey," Frank murmured, pulling her tightly against him. "I'm so sorry for the lost time. I'm so sorry I allowed money and fear to control me. I'm not saying there won't be any future problems, but I am assuring you that this issue won't be one of them. I see the error of my ways. I know what it nearly cost me."

"Thank you, Frank. Thank you for the best Christmas of my life. Say, I have an idea." She scooted away from him and went to the Christmas tree. "Let's open our presents. I have something for you, but I have to admit, it was Gramps' idea."

"Why should we open our presents now?" Frank questioned curiously. "I kind of liked the snuggling we were doing."

Lynn cocked her head and grinned. "If we open our presents now, we won't be in any hurry to get up in the morning."

Frank jumped up from the couch so quickly he made Lynn squeal in surprise. "Then open mine first," he declared, reaching for a rectangular gift box.

Lynn laughed. "I'll open mine, while you open yours." She handed him the wrapped present and took the box.

"It's a deal."

They opened their gifts, and Lynn couldn't help but gasp at the contents of her gift box. "Oh, Frank. It's exquisite." Inside was an antique jewelry box.

"Lift the lid," he encouraged.

She did so and listened to the music box rendition of "Silent Night." "I love it," she whispered.

"I hoped you would," he said, reaching out to take hold of her hand. "I have something else for you at home, but this just seemed to speak your name."

"What do you think of your present?" Lynn asked, straining to control her emotions.

Frank finished unwrapping the paper and laughed out loud.

"What?" Lynn questioned. "Gramps said it would be perfect."

"It is," Frank replied.

"Then why are you laughing?"

"Omar told me I'd better set my priorities straight if I planned to have a family. He said, I'd need to get a good photograph album if I insisted on keeping my job and seeing anything of my family."

Lynn stiffened slightly at the mention of children. She wanted to bring the subject up herself. Wanted to tell him that she'd decided to have a baby as soon as God allowed them to conceive. It seemed such a delicate subject, however, that she'd just not gotten around to it yet, and now Frank was speaking of it and she didn't know what to say.

Frank sensed her mood and put the album aside. Reaching out, he took the music box from her hands and put it with the album. Pulling her with him to the couch, Frank drew her into his arms. "There's something else I want to say," he told her, pushing her back just far enough so he could see her face. "You don't have to have a baby—if you don't want to. I was wrong to badger you about a family. Children should come into a home where they are wanted by both parents. I would never force you to have my baby, and I just want you to know that, here and now."

Lynn smiled, knowing what it had cost him to say those words. "Frank, I want to have your baby. I want to have lots of your babies. I just wanted to have them with you."

He reached up to touch her face and Lynn felt her pulse quicken. "I think that's a workable situation."

"You think so, eh?" Lynn teased.

"It would make a rather nice Christmas present, don't you think?"

Lynn laughed out loud, then realized Omar was just upstairs. "Perhaps, we should take this to my room."

Frank had her up on her feet before she could say another word. Pulling her against him, he kissed her passionately. Lynn melted against him, relishing the feelings of desire that washed over her. No one else existed in the whole world. There was no one but this man—this moment—this love.

Before she knew it, Frank had started walking her towards the stairs. His embrace remained tight, however, and before she could protest, he'd swept her up into his arms.

She giggled out loud.

"Well, it looks like I got my Christmas wish," Omar said, from the top of the stairs.

Lynn felt her face grow hot and Frank just laughed. "Guess we got a little noisy, huh?"

"Sorry, Gramps," Lynn added.

"I'm not," Omar said with a laugh. "I couldn't be happier. Looks like we all get a Merry Christmas."

"Yes," Lynn replied. "And no more silent nights."

epilogue

After two years of acting as Bridgeton National Life's vice president, Frank came to realize just how much he'd missed out on during his years of travel. He was content in a way he could never hope to put into words. God had blessed him over and over, and when all had seemed hopeless, God had seen him through the worst of it and had given him more than he could have ever imagined possible.

Stacking firewood into a sling, Frank whistled a Christmas tune and headed back into his new house. He heard Lynn's voice coming from the living room and laughed to hear to her rearranging the words of yet another Yuletide carol.

"O Christmas tree, O Christmas tree, instead of one baby, I got three."

Frank laughed and looked from where Lynn danced around throwing tinsel on the Christmas tree, to where his triplet daughters sat clapping and laughing at their mother's antics.

To say, they had been surprised by the arrival of triplets was putting it mildly. To say they'd been blessed far beyond comprehension was also an understatement.

"So how are the Murphy women?" Frank questioned,

unloading the wood beside the fireplace.

"We are all just fine," Lynn replied. "The girls think they completely understand this tree business and have decided that next year they will handle the decorating themselves."

Frank laughed and came to embrace his wife. "I'm sure they will give us plenty of help throughout the season. After all, they are starting to walk with rapid agility."

Lynn nodded. "They are something else, aren't they?"

"I'm amazed at this thing which you have done, Mrs. Murphy," Frank told her, giving her a light kiss on the lips. "I never fail to be amazed, even now over a year after their birth."

Lynn pulled back, a mischievous grin on her face. "You think this is something, wait until you see what I do *next* time."

Tracie Peterson

The acquisitions editor for **Heartsong Presents**/Barbour Publishing, and best selling author of over thirty fiction titles, Tracie Peterson lives and works in Topeka, Kansas. First published as a columnist for the *Kansas Christian*, Tracie resigned that position to turn her attention to novels. She has over twenty-three titles with the Heartsong Presents book club and stories in four separate anthologies from Barbour. Other titles include a historical series co-written with Judith Pella and published by Bethany House, and two Portraits romances from Bethany. She is also the author of an upcoming series from Bethany, entitled *Westward Chronicles*. Voted favorite author for 1995, 1996, and 1997 by the **Heartsong Presents** readership, Tracie is also a wife and the mother of three wonderful children.

Hearts United

Debra White Smith

Dedication

To all my spectacular friends at Inspiriational Writers Alive! East Texas Chapter—especially Maxine, Judith, Shirley, Rob, Bob, and Winnie. You guys are beyond wonderful!

Chapter 1

Dr. Ian Lowderman rested his athletic frame on the edge of his Aunt Felicia's hospital bed. Tenderly, he placed her limp, pale hand in his and noted her pulse, weaker and slower than last night. Two weeks ago he never dreamed she would be in the ICU ward at Southwest Texas Methodist Hospital; that he would be her surgeon's consulting physician.

With a groggy smile, Felicia opened tired eyes to stare languidly at her nephew. "Come to check on me again?" she whispered.

"How's my girl?" he teased, forcing a grin against his tightening throat.

"Don't patronize me." Her faint words contradicted her normally spunky spirit. The usual spark in her deep-set brown eyes was no longer there.

A compulsive swallow, and Ian rolled his eyes. "Even from her hospital bed, she keeps me in line."

"You mean from my death. . .deathbed, don't you?" The words squeezed through her throat, dry and cold. Their resolve penetrated her sallow, grayish face. In her soul, his aunt of only fifty was planning to die. The pain, the postsurgery depression had finally overtaken her. When nature was at the peak of its autumnal beauty,

Felicia was withering away like a late rose caught in an early frost.

"You aren't going to die," Ian insisted, his tone much sharper than he intended. Ian gripped her hand as if he could infuse his own life into her. "Listen, Uncle Ed needs you. The church needs you. Your son needs you. I need you."

"But I'm just so. . .so tired." A dry cough wracked her.

Desperately, Ian wished he could reverse the last week. Wished he could have prohibited her from beginning that trip to Oklahoma City to visit her new granddaughter. Wished he could have stopped that car accident that proved fatal for two other drivers. Poor dear, she never even got out of San Antonio.

Aunt Felicia had escaped with a ruptured spleen, lacerated intestines, and a broken leg. The surgery saved her life. But her diabetes severely complicated the healing. Her chance of recovery seemed to diminish with every breath.

She had been a second mother to him. Even though she was his aunt by marriage, Ian had felt closer to her than he did to his dad's own brother, Ed. Growing up, he spent as much time at her house one block down as at his own house.

His mother deserted him and his dad when Ian was only ten. He still remembered all the lonely nights his Aunt Felicia quieted his sobs. Then, the pain dulled with time, and his aunt had created new, happy memories to replace the old ones.

A pastor's wife. An encourager. An angel of mercy to those in need. Never complaining. Always smiling.

In short, everyone fell in love with the slightly overweight woman. Regardless of her auburn hair and creamy skin, she wasn't a raving beauty. But oh, what a beautiful spirit.

Why was she giving up? It seemed so unlike her. Perhaps the pain. Because of her broken leg and lacerated intestines, she had been in extreme pain from the onset. Even though Ian had blazed through medical school and proven himself a brilliant surgeon, he had never experienced the physical complications she now endured. Despite his medical training, Ian knew in his soul he couldn't comprehend her suffering.

"Would you let me pray for you?" he asked, his voice quivering.

A slight nod. Surrounded by the white sheets, I.V. tubing, and the antiseptic smell of the ICU, she looked more forlorn than she had when Ian entered minutes before.

"Dear Lord—" Ian hesitated, choosing words and immediately dismissing them. Most of his thirty-five years he had relied on Aunt Felicia. "Dear Lord—" What did you pray when a loved one was slipping through your fingers like sand? "—please be with Aunt Felicia. She needs You. Lord, don't—don't let her give up. We. . .we need her." Ian's voice broke.

"Amen," Aunt Felicia whispered. A lone tear slipped down her temple. "I'm sorry, dear, but I need. . .I need sleep." She closed her eyes, her labored breathing becoming more rhythmical as sleep claimed her.

Ian tried to force himself to open her chart and stare objectively at her diminishing vital signs. But the overwhelming urge to groan, throw the chart across the room, and demand a resounding "why" from God almost wouldn't be denied.

He had seen the signs more than he cared to remember. She was dying. She needed a miracle.

Feeling as if an autumn chill settled in her bones, Andrea Dillon paced in front of the ICU ward. The last twenty-four hours had been like emotional suicide. Yesterday morning, she dialed Felicia Lowderman's number. When Andrea asked for Felicia, her husband stated that she was in the ICU at Southwest Texas Methodist Hospital. Unsure whether she should tell Felicia's husband who she was, Andrea opted to thank him kindly and prepare to leave. During her journey from Houston to San Antonio, Andrea was washed in a sea of feelings—horror, despair, worry.

In a daze, she checked into the hotel closest to the hospital and spent the night and morning impatiently awaiting visiting hours. Now, she stood outside the ICU ward, fighting tears, fidgeting, desperate for that moment when she could hold her birth mother's hand.

Her birth mother.

For five years, she possessed her birth mother's address and phone number. After tracing Felicia Brown Lowderman, Andrea had written. When Felicia joyfully responded, Andrea experienced an onslaught of emotions she hadn't anticipated. Fear. Uncertainty. Anxiety. And a resurrection of resentment for the person who rejected her at birth. The irony of her resentment was that through Felicia's rejection Andrea received the best Christian parents any kid could want.

Eventually, Andrea wrote a letter back to Felicia. A letter which broke contact. A letter, asking Felicia not to respond. Five years ago, she simply hadn't been ready to handle a relationship with the woman who had rejected her as a helpless infant.

A recent, recurring dream had beckoned Andrea to reverse her decision. For six nights, the dream persisted. In that dream, her mom, a faceless wraith wearing a hospital gown, had teetered on the precipice of a cliff, clutching, calling, clinging to Andrea. As much as Andrea tried to save her, the specter toppled over the edge, screaming for Andrea until the sea-bathed stones embraced her crumpled body in their spiky arms. Andrea knew; she knew somewhere deep in her soul that her birth mother was praying for her to come.

Today. Today Andrea would meet her. Did Felicia, like Andrea, possess a cloud of unruly auburn hair? Did she likewise have a freckled nose? And were her eyes, like Andrea's, as brown as rich chocolate? Soon, Andrea would know.

Other speculations plagued her. Would Felicia be glad to see her? And what about Felicia's family? Would they resent Andrea's intrusion? Did they even know about Andrea? The brief communication they had shared only five years before never answered these questions.

The dream must have been God's way of urging Andrea toward re-establishing the contact. She would have to trust God to take care of what could become a volatile situation.

Please Lord, don't let her die. Not before I've had her in my life. Please keep her alive. Somehow help me help her.

Another glimpse at her sporty wristwatch, and Andrea decided that 9:55 was close enough to the 10 a.m. visiting time. A deep breath, a square of her shoulders, a blot against the threatening tears, and Andrea stepped toward the metallic swinging doors.

But someone exited before she could enter. A tall, sandy-haired someone with blond lashes, blond brows, and a scowl that would stop a hurricane in its tracks. A someone with broad shoulders, pale gray eyes, and a bulky physique. A someone who looked as if he belonged on a Viking ship rather than in surgeon's scrubs.

If Andrea hadn't been so distraught, she would have stopped to take a second look.

His clipped, almost rude, "Excuse me," barely penetrated her consciousness.

"Excuse me," she echoed, trying to sidestep his path.

Just as she reached for the door, she felt his scowl virtually piercing the base of her neck.

"May I ask your name?" he bit out.

Blinking, Andrea turned to stare up at him in blank surprise. "What?"

"Your name. What is it?" A light, intense and protective, glittered in the depths of his pale eyes.

She bristled, resenting his tone, resenting him in a strange way. So odd. She had never even met the man. "Andrea. Andrea Dillon." And, as his face registered shock, fear, dismay, Andrea didn't try to stop her next words. "And your name?"

"Dr. Ian Lowderman."

"Lowderman?" Her blood felt as if it drained to her knees. Her palms produced a clammy film of sweat. Lowderman was her birth mother's married name. Could this giant of a man somehow be related?

"You know me?" His eyes narrowed in speculative glint, as if he were testing her to prove some assumption.

"No. I know the name. I'm here to visit a Felicia Lowderman. Are you related to her? She's—she's my—I'm her—"

"Her daughter?"

"How did you know?"

"I'm her nephew. By marriage. Several years ago she told me about placing a daughter named Andrea for adoption. Plus, you look almost exactly like Aunt Felicia. Except—"

"Except what?" Andrea asked, simultaneously elated by his words and frightened by his increasing scowl.

"Never mind," he clipped. "Do you understand just how sick she is?"

"I know she's been in a serious car accident and is—is in critical condition." Andrea battled burning tears. An urge to punch this tall, arrogant man right in the gut stomped through her mind. The last week of that dread nightmare, the last twenty-four hours of pure anxiety had been bad enough without being interrogated by some overgrown Viking.

"Yes. And I'm her consulting surgeon. I don't believe she needs any more upheaval than she's already had. I've just told the nurses to restrict all of her visitors to her husband and son only."

"But you can't—"

"Yes I can," he said in a measured voice.

"But I'm her daughter. I want to meet her before—if she were to die—I—"

"She might be dying," he rasped as if the admission wrenched his very soul. The unshed tears filling his eyes took away Andrea's urge to punch him. "I asked the nurse to call Uncle Ed in now."

"Then that's all the more reason for me to see her."

"No," he shouted. A passing orderly exposed them to a curious glance. "No," Ian whispered urgently. "Your seeing her might send her into cardiac arrest. Her blood pressure is dangerously low as it is."

Andrea had deliberated these very issues before leaving the hotel that morning. But some urgent, desperate force propelled her to see her birth mother. She agreed in theory with Dr. Lowderman, but simply had to see Felicia or be prepared to die of misery. "My seeing her also just might give her the strength to pull through," she reasoned.

"You don't even know if she wants to see you."

"She wants to see me." Andrea gritted her teeth, the dream still plaguing her.

"There's no way you can know that." He bent to point his index finger right at her nose.

"I know that I made brief contact with her five years ago, and she was more than willing to see me then."

"And you didn't meet her?"

"No." A blink, and Andrea focused on the wisps of reddish blond hair peeking past the neckline of his scrubs. She in no way felt compelled to bear her private feelings to this man. Her emotions were none of his business. Besides, as much as she hated to admit it, Dr. Ian Lowderman was a bit intimidating.

Andrea had always been chunkier than most of her friends, and her athletic build had given her the advantage in school sports. At five-nine, one-hundred-sixty pounds, she wasn't overweight, but she had never felt petite.

Until now.

This man stood at least six-six, and although he didn't appear overweight, his large frame probably tipped the scales close to two-seventy-five.

Impulsively, Andrea stepped backward and conjured every scrap of bravado she possessed. She had gone nose-to-nose with some of her male colleagues several times, never once flinching. She could do it again.

Despite his height and demeanor, Andrea was still determined to see her birth mother—even if she had to sneak in. But her usually expressive face must have spoken her motives.

"I hope you aren't planning to ignore me," he said through tight lips. "If you're like most of the women I've dealt with, you're willing to go to whatever lengths necessary to get what you want, even if it means putting the health of another in jeopardy."

Andrea winced at the venom dripping from his every word. How could he be so unfair? He had never even met her. *The jerk!* "That's not true. If you'd just let me explain—" Regardless of her resolve to fight, Andrea trembled. Too much stress. Too much worry. Too much conflict. And the tears she had held at bay since yesterday morning threatened to gush forth like an angry, hot geyser.

Chapter 2

Ian couldn't believe his actions. In dismay, he listened to himself insult a woman he had never met. And as much as he tried to stop his heated words, they exploded like a volcano.

What was wrong with him?

Aunt Felicia. Her condition so unnerved Ian, so drove him to protect her that he lost all sense of respect for Andrea's feelings.

But Aunt Felicia wasn't the only reason. Because of his mother's desertion, Ian had long ago stopped trusting women, had long ago cast them all into the same mold, whether that was fair or not. Except Aunt Felicia.

Forcing himself to focus on Andrea who abruptly brushed aside a tear, Ian softened. *Poor woman. Her motives just might be pure.*

Regardless of her motives, Ian had to hold his ground. Aunt Felicia was so weak, she simply couldn't withstand the emotional turmoil of seeing a daughter she bore thirty years before. Ian made a spontaneous decision. "Come on," he said, placing a gentle hand on Andrea's hunched shoulder. "Let me buy you a cup of coffee."

The mute fury flashing in her eyes didn't surprise him. Neither did the way she jerked from his touch.

"No thank you," she said through clamped teeth. As if one more second of his presence would nauseate her, Andrea turned and ran toward the opening elevators.

"Andrea. . . Andrea. . ." Ian rushed after her. Ignoring the penetrating stares of the trio of disembarking passengers, Ian stepped onto the elevator only seconds after she did.

She bolted toward the closing door as if he were a deadly poison to be avoided.

"No, wait." He grabbed her arm, and the elevator doors hissed to a close.

"Let go of me," she demanded, rage and fear marring every feature. With three backward steps, she plastered herself against the elevator's wall and glared up at him like a defiant mouse caged with a rattlesnake.

Ian flinched, feeling more and more like a cad. Even though he didn't plan on pursuing a relationship with any woman, he had never planned to frighten one either. Ian wasn't about to leave her until he could repair the negative impression. "I'm not going to hurt you."

"Well you better not, mister." Her voice held a threat of her own.

Silently, he reached past her to push the button for the first floor. "We both could use some coffee."

"I'm not going to have coffee with you," she said obstinately. "I'm going back to my hotel room."

"Please," Ian added, trying for all he was worth to infuse a plea into his eyes. "At least let me tell you about Aunt Felicia."

She lowered her stubborn gaze. And despite himself Ian was taken with her freshness. As he'd already told her, Andrea looked exactly like her mother. What he hadn't told Andrea was that, while her mother bordered on plain, Andrea possessed a certain charm, a certain tilt of her pouty mouth that arrested his attention.

Not that any of that mattered. He was committed to bachelorhood, married to his practice. He simply couldn't allow himself to be vulnerable, to be abandoned once more. At the tender age of ten, Ian had vowed to avoid all women. Except for an occasional relapse in adolescence and college, he had stood by his vow.

"I won't bite," he added, trying to focus on his aunt's welfare rather than Andrea's charm. "I promise."

Five minutes later, Andrea sipped a cup of hot, black coffee and stared in brooding silence as Ian stirred two packages of sugar into his own coffee. Why she listened to his contrite apology and softened voice she would never know. One minute she had been thinking pigs would fly before she would share coffee with him. The next minute, she heard herself placing her order. He had insisted he pay. She let him.

With the noise of clinking dishes in the background, Andrea nervously fingered the spoon resting on the circular table. Even though she survived occasional bouts of shyness, Andrea had never been so completely without words. All she could do was fidget with the buttons on her tailored shirt.

As the minutes stretched like gaping canyons between them, Ian seemed oblivious of Andrea's presence. Finally, he sipped his coffee, cleared his throat, and exposed her to a sheepish grin.

"Dr. Ian Lowderman." He extended his hand across the table; a large hand, dotted with freckles.

Andrea wasn't sure whether she should actually shake it. The man was insufferable, and that was an understatement. Then, she found her hand in his before she realized it. "Andrea Dillon. Dr. Andrea Dillon." Andrea couldn't deny the satisfaction of seeing the surprised spark in his eye. "I just finished my internship at Texas Children's Hospital."

"A pediatrician, then?"

"Yes." Andrea, shifting restlessly, didn't plan to sit here all morning exchanging empty pleasantries with this difficult person. She wanted—she was going—to see her birth mother. The sooner she shook him off her trail, the more likely she was to get into ICU. His opposition had only heightened her resolve. He might be the attending physician, but that didn't mean he understood the spiritual force urging Andrea to speak with Felicia.

"Do you really think Felicia is going to die?" Andrea's voice caught, and she suddenly felt as if she had lost her birth mother twice. Once at birth. And now.

"If she doesn't start fighting, she will. That's why I'm so—I was so—I guess, protective of her. You're a doctor. Surely you understand."

"Yes. I totally understand. And please don't think that I haven't thought of the strain my visit might put on her. But there is something else at work here. I have been experiencing a recurring nightmare for a week. Felicia appears in a hospital gown. She is falling off a cliff and calling for me to help her. At the end, I see her crushed on the rocks below. As I've already told you, I briefly contacted her five years ago. But because of some—some—emotional issues, I felt that I couldn't continue the contact. I hadn't even planned to contact her again. Then the dream. . ."

"Oh." Thoughtfully, he gazed at her as if he might be actually considering her request.

"I don't know whether or not you believe in God, Dr. Lowderman—"

"Ian."

"Okay, Ian. I don't know whether or not you believe in God—"

"I do," he said, that defensive edge back. "As a matter of fact—"

"Well, I believe God has been trying to show me something in that dream. I believe my mother needs me. I might be the person that will help her start fighting to survive."

"I can see why you'd feel that way." Ian seemed to be struggling to keep the edge from his voice. "But I cannot get past the fact that her seeing you just might so stress her that her heart could fail," he snapped, losing the battle to remain calm. A discouraging scowl seized his face. "You know that. What's the matter with you?"

"There's nothing the matter with me." Andrea's voice rose. "What's the matter with you? Are you so blinded by your own opinions that you'd let your aunt lie there and die rather than realize that God is at work here?"

Two doctors at a nearby table glanced their direction, then discreetly resumed their conversation.

Ian, seeming determined to control himself, focused on his steaming, fragrant coffee.

Her eyes still stinging from the threat of tears, Andrea had never been so frustrated in her entire life. What would it take to get through to this man? He said he believed in God. Either his belief was limited or he thought she was lying.

"All right." His pale gray eyes seemed to penetrate her very soul. "I'll consider letting you in there. . . ."

She blinked in surprise.

"Only after Felicia improves. Maybe in a couple of days. But there are several things you need to think about."

"Okay." She refused to break his gaze.

"First. . ." He hesitated.

A perverse joy danced through Andrea's mind. The man could actually be uncertain. His next words annihilated her joy.

"I assume you know Ed is Aunt Felicia's husband?"

A nod.

"Well, nobody on Uncle Ed's side of the family knows about you except me. Second, Uncle Ed is a minister. He and Felicia have been with this congregation almost twenty years, and . . ." He trailed off meaningfully.

"What are you implying?" Andrea wanted to force him to say what she knew in her heart. Andrea hadn't been wanted thirty years ago. She had been rejected by the very person who had given her life. Perhaps the reason Felicia had complied with Andrea's request to end contact five years ago was because Felicia had so much to lose should her husband's congregation discover she gave birth out of wedlock.

Suddenly, all the shame, all the fury, all the feelings of worthlessness which had tormented Andrea through adolescence erupted anew. Breathless, she reeled with each onslaught of raw pain. Only after she radically connected with God during a senior high youth camp had Andrea found relief from some of the pain she had so skillfully hidden with good grades and sports awards. She discovered a new worth in knowing that, regardless of her birth mother's rejection, her Heavenly Father loved her; loved her enough to give His life for her.

But with this—this Viking sitting across from her, implying that Andrea's presence would ruin her birth mother's life, Andrea felt all the old rejection once more, only on a deeper level. Not only was she rejected as an infant, but she was also being rejected as an adult. New tears threatened. Andrea bit her lip. Her real mother had warned her that perhaps her birth mother wouldn't be ready for a visit. What if Felicia, or perhaps Ed, refused Andrea's attempts at friendship? Fleetingly, Andrea wondered if that wound would be too deep for even God to heal.

"I think you understand what I'm implying," Ian said, with surprising gentleness. The gentleness flowed from his eyes and communicated a compassion that, only minutes ago, Andrea would have sworn he couldn't feel.

A hard swallow. Andrea forced herself to composure, forced herself to focus on the issue of the moment. "Don't think I haven't already thought about part of this. I didn't know that Ed was a pastor. But I do understand that there's a possibility—" Her voice quivered. She purposefully cleared her throat. "—a possibility of no one accepting me. Please understand," she added, trying to remove every threatening thread from her voice. Perhaps, somehow she could break down his defensive wall. "I—I hadn't planned on just dropping in like this. Because of the dream, I called yesterday morning, planning on talking with Felicia to simply make sure that she was okay. But then—then when—when Ed told me. . .I just couldn't sit in Houston with her on her deathbed."

"I understand that," he replied evenly. "But I have to do what's best for her. How would you feel if immediately after your visit today she went into cardiac arrest?" His penetrating stare dared her to move one muscle. "If you still insist on seeing her, even after knowing how it might change her life, I will consider letting you visit in a couple of days. That will have to be enough for you."

Andrea, forcing her face into an impassive mask, said nothing. No matter what she did, he wouldn't listen to her; he wouldn't admit that Felicia desperately needed her today; he wouldn't understand that Andrea was more sure of this than she had been of anything in her life. Even though she was risking being rejected, some unexplained force drove her to see her birth mother; see her now.

"Okay," she said simply.

Eyes narrowing in speculation, he stood. "I've got more rounds to make and a surgery scheduled in a couple of hours. Would you like me to walk you to your car?"

"No. I'm going to finish my coffee first. Thanks anyway." Andrea attempted the most miserable expression she could conjure. Dr. Ian Lowderman didn't know whether or not to trust her. She wouldn't let her expression substantiate his doubts. For if he knew what she was planning, he wouldn't let her out of his sight.

Chapter 3

Many years had elapsed since Ian had risked taking a woman in his arms. As he boarded the elevator and caught a glimpse of Andrea's forlorn face bent over her coffee, he fought the urge to run back to her, wrap his arms around her, and cradle her head against his shoulder. Ian had once again felt like a cad when he informed her of Ed's being a pastor. She maintained amazing composure if the pain in her eyes indicated the agony his words inflicted. But his first allegiance was to his aunt and uncle. He would go to any lengths to protect them, to guard their spotless reputation.

Like a weary warrior, Ian rested his forehead in his palm and tried to erase Andrea's image from his mind. Something about her arrested him. Ian tried to remind himself that he had suffered greatly at the hands of a woman. But he couldn't even recall what his mother looked like. His thoughts were centered on Andrea.

A real trooper. Andrea Dillon was a fighter. Ian sensed she was seldom thwarted. That awareness brought a combination of admiration and concern. Another scowl, and he rubbed his face. Would she abide by his orders? Regardless of her own medical knowledge, she seemed convinced that God was compelling her to see Felicia. Perhaps he should make another stop by ICU to tell the nurses to keep Andrea out of Aunt Felicia's room. As much as Ian would like to allow Andrea to visit Felicia, he would never forgive himself if the stress were too much.

Immediately, he checked his expensive Swiss watch, one of the few luxury items he allowed himself. There were too many lonely children at the boys' home for Ian to waste money on himself. When he noted the time, Ian produced a frustrated growl. His next surgery was sooner than he thought, and he desperately needed to make his rounds. No time for a return trip to ICU. He would have to hope he intimidated Andrea enough to keep her away from Felicia. For now, anyway.

A tiny, taunting doubt scurried through the back of Ian's mind as he remembered the stubborn tilt of Andrea's chin. Had anyone ever really intimidated Andrea Dillon for very long?

Thirty minutes later, Andrea exited a doctors' lounge, dressed in scrubs, her hair tucked neatly under a surgeon's cap. Before leaving the cafeteria, she asked a nurse a few harmless questions and, in a matter of minutes, discovered the closest doctors' lounge in which to change her clothing.

Assuming her "I'm the attending physician" persona, she slipped into ICU, past the nurse's desk, and toward room number 410. Andrea hoped the room number the receptionist had given her was still the correct one. She also hoped Felicia's room was void of staff or guests.

Dear Lord, she prayed, her knees trembling, her stomach in knots. *I'm not really sure You bless those who are sneaky. And I'd hit the ceiling if I were Ian Lowderman. But I've got to do this. I've got to see her. Please, please don't let my presence overexcite her. Please keep her calm.* A compulsive swallow. *And me too, Lord. Keep me calm, too.*

Silently, Andrea stepped into the room alight with sun rays squeezing through the half-opened blinds. For the first time, she gazed upon the woman who gave her life. Andrea would know the sleeping woman in a crowd of thousands. Ian was right. She was almost Andrea's double. Only older. And more tired. And. . . and almost gray.

Stifling a sob, Andrea dared to move closer, to gingerly take Felicia's limp hand in hers, to lovingly, cautiously stroke a strand of auburn hair, so like her own. How often had Andrea wondered about this moment, never imagining that Felicia would be surrounded by an IV and monitors and antiseptic smells; smells to which Andrea had thought she was immune; smells which now twisted her stomach in nausea.

Oh Lord, she prayed again. *Please don't let her die. You mustn't let her die. Not before I've had her in my life.*

Like an angry, roaring waterfall, an overwhelming surge of guilt pounded Andrea's spirit. Five years ago, she had rejected Felicia. Why hadn't she given her a chance?

Felicia's lids fluttered open to reveal sunken brown orbs cloaked in the fog of approaching death.

Andrea removed the surgeon's cap.

No words. Felicia only smiled slightly, squeezed

Andrea's hand, and closed her eyes once more. Then, a whisper as wispy as angel's hair. Andrea leaned forward and strained to hear. "I prayed you'd come."

"I know." Andrea choked back the tears, forcing herself to be strong. Instinctively, she tightened her grip on Felicia's dry hand, determined to hang onto any promise of life her birth mother might possess. "I love you," she rasped, momentarily reliving all those adolescent years she swore hatred for Felicia. "And I—I need you."

No response. Only the faint smile, then rhythmical breathing.

Even though Andrea wanted to stand by Felicia's side all day, she knew she must escape before being discovered. If she were careful, perhaps Andrea could visit several times today without getting caught.

"I'll be back soon," she whispered into Felicia's ear, then placed a tender kiss on her forehead.

Biting her bottom lip, Andrea brushed aside her warm tears, gave Felicia's hand one final squeeze, and turned to leave.

But someone was blocking the doorway. A tall, sandy-haired someone with blond lashes, blond brows, and that same scowl; the scowl which would stop a hurricane in its tracks.

Ian Lowderman. Again.

He didn't say a word. He didn't have to. The red flush under his light tan, his clenched jaw, his drawn brows said it all.

Andrea suppressed a groan then fought the urge to guiltily look away. An assured lift of her chin, and she weathered his irate glare with a bold stare of her own.

She couldn't blame him for being furious. But whatever fury he vented was worth seeing Felicia.

Without a word, he grabbed her upper arm, practically dragged her out of the room, and marched her to the nurses station. "I've already told you once, I want someone in Felicia Lowderman's room constantly," he clipped to a young nurse. "I want vital signs on her every fifteen minutes. And no one—*no one* is supposed to see her but her husband and stepson. Do you understand?"

"But her surgeon said—"

"I don't care what her surgeon said." His words pierced the room like high velocity bullets, and the nurse cringed.

Andrea, trying to twist from his grip, felt enormous pity for the poor woman, for the whole staff. Like a crew of privates before an overbearing general, all six attending nurses seemed to be holding their breath until the doctor exited.

At last, Ian strode toward the swinging doors. Andrea trotted to keep up with him. Never, had she experienced such an onslaught of contradicting emotions. Overwhelming love for Felicia. Relief, that she saw her birth mom. Frustration, that she had been caught. Rage with Ian Lowderman. Yet Andrea knew in her heart Ian wanted the best for his aunt. She shouldn't be angry with him for that. Nonetheless, Andrea had the undeniable urge to punch him in the gut again. Especially for the way he was hauling her along like so much excessive baggage.

When they were through the doors, Andrea purposed to take his treatment no more. "Let go of me."

She tried to pry his fingers from her arm.

"Not until I remove you from the premises," he said, his voice strangely calm; a calm like the lull before a tornado.

Then a new emotion struck her as he passed the closed elevators and slammed open the door of the nearby stairwell. Fear. Would this hulk of a man physically injure her? Under normal circumstances, she didn't figure him the violent type, but these were definitely not normal circumstances.

"I'm not going down these stairs with you," she barked out. "And if you don't let go of me, I'm going to scream my lungs out and have you arrested for—for—"

"For what?" He abruptly released her and bent until his nose almost touched hers.

Speechless, Andrea peered up at him.

"For stopping an obstinate woman from killing my aunt? For ending the impersonation of a surgeon? For catching you violating visitation rules? Now you really have a cause to scream, don't you?" Gradually, his voice rose until it echoed off the stairwell. "I think I'm the one who ought to scream!"

Terror. Andrea's fear had escalated into terror. The kind of terror that melts every fiber of bravado into mute rigor mortis. She could do nothing but stand like a wide-eyed statue; stand, until Ian's face slowly drained of color; stand, as his eyes filled with unshed tears.

"You just better hope your visit doesn't kill her," he snarled, his face still inches from hers.

"It won't," she whispered, astounded that she could even speak. What astounded her even more was that her terror had transformed to pity. Ian might have his faults, but Andrea knew without any doubt that he loved his aunt; loved her deeply.

"She's the only mother I've got." His eyes, so clear, so piercing, turned to those of a vulnerable schoolboy. Andrea recognized some of her own feelings of rejection.

Impulsively, she reached to stroke his face, more as a communication of one survivor to another than anything else. The minute her palm encountered his jaw's blond stubble, Andrea knew she had stepped into a realm she never dreamed of entering. All the energy of his rage seemed to flow into her hand and jolt her arm in an electric-like shock. She couldn't let go.

Ian's eyes widened, his brows arched, and his hand covered hers. Then, before Andrea could pull away, he turned his lips to her palm and bestowed a lingering kiss at the base of her fingers.

A gasp. And Andrea jerked away to stumble against the wall. She held his gaze. Afraid to look away. Afraid not to.

"I—" Ian's searching, confused expression reflected the turmoil churning within Andrea.

How had this—this awareness sprung up between them in such short time? One minute Andrea feared Dr. Lowderman might become violent, and the next minute, she feared he was going to take her in his arms.

He might still do that. The way he lingeringly contemplated her mouth, she had no idea what to expect.

Then, as if he were exerting great effort, Ian stepped away and scrubbed his hand through his curly, cropped hair. "I'm sorry I—I blew up on you like that."

His voice tight with emotion, he concentrated on his white canvas shoes. "I know it's probably hard for you to believe, but I'm a Christian, too. And just for the record, this is the first time I've ever acted like this. . ." He hesitated uncertainly as if he were talking about the kiss, not the yelling.

"Well," she rasped, amazed that she even recognized her voice. "This is the first time for me on all this, too."

With a tight smile, he opened his mouth to speak again, but Andrea would never know what he was to say. An urgent message over the intercom sent them both racing into the hallway.

"Code blue to ICU. Code blue to ICU."

Chapter 4

As Ian rushed toward ICU, Andrea dogged him, her mind reeling with shock. In one second, she relived her nightmare, saw Felicia's body crumpled against the jagged rocks. The dream had become a reality. Felicia was dying. Andrea was to blame.

Before Ian burst through the ICU doorway, he turned to Andrea like a pit bulldog on a defenseless rabbit. "Don't even think I'm going to let you back there," he ground out. "This is your fault! And if you have any sense left in that head of yours, you'll leave before the rest of the family finds out."

Andrea flinched with the fury of his accusation. Ian's words produced the final breaking of the dam holding her grief at bay. As he ran toward Felicia, Andrea collapsed against the wall, covered her face, and slid to the floor. One anguished sob after another racked her spirit. Why would God urge Andrea to Felicia, then allow Felicia to die? Too distraught to even pray, she groaned, coughed, pulled her knees to her chest, and rested her forehead on them. As she spun and spun and spun in the tornadic agony wrenching her soul, Andrea felt as if she were the only person in a very cold universe.

Then the rush of feet. The staff was responding to the code. Andrea didn't even look up. She couldn't. She couldn't face anyone who might soon learn what she had done. Once the rush ended, the sound of footsteps echoed from ICU. Slow, steady footsteps which approached then stopped only inches from Andrea.

A consoling hand rested on her shoulder. "Andrea?"

Ian.

She cringed against looking at him, but dared peer up through blurry tears.

"The code wasn't for Aunt Felicia," he whispered, a mask of regret softening the intensity of his eyes.

The shock of the good news sent Andrea into another onslaught of crying.

"Come on," he muttered, pulling her to her feet.

Andrea didn't question where he was taking her. She allowed Ian to lead her where he would. When they stopped, they were in the very doctors' lounge where Andrea had donned the scrubs. Thankfully, they were alone.

Eventually Andrea's tears abated and she became overwhelmingly aware of where she stood. In the haven of Ian's arms. A complicated man whose feelings ran deeply. A man whose strength seemed to fuse Andrea's very being.

"Andrea, I. . ." He hesitated, his voice thick with tears. "After I discovered the code wasn't for Aunt Felicia, I checked on her. She's asleep, but her cheeks have taken on color again, and her vital signs have already slightly improved."

Andrea produced a wobbly smile. Blotting at her

wet cheeks, she pulled back to peer into Ian's face. And that flabbergasting jolt of electricity returned. He was too close, and every coherent thought vanished from her grasp.

"Andrea?" he questioned, the confusion mounting in his own eyes.

As if another force urged her toward him, Andrea didn't hesitate when Ian's lips lowered to hers. The kiss, a mere wisp of a touch, might have appeared meaningless. But it stroked a cord in Andrea which no man had yet discovered. Romance was the last thing on Andrea's mind when she entered the hospital that morning. Now she wondered exactly what God had planned for her. Did it involve more than the issues with Felicia?

Once again, Andrea peered into fathomless pale eyes that churned with as many questions as Andrea herself experienced. And a "where do we go from here" claimed Ian's every feature.

"I'm so sorry I was so cruel. I have been nothing short of a—a jerk from the start," he finally said, grabbing a tissue and blotting her cheeks. "If there's any way you can forgive me—maybe it would help you to know I feel half-crazed with grief—"

"If I were in your shoes, I would have been just as furious," Andrea candidly admitted through diminishing sniffles. "I'm sorry too. But I guess not sorry enough not to ignore your orders." A half-smile.

"Maybe you were right. Maybe it was for the best." After several silent seconds, Ian awkwardly stepped away from her and settled onto the arm of the overstuffed couch.

Andrea sensed him deliberately erecting a barrier between them. Feeling cold, forlorn, lost at sea, she grappled with what to do next. That kiss. It seemed to rebound back and forth between them like an unspoken echo. Finally, Andrea decided the best thing would be to simply disappear into thin air. If only she could.

"I'll be checking on Aunt Felicia off and on all afternoon," he said in a voice sanitized of all emotion. "If she continues to improve, I don't have a problem with your seeing her again tonight."

"Okay," Andrea squeaked out, concentrating on the room's simple decor. "I appreciate that more than you know."

And the kiss continued its merciless echoing. Andrea had come up against something she had never encountered—a man she responded to like an impatient thunderstorm, overwrought with lightening.

At last, Ian stood and turned for the door. Narrowing his eyes, he peered toward her. "I'll let you get changed. What hotel are you staying at?"

"The Omni off I-10 and Wurzbach."

"Okay. I'll call later."

So that was it. Ian was going to simply walk away as if nothing had happened. A tiny tendril of relief sprouted in Andrea. Maybe that was for the best. If she were fortunate enough to be apart of Felicia's life, she and Ian might often be in the other's path. Although Andrea couldn't deny her attraction to Ian, she also didn't want to entangle herself in his world. She knew in her gut that Dr. Ian Lowderman had some serious issues to wade through. Andrea didn't feel she was equipped to do any wading at this point in her life.

As Ian reached for the doorknob, he hesitated and turned back to Andrea, his face impassive. "I hope you won't misinterpret my intent," he said evenly.

Andrea stretched for his meaning, so vaguely implied. Was he talking about allowing her to visit Felicia or that kiss still tormenting Andrea's peace of mind? "Intent?"

"Yes. I think you need to know that I am a bachelor and always will be. I'm neither looking for nor interested in—"

"Rest assured, Dr. Lowderman," Andrea ground out. "I pose no threat to your bachelorhood. Don't flatter yourself."

He scowled. But the scowl did little to hide the spark of surprise flashing through his eyes.

She returned the scowl. She had learned in personal confrontations the one who looked away first was often the loser. She refused to be the loser. Andrea would glare at the man until they both turned to statues.

A short plump doctor entering the lounge disrupted their standoff. Silently, Ian stepped through the doorway, and Andrea opened the metal locker where she had stashed her clothing. With mammoth determination, she pushed Ian from her mind and focused on the next visit with Felicia.

Within a month, Andrea was privileged to help Felicia prepare to go home. A warm glow engulfed her as she recalled Felicia's miraculous rebound. Many times Felicia gave credit to Andrea and Andrea passed the praise to the Lord.

The doctors were amazed.

The staff was amazed.

Felicia's family was amazed.

The whole thing had been nothing short of a miracle. And when the miracle began Andrea's recurring dream had thankfully been no more.

"So what do you think?" Andrea asked, pulling a colorful house dress from her shopping bag. "I thought you'd enjoy wearing this home."

"There was no need for you to do that," Felicia said. "Ed is supposed to be bringing something from home."

"I know, but," Andrea shrugged. "I wanted to do something special."

With a flush of happiness on her cheeks, Felicia reached for Andrea's hand, and Andrea sat on the edge of the hospital bed. "You have no idea what you mean to me," Felicia said through tears. "You're being here is more than I ever dreamed was possible."

"You don't have to—"

Felicia raised her hand to stay Andrea's words. "There are some things I've wanted to tell you all month but haven't had the strength to say. I think now is the time, before it all gets lost in the bustle of going home."

"Okay," Andrea whispered. Suddenly, the old resentment Andrea had harbored seemed foolish in the face of the love shining from Felicia's eyes.

"I prayed from the minute I placed you for adoption that one day you would return to me. Turning you over to that nurse for the last time was the hardest decision I ever made in my life. But after a lot of prayer, God gave me peace about it. I knew you were in a home with a mom and dad that could take care of you better than a single college girl like me ever could. It was a sacrifice, but I felt I was making the best choice for you." Her gaze drifted out the window, toward the golden, November trees. "Every year, I made you a birthday cake and imagined you sitting across from me. I would sing 'Happy Birthday' to you, then blow out the candles." A sigh. "I guess it was my way of trying to deal with it all. And my dear, sweet Ed was like a rock every year. Your birthday was always the hardest time for me."

Salty tears pooling in the corners of her mouth, Andrea spontaneously wrapped her arms around Felicia. "I've wanted to tell you how sorry I am for breaking contact five years ago. I—I just couldn't—"

"It's okay. You don't need to explain a thing."

For what seemed like hours, the two silently hugged, gently cried. Somehow this time of sharing began to complete the healing which God initiated many years before.

Through companionable laughter, they pulled apart, and Andrea smiled into her birth mother's eyes. "If it's any help to you, I'm so thankful for my parents. They've been the best parents any kid could hope for."

"Yes, I already know that. The Lord showed me that years ago or I would have never had any peace. And you—look at you—you alone attest to your family. All grown up. Self-assured. A doctor now. What more could I ask for?"

As the two continued their amiable chatter, a question began a slow tolling in the back of Andrea's mind. Was there anything her parents could have done to ease her resentment toward Felicia? Andrea hadn't even learned she was adopted until she was in junior high. Why hadn't her parents told her before then? Why all the secrecy? Their secrecy made Andrea feel that adoption was something to be ashamed of. That perhaps she was shameful. Not that her parents ever treated her as anything but a treasure, yet still. . .

Andrea, pondering her thoughts, was zipping Felicia's duffel bag when the room's door swung open. Ed Lowderman stood in the doorway. Andrea's self-proclaimed champion. That tall, angular, ever-smiling man who had encouraged Andrea to call him "Uncle Ed." He had come to take his wife home. With a ready smile, Andrea prepared to greet him. But the greeting stilled on her lips when Ian walked in behind Ed.

Chapter 5

Since their encounter in the doctors' lounge Andrea had seen Ian only twice. Each time, they had passed in the hospital hallway with nothing more than a brief acknowledgment. A few times when she rang Felicia's room from Houston, Andrea had spoken with Ian. Their conversations had been short, to the point, and distant, on both sides. After each encounter, Andrea desperately wished to squelch the effect Ian had on her pulse. But she couldn't. Despite his complicated, difficult personality, despite her better judgment, Andrea found him fascinating.

Now here he was, just as commanding as he had been the first time Andrea saw him. Walking into the room behind Ed. A pleasant smile lighting his face. But he still hadn't noticed Andrea.

She had always considered herself a strong woman who made decisions based on reason. Having determined to finish medical school, Andrea left little time for romance. Still, she had known somewhere in the back of her mind that the man she married would have to be a force.

Ian Lowderman was a force.

She swallowed against a dry throat and wished her

mind wouldn't run in that direction. She had a pediatric practice to establish. Marriage was not something she was interested in at the moment. Especially not with Ian.

Feeling like a cornered fox at the mercy of a baying hound, Andrea didn't know where to turn or what to do. But one thing was certain. This hospital room was too small—way too small—for her and Ian both.

Just as she was preparing to make her escape, Ian spotted her. His pleasant expression hardened. His eyes slightly narrowed. His mouth stretched tight. Whether he was angered or shocked, Andrea couldn't determine. She didn't even want to determine. She just wanted to escape!

"The car's waiting on you at the front door, Madame," Ed said with a feigned British accent. He bowed as if Felicia were the queen of England.

"Thank you, James," she teased with a aristocratic nod of her head.

"Er. . . I'll just take your duffel bag down while Uncle Ed and Ian arrange for your wheelchair."

"I didn't realize you and Ian had met in person," Felicia said, eyeing her daughter and nephew speculatively.

Andrea felt like biting off her own tongue.

"Yes, we met briefly when Andrea first arrived to see you," Ian said in a strained voice.

"Oh," Felicia said.

Andrea bent to bestow a quick kiss on her mother's forehead.

"Why don't you wait and just go down with us, Andrea?" Felicia asked.

"Uh. . . I've got to get my car out of parking anyway."

She felt Ian and Ed watching her. "I'll just pull around to the front and wait there. Then I'll follow you home as planned."

"Okay." Felicia glanced back to Ian, then to Andrea, a knowing glint in her eyes which made Andrea a bit uncomfortable. What did she suspect?

Ian tried to resist watching Andrea leave, but the effort was wasted. She was by far more attractive than she had been the first time they met. That day, her face had been distraught, drawn, and drenched in tears. Still, she had almost blown his socks off. Ian wasn't used to having his socks blown off. The whole thing made him more than uncomfortable. And Andrea had just left him "sockless" again.

He pictured her walking down the hallway, toward the elevators. If Ian hurried, he just might catch her. But in the background, he heard someone speaking his name.

"Ian. . . Ian. . ."

He dragged his thoughts from Andrea and focused on his aunt. "Yes?" he replied absently.

"I was just asking if you wanted to have lunch with us."

Both Ed and Felicia studied him.

"Uh. . .yes. That would be nice." Ian imagined Andrea pushing the elevator's button and waiting. If he hurried, he still might catch her.

"Good," Ed said, his lean face a collection of pleasant smile lines. "I can go to the deli, and—"

"Okay." Ian imagined Andrea stepping onto that elevator. She was getting away from him. "I'll be back."

Without a backward glance, he rushed from the room.

In less than a minute, Ian caught sight of Andrea, entering the empty elevator. Silently, he stepped in beside her. She appraised him, a spark of surprise lighting her eyes.

"Hi," he said.

"Hello."

The door slid shut. Ian felt as if he were trapped in a room devoid of oxygen. And without oxygen, his brain was failing. He had no idea what to say.

Andrea fidgeted with her keys which made an impatient clinking sound. The door hissed open on the ground floor. The shadowed parking garage greeted them.

Ian stood aside for Andrea to exit. He followed closely, matching her pace. "I never have gotten the chance to thank you for all you've done for Aunt Felicia." At last he had found some words.

"I just did what God prompted me to do. He's the one who did the work."

"I know. But you had the guts to do what He wanted even in the face of—"

"Your opposition?" She darted a triumphant glance his way.

He narrowed his eyes. "Exactly."

"So are you finally admitting you were wrong?"

"I think you would have done the same thing in my shoes."

"Probably." Andrea halted beside a sporty red car. "You know, I'm surprised at your following me, Dr. Lowderman," she said with a smirk. "Aren't you afraid I'm going to propose?"

"You could have gone all day and not said that," he bit out, irritated with her but more irritated with himself for his own weakness in following her.

"If I remember correctly, the thought originated with you in the doctors' lounge." She inserted a key into her car door and disengaged the lock with a decisive click.

"I was just being honest," he said evenly, trying to control his temper.

"If you were really honest, you would have never. . ." As if her own words caught her off guard, Andrea averted her attention to opening the car door.

"Never what?" It was his turn to goad.

"Never mind." With purpose she deposited Felicia's duffel bag in the back and sat in the driver's seat. Andrea seemed determined not to look at him again.

"I guess this is my cue to get lost."

"Uncle Ed and Felicia will be waiting on us."

"Then why don't I just ride around with you?" Ian couldn't believe his own suggestion.

But it certainly arrested Andrea's attention. "If you insist."

In seconds, Ian settled into the bucket seat. "You know, there's no reason for us to be enemies."

"Who says we're enemies?"

Ian ignored the comment. "If you're planning to visit Aunt Felicia regularly, we most likely will bump into each other. We might as well start practicing being amiable now."

She exposed him to brief, quizzical scrutiny.

Despite his words, in his gut Ian knew he wanted

much more than friendship from this intelligent, attractive doctor. She drove from the garage and into the sunlight, and he couldn't resist the urge to admire her profile. Andrea Dillon wasn't the kind of woman anyone would want to put on the cover of a magazine. But Ian had never gone for that type anyway. The thing he found so fascinating about Andrea was that she had the grit to match him word for word. She had yet to back down. And if the truth were known, Ian had anticipated their next meeting since their encounter in the doctors' lounge.

The whole situation simultaneously thrilled and daunted him. What he told Andrea after their kiss had been truth. Ian wasn't interested in marriage. Not even a little bit. He wasn't sure he could trust—really trust—a woman enough to get married. Not after his own mother's desertion. He imagined himself like his father, trying to raise a boy on his own. Not something Ian wanted forced upon him.

So where did that leave him?

A bachelor who donated most of his leisure time and a chunk of his money to a home for boys trapped in the foster-care system. He had plenty of sons of all ages. A home full, for that matter. His work there fulfilled his needs for fatherhood.

But what about his other needs?

He reflected over the past few years. Ian had immersed himself so much in his career and that boys' home that he had been able to suppress those needs. Until now. Another glance toward Andrea. The pouty turn of her lips. That no-nonsense gleam in her eyes. Her cloud of unruly auburn hair. Ian restlessly shifted in the seat. This little red car had suddenly grown too small.

As Andrea slowed to a stop behind Ed's worn sedan, Ian wondered how soon she would be returning after this visit. Would Andrea spend the holidays with her birth mother or her adoptive mother? Ian had no idea whether he wanted to see her or avoid her. "What are your plans for the holidays?"

"The holidays?" she echoed as if the concept were totally foreign.

"Yes. Thanksgiving's in three weeks. Then Christmas is around the corner. I was wondering whether you'd be here or in Houston."

"What's it to you?" she challenged, a taunting gleam in her eyes.

"Are you trying to be difficult on purpose or does it just come natural?"

"It's natural." Andrea pushed the floor gear shift into park and turned off the engine.

"Just so we understand each other."

They got out, each slamming the car doors, and the sound echoed off the hospital's covered driveway.

Andrea rounded the car and leveled a determined gaze at him. "I don't know what kind of game you think you're playing, Dr. Ian Lowderman, but—"

"Who says I'm playing a game?"

"I do. Because you are. But I think you need to understand something very important about me." She pointed her index finger at his nose.

"Which is?"

"You aren't the only one not interested in marriage. So you can stop wasting your time."

Ian crossed his arms and leaned against the car. "Do I detect a note of hurt pride in your voice?"

"What are you talking about?"

"I'm talking about the fact that you've alluded twice to my comment in the lounge about marriage."

Her cheeks flushed, and Ian began to think he had scored the final point. But the victory was short-lived.

"I just want to make sure you understand that your bachelorhood," she waved her hand for emphasis, "is not at risk with me and never will be."

"Now that we have everything out in the open," he drawled. "I would like you to answer my question about the holidays."

"Most likely, I'll spend the core of the holidays with my parents." She paused to expose him to satisfied smirk. "Happy now?"

Ian opened his mouth to retort, but Ed's jovial call halted his words.

For Andrea, the next several minutes were a bustle of activity. Settling Felicia in the car. Making her comfortable. Arranging her luggage and numerous plants. All the while, she felt Ian's powerful presence. Trying to read that man was like trying to read Chinese.

By the time she collapsed behind the steering wheel of her trusty car, Andrea was exhausted. The whole month had been like an emotional roller coaster. And the last ten minutes of conversation with Ian had required every scrap of wit Andrea could muster. The man had a way of bringing out the worst in her, but she refused—she absolutely refused—to allow him to get the upper hand. Why had he followed her to her car in the first place? Andrea had almost fainted when he stepped into the elevator.

As she watched him fold his "Viking" frame into the back of Ed's sedan, Andrea began to pray like mad. *Lord, I think You know how thankful I am for everything You've done with Felicia. But Ian? Why did You have to throw him in the picture? Why couldn't he be safely married with a wife and two kids? Then I wouldn't have this problem. You know I don't feel like it's the right time for me to settle down. I wasn't even looking for a romance. And we both know Ian isn't. Or at least he says he isn't, but the way he acted today. . . He is really strange, Lord. I think he's got problems that are too big for me, and I don't believe I want to get tangled in them. So. Would it be too much to ask if You could just conveniently keep him out of my path? I would really appreciate it.*

The sedan began pulling away from the hospital. As Andrea followed, a very disturbing thought exploded into her disjointed prayer. *You have never once asked God what He wants in your relationship with Ian.*

A groan.

What if Ian was the man God had chosen for her?

NO!

Andrea refused to think in those terms. She pictured herself falling madly in love and having Ian break her heart because he wouldn't commit to marriage. A risk Andrea wasn't willing to take. She had other heartaches to mend, like confronting her parents with questions of why they weren't more open about her being adopted. That was enough for one woman to have to deal with. Ian, no matter how arresting, simply couldn't be a part of Andrea's world.

Chapter 6

One month later, Ian sat on the balcony of his lonely town house, overlooking the shadowed San Antonio streets as the dawn awakened them. Absently, Ian stroked his Siamese cat, Simon, who snuggled into the crook of Ian's arm and purred with pleasure. Ian had discovered the motherless kitten one morning two years ago. Simon pitifully meowed until Ian took him in, fed him, and provided him a spot to sleep. Now Simon thought he owned Ian. Up until a few weeks ago, the cat supplied ample company for him. But lately, Simon lacked appeal.

Ian missed Andrea.

He barely knew her, yet he missed her.

She had called Felicia last week before Thanksgiving dinner was over. Ian knew the caller was Andrea because of Felicia's reaction. Still, Ian never inquired about her. He didn't want to give his aunt and uncle anything more to speculate over. They were already speculative enough.

Ian had taken the week after Thanksgiving off and planned to do some minor repairs around the house, then spend a few nights at the boys' home. But here he sat. The first morning of his week off, staring at the bejeweled sunrise, thinking of Andrea.

Ian could call her.

Aunt Felicia had her number.

Restlessly, he debated the issue as a cool autumn breeze teased his thoughts. The mellow smell of his gourmet coffee, steaming on the wicker table, tempted his taste buds. Ian took the cup, sipped the dark, rich liquid, and his dilemma continued.

If he called Andrea, she would think he wanted to begin a relationship. She had already "put him in his place" on that issue. But Ian wondered if her rejection was a result of his saying he was a confirmed bachelor. Despite what she said, Ian suspected he hurt her pride.

At last, Ian decided to pray. *Father, I need help. I've met a woman that makes me want to forget my childhood wounds. I don't know what to do. If I release the pain, then I'll be vulnerable. Just as vulnerable as my father. . .*

For the first time in his life, Ian began examining—closely examining—the wound that his mother left. Would it ever heal? Was Ian fated to a life of pain? He had spent most of his adult years covering that wound with a busy schedule and a string of accomplishments in academics, sports, and medicine. Now, examining the wound in the morning light, Ian saw that covering it had only made it worse. Somewhere deep inside, Ian needed to be healed. But how? How could God remove the pain that had ravaged his soul and left him forever scarred?

Once more, Andrea waltzed through his mind.

Was she the woman for him?

If so, how would Ian ever embrace her when he had yet to embrace his own healing?

Still, he needed to talk with her. He needed to see her. A force deep within drew Ian to Andrea like a moth to a candle.

He placed Simon in the other wicker chair and swallowed the remainder of his coffee. Ian would call Felicia. Then, he would call Andrea.

After her morning walk in the park, Andrea entered her sparsely furnished apartment, depositing her mail on the petite breakfast bar. She had looked forward to this day for years. The beginning of establishing her practice. Today, Andrea would be interviewing a group of pediatricians for a possible spot in their practice. One of the doctors was retiring. That hopefully left room for Andrea.

The phone rang just as she was stepping into the shower. She started to let the answering machine catch it, then thought better of it. Her father hadn't been feeling well last night, and Andrea was concerned. Perhaps this was her mother calling.

Grabbing her flannel bathrobe, Andrea retrieved the cordless phone from her cluttered bedroom. "Hello," she said, anticipating her mother's soft Texas drawl.

"Andrea?"

Her stomach dropped to her feet. How many times had she thought of Ian in the last month? It would be easier to count the number of times she hadn't been thinking of him. She had desperately wanted to ask about him when she called Felicia at Thanksgiving, but had refused to show her weakness. During the Thanksgiving holidays, Andrea's mother had commented on how distracted she seemed. Yes, Andrea was distracted. Distracted by Ian. But also distracted by the issues that lay between her and her parents. Issues which she had no idea how to broach.

"Andrea?" Ian repeated. "Are you there?"

"Yes—yes," she stammered. "You just took me off guard."

"Are you working today?"

"Uh, no. I'm interviewing for a position, actually."

"Morning or afternoon?"

She sat on the edge of the unmade brass bed and wondered what Ian had up his sleeve. No telling. The man was unpredictable, to say the least. "Morning." She checked the clock on her oak night stand. "8:00" glared at her in glowing red. "In a couple of hours, actually."

"So. . ." He hesitated, and Andrea thought she detected a hint of vulnerability in his voice.

Oh please, Lord, she prayed urgently. *Don't let him ask to come here, not sounding like this. I don't think I can tell him 'no' if he sounds vulnerable. You know I can't handle being with him. He makes me crazy.*

"Want some company?" Ian finally asked.

"You mean today?" She wanted to stall the request. Maybe if she stalled long enough Ian would have time to snap out of the vulnerable mode and back into his arrogant mode. Then she could easily refuse him.

"I'm off this week. I was thinking maybe I'd drive over and we could have lunch and go to a museum or something."

Still vulnerable.

"A museum?" *Oh Lord, let him say something I can*

challenge. I can't handle him in this mood.

"Yeah."

"Uh. . ."

"Museums are a great place to get to know somebody. Don't you think?" His final words were so soft, they seemed more like a caress than a question.

Andrea swallowed hard and clutched her midsection. Did Ian want to get to know her better? What was he implying? Had he missed her as much as she missed him? Andrea wouldn't dare admit it to a living soul, but the last month had been nothing short of a mountain of torment. Ian had haunted her dreams and almost every waking moment.

But he was the unattainable. Or at least he claimed to be. His actions, however, did little to support his claims. The last time she saw Ian, Andrea had accused him of playing games. Was this invitation another move in one of those games of his?

"So, do I take your silence as a rejection?" he said, his voice heavy with disappointment.

"No. Not in the least. You just took me by surprise, that's all." How could Andrea be agreeing to spending the afternoon with Ian Lowderman? Had she lost her mind?

Chapter 7

By five o'clock, Andrea was once more exhausted. Simply put, Ian drained her of every ounce of energy. This time, she felt no need to verbally spar with him, but she did feel the need to be on guard. Trying to second-guess the man was like trying to catch the wind. All afternoon, he had been the perfect gentleman. Charming. Considerate. Attentive. In his pale eyes lurked an attraction which both daunted and thrilled Andrea.

But where did they go from here?

Presently, they had arrived back at her apartment, and Ian sprawled on her overstuffed couch as if he planned to be a fixture for the evening. In the kitchen Andrea poured colas in two glasses and debated what to do next. Should she politely sip her soda with him until he left or invite him to stay for dinner? The whole scene was laced with comic irony. Sipping sodas with Ian Lowderman was like camping on a volcano. So much tension lay beneath the surface that the wrong move might plunge Andrea into a pit of lava. As she stared blankly at the fizzing colas, Andrea simultaneously wished Ian would leave and wished he would stay.

When she heard him stand and walk into the kitchen, she stiffened. What was he up to? He stopped just behind her, so close Andrea could feel his warmth. Slowly, Ian placed his hands on her shoulders. Swallowing hard, Andrea closed her eyes. Ian hadn't touched her all afternoon. A couple of times, she knew he had contemplated taking her in his arms. But they had been at the Museum of Natural Science, replete with a planetarium and live butterfly exhibit. Not exactly the most romantic spot on earth. At first, Andrea had been thankful for the safety of a public place. Yet, by the time they left, she yearned for his touch, despite her better judgment. Now, he was standing behind her, caressing her shoulders. Andrea knew she was going to dissolve into a warm, delicious heap right here in her own kitchen.

"Andrea," he muttered.

"Yes."

"We need to talk."

"We've talked all afternoon," she said, amazed at the even tones of her voice.

"Not really, you know."

He turned her to face him. Andrea looked into eyes that were a churning mixture of pain and confusion. He produced a sad smile and stroked her cheek. Andrea caught her bottom lip between her teeth. If he kissed her she would drown in her own emotions. How could this be happening? How could she be letting Ian twist her heart into a knot so tight it would never unravel?

"I really enjoy being with you," he finally said.

Another swallow. "And you aren't afraid I'll threaten

your bachelorhood?" Her sarcastic attempt at humor failed miserably.

"Actually, I am afraid of exactly that."

"Oh." She was drowning in her own emotions without the kiss.

"I think I could fall in love with you, Andrea Dillon."

"But we haven't known each other long enough."

"Don't tell me you don't feel it."

Andrea silently held his penetrating gaze.

"Did you miss me this month?" he rasped, pulling her next to him.

"Yes," she admitted, her voice muffled against his oversized sweatshirt. His heartbeat seemed a reflection of his character. Strong. Determined. Willful. Andrea drank in his every nuance, wanting to absorb the very essence of who he was. At last, Ian cupped her chin in his hands. Their kiss rocked the universe.

When Ian pulled away, his eyes were twin pools of uncertainty. "When we last parted at the hospital, I never intended to contact you again. But it was like I took you home with me. You wouldn't give me a moment's peace."

"I felt the same way."

Ian closed his eyes as if he were grappling for his next words. "Do I dare be totally honest with you?"

"I wish you would. You are a complete enigma to me." She stepped out of his embrace, picked up the liter of cola, and nervously added more liquid to the waiting glasses.

Andrea needed about a mile of space between her and this giant of a man. She would have to settle for a few feet.

He moved to her side and leaned against the counter. Thoughtfully, Ian peered out the kitchen window, toward the Houston skyline. "When I was ten, my mother left my father and me. She divorced my dad, and we never saw her again," he said in a hollow voice, as if the words had been long stored in a musty closet. "It's been twenty-five years. You would think I would have gotten over it by now." The grief, so heavy in his voice, seemed to emanate from him like an old, dense, tired fog.

Andrea, moved by his pain, laid her hand on his arm. What could she say? "I'm sorry" seemed trite and more than inadequate. So she remained silent and hoped the silence spoke her empathy.

"Because of that, I vowed I would never get married. I felt that I'd be setting myself up for the same heartache. And I simply couldn't stand the thought of having my guts ripped out all over again."

"Do you know why your mother left?" Andrea asked gently, all the while trying to stay the tears stinging her eyes.

A humorless chuckle. "Yes. My father finally told me when I was an adult. I learned some rather startling facts about my conception."

"Oh?"

"It seems my parents had to get married. After ten years of marriage, my mother was still young and adventurous and wanted freedom. Being cooped up with a husband and a boy wasn't enough for her. Dad never mentioned it, but I don't think my mother ever loved him."

"And you didn't hear from her again?"

"No. Dad found out she moved to New York. That's

all we know. I think that's all she wanted us to know."

"I guess we have a lot in common when you think about it." Andrea sighed and rubbed her forehead. "Both conceived out of wedlock. When we were adolescents, we had no idea where our mothers were."

"But you found yours."

"Yes." Andrea picked up the colas and handed one to Ian. She took a sip of the cold, sweet liquid and tried to swallow against her tightened throat. "And I've debated about how much I should visit Felicia. What you said when we first met about their congregation finding out—"

"Andrea, I never intended that to hurt you. I simply—I just didn't want—"

"I know." She shrugged. "Your first allegiance is to Felicia."

"Since I was ten, she's been the only mother I've known."

"But I have another mother, don't I?"

"I didn't mean to imply that I resented your contacting Felicia." Ian took her hand and led her toward the living room. "The only hesitancy I had was about it disrupting her life. But your seeing her hasn't seemed to disrupt it at all. Actually, I'm really glad you've stayed in contact with Aunt Felicia. She's a different woman than she was, even before the wreck. There's a new spark in her eyes that has never been there."

"Well, it's helped me come to terms with a lot of issues from my own life." They set on the floral sofa. "But it's also opened up a new can of worms with my parents."

"Oh?"

"Yes. I've been really angry with them for not telling me before junior high that I was adopted. And the only reason they told me then was because a relative let it slip out. The whole thing made me feel like adoption was somehow shameful. That maybe I was shameful. I've wanted to confront them, but I don't know how." She set the base of her glass on her thigh and examined the wet circle it left on her jeans. "I think if they had just been honest with me from the first that it would have saved me a lot of resentment toward Felicia, and now, toward them."

He drained his cola and set the glass on the medical journals scattered across the coffee table. "Do you think maybe they didn't know how to handle the whole thing? I mean, adoptions thirty years ago weren't handled like they are today. Maybe they did the best they could with the knowledge they had."

"Well it wasn't good enough," Andrea snapped airily. Abruptly, she stood to walk toward her piano where the latest family photo greeted her. Amazingly, Andrea favored both her parents. Except for a few flecks of gray, her father's wavy auburn hair was the exact shade of Andrea's. And Andrea's upturned nose seemed a replica of her mother's. God had placed her with this marvelous couple. There was no arguing the fact. But even with God's miracles, human beings still had a way of making wrong decisions.

"I'm sorry," Ian said.

He was behind her again. *Why does he keep doing that?* His nearness left her feeling as if she were trapped without one trace of oxygen. "No, I'm sorry."

She smiled her apology. "I shouldn't have snapped at you." Andrea, studying the toes of her western boots, sensed Ian peering at her.

So. He had told his story. She had told hers. Now what? It seemed Andrea was perpetually asking that with Ian.

"How did your interview go?" he asked.

"What?" His sudden change of subject jarred her thoughts.

"Your interview today. I never asked you about it."

"It went fine. No, it went great."

"Good. Maybe the position is yours then."

"If you want the truth, I really feel like it is."

They stood in silence until Andrea felt him erecting that wall of his once more. The same wall he had erected in the doctors' lounge. Dr. Ian Lowderman was probably about to make his exit. At least now Andrea could finally see the reason for his infuriating actions. Ian was grappling with some serious pain. Pain that left him terrified of commitment. His terror left Andrea more than frustrated.

"Well, I guess I need to head back to San Antonio."

"I knew you were about to say that," Andrea replied, a hint of resentment in her tone.

His right brow arched. "Oh?"

"Yes." She gritted her teeth and suddenly wanted to punch this man, half again as big as she was. He had disrupted her from the moment she met him. He had inhabited her thoughts for a solid month. He popped into her life for a day, just long enough to twist her heart into a knot and declare he couldn't commit to a relationship.

Then, he rebuilt his blasted wall and was going to return to his world. When would he be back? Would he ever be back?

"I've figured out that's the way you operate," she continued, an edge to her voice.

Narrowing his eyes, Ian glared down at her.

Andrea didn't flinch.

"What's that supposed to mean?"

"You figure it out."

"I guess I can forget a return invitation?"

She felt that wall of his wavering between them. Andrea blinked in surprise. "You mean you would come back?"

His lips curved into a sad, uncertain smile. "I don't know."

Andrea turned her back and started toward the kitchen.

He grabbed her arm.

"I can't do this, Ian," she said tightly. "Either we're on or off. I'm sorry about your childhood, but I cannot be the victim of your fear to commit."

Ian released her. "Okay. If that's the way you feel."

"It is the way I feel."

Silence.

Ian walked toward the door.

Andrea didn't dare look at him. One look, and she might throw herself in his arms and beg him not to leave. After a lengthy pause, he opened the door and quietly exited.

Chapter 8

Andrea sat in the parking lot of Calvary Community Church, her palms moist against the steering wheel. Three weeks had lapsed since she had seen or heard from Ian. Everywhere she turned, the trappings of the season greeted her but left her feeling hollow. Christmas was only four days away. Andrea planned to spend this weekend with Felicia and Ed and be with her parents during the rest of the holidays.

This afternoon, Felicia had given Andrea directions to this modern, brick church. Tonight, the Christmas play was receiving its final practice before the performance tomorrow evening. When the practice was over, Andrea would follow Felicia and Ed home, spend the night, and return for Sunday worship the next morning. She had never attended church with her birth mother, and Ian's initial warning haunted her. Andrea had tried to swerve Felicia in her insistence that Andrea go to their church. What if the congregation learned of Andrea and Felicia's true relationship? But Felicia said she had nothing to hide and nothing to be ashamed of. God had forgiven her.

Yet another thought haunted Andrea. Being with Felicia and Ed most likely meant encountering Ian.

How would Andrea ever handle all the tension? If the man made even the slightest attempt to hold her, Andrea knew she wouldn't have the strength to refuse. In short, Andrea had finally admitted to herself that Ian was exactly the kind of man she wanted to marry, and she could fall in love with him very easily. Perhaps she was already falling in love. All month, she had prayed that God would obliterate Ian from her mind. But it seemed that God didn't hear that prayer. Instead, Ian demanded her every spare thought. The only time Andrea didn't think of him was when she was busy with patients in her new practice.

With more worries than bravado, Andrea opened the car door to be greeted by the cool December night. No chance of a white Christmas, not in south Texas anyway. But at least the weather was cold. Andrea could remember many years wearing shorts the week of Christmas.

The dimly lit parking lot was half full of various cars, and the church windows glowed with inviting light. Andrea had purposefully waited until the practice was almost over before journeying inside. This had been her Saturday to be on duty at the children's clinic, and she hadn't been able to leave for San Antonio until late afternoon. As her western boots crunched against the occasional piece of loose gravel, Andrea thanked God for opening the position up for her at the children's clinic. So far, she had thoroughly enjoyed practicing there.

Someone exited the church's side door, and Andrea debated about whether to go around the church or try to enter the front glass doors. The front doors might be locked. As the shadowed figure rounded the corner, she approached him to make her inquiry.

"Andrea?" a soft male voice called.

She stopped and closed her eyes as her heart dropped to her knees. Ian. She knew she would see him. But not so soon. And not in the shadows.

"Yes, it's me."

"Aunt Felicia sent me out to see if you might be here. She's worried about you."

"I've been here about half an hour. I was just waiting until I felt like practice was almost over. I hated to barge in."

He stopped within inches of her.

Andrea felt as if she was spinning in a whirlwind of emotion. The deepest part of her wanted to wrap her arms around Ian and never let him go. Yet, on another level, she wanted to run back to her car, lock the door, and race to the haven of her Houston apartment.

"How have you been?" he asked.

"Fine," she choked out.

"Did you get the position?"

"Yes. I started a few days after I last saw you." Why did Andrea mention his visit? The whole thing popped back in her mind in vivid color. Their pleasant lunch. The museum. The return to her apartment. That universe-rocking kiss.

"Andrea," he began uncertainly. "I've missed you." He stroked her cheek with the backs of his fingers. "You're all I can think about."

Biting her lips, Andrea closed her eyes and relished his touch. Then Ian pulled her to him, and she was lost in his arms once more. The sound of approaching footsteps jolted Andrea back to reality.

"Ian? Andrea?" Felicia's voice floated from nearby.

As if they were school kids caught kissing on campus, the two abruptly ended their embrace.

"Felicia!" Andrea called, forcing her voice into normal tones. She walked toward her birth mother, wondering all the while if her wobbly legs would fail her. Andrea hadn't seen Felicia since she helped her home from the hospital. The hug they exchanged was packed with the power of years of separation.

"It's so good to see you again," Felicia said, tugging Andrea toward the church's side door.

In seconds, they were inside a well-lit hallway with Ian close behind. The bustling sounds of Christmas play practice echoed from the sanctuary. Several church members scurried here and there as if they were chasing Christmas from corner to corner.

One elderly lady stopped and laid a hand on Felicia's shoulder. "Do we have a visitor?" she asked. Her curious, dark eyes appraised Andrea and Felicia in a way that left Andrea a bit uneasy.

Once again, Ian's initial warning about Ed's ministry being affected because of Andrea gnawed at her. If the church members discovered their pastor's wife had given birth out of wedlock, would they reject Ed and Felicia?

"This is Andrea Dillon," Felicia said with a smile.

As the gray-haired, erect woman continued her speculative appraisal, Andrea tensed. Would Felicia explain their relationship?

"Nice to have you, Andrea." The woman's wrinkled mouth curved into a stiff smile. "I'm Stella Jones."

Feeling Ian tense behind her, Andrea cringed inside as she shook Stella's cool hand. Was coming to Felicia and Ed's church such a wise idea?

Felicia, smiling joyfully, seemed completely unaffected. As Stella uttered the correct pleasantries and continued on her journey up the hallway, a teasing twinkle lighted Felicia's brown eyes. She glanced toward her nephew. "I didn't know you had started wearing lipstick," she said, her eyebrow cocked at a knowing angle.

Ian guiltily dashed away the traces of Andrea's lipstick, and Andrea wanted to groan. Her face heated.

"Well," Felicia continued, an amazed light in her eyes. "I guess you two. . .have more in common than I suspected."

In that moment of embarrassed silence, Andrea forgot about Stella Jones.

This whole thing was crazy. How had Andrea's life gone from its normal habitual routines to this series of upheavals in a matter of months? She had not only contacted her birth mother, with all the emotional baggage that entailed, but she was also having to deal with a nerve-racking relationship with a complicated man.

"Felicia," a young woman called from the edge of the sanctuary. "We need you."

"Sorry, Andrea," she said, squeezing her daughter's hand. "I'm the co-director. We're almost through. You're welcome to sit on the back pew. I hope you don't mind waiting."

"No, I don't mind." Andrea wanted to beg Felicia

not to leave her alone with Ian.

"Now you behave yourself." Felicia shook her finger at her nephew.

"She is an unrepentant tease and always has been," Ian said as they watched Felicia slightly limping toward the sanctuary.

"How is she doing?" Andrea asked, glad to have any diversion. "She keeps telling me on the phone that she's great."

"She is great. Her doctors still can't believe it."

"That's wonderful."

"Yes."

Awkward silence. And Andrea studied her jeans and boots.

Ian cleared his throat.

She glanced up at him.

"Could we talk?" he asked, a hint of vulnerability in his voice.

NO! Andrea wanted to scream. "Sure," she said, knowing she was hopeless in the face of Ian's vulnerability.

"There's a room just off Uncle Ed's study."

She followed the powerful man, who was dressed in sweats. Felicia had mentioned Ian a few times in their phone conversations. Even then, Andrea suspected that Felicia knew more about their relationship than either Ian or herself had shared. Now, she was certain that Felicia had inserted those tidbits about Ian on purpose. Felicia said that Ian turned down the chance to play professional football for a career in medicine. She also told the story of Ian's devotion to a particular home for boys. As Andrea trailed him through the church office toward a door marked "Prayer Room," she wondered if there was any end to Ian's many facets.

He clicked on the light which revealed a tiny room resembling a sanctuary. A few pews. An altar. A cross above the altar.

Ian closed the door behind her and hesitated. "I was wondering if you would pray with me, Andrea?" he asked reverently.

"Pray with you?" she echoed, astounded at his request. One minute he had dazzled her with a kiss and the next minute he wanted prayer. The man was beyond unpredictable.

"Yes. You know I have a problem with trust."

She shook her head.

"And I've gotten to a point in my life where I really want to trust." His eyes spoke what he didn't say. *You, Andrea. I want to trust you.* "I've decided that I'm really tired of carrying around this pain." He closed his eyes and took a deep breath. "God has shown me I need surgery of the soul. I'm not exactly sure what all that entails, but I promised Him the next time I saw you I would ask you to begin praying with me."

Tears. They crept up on Andrea, filled her eyes, and began streaming her cheeks. Never had a man asked her to seriously pray with him. Absolutely never. *Oh Father,* she pleaded, *I don't know what You're doing here, but You've got to give me some guidance. I could lose my heart quick, and I really don't want it to get broken.*

"I'll pray with you," she whispered. "If you'll pray with me."

"Still haven't confronted your parents?" he asked as

if he could read her mind.

"No. And I'm beginning to wonder if I should. Maybe you were right. Maybe they just did the best they could. They are absolutely wonderful, Ian. Really. And if I'm not going to confront them, I need to be released from this resentment that I can't seem to shake."

Ian took her hand in his. "I'll pray for you."

Together, they knelt at the altar and began pouring out their souls to the One who created them. After a river of tears, Andrea felt Ian distance himself from her. First in his spirit. Then physically. Eventually, he stood and quietly walked away.

Ian parked his decade-old truck, got out, and walked toward his town house. He felt like a cad, leaving Andrea like that. But he hadn't bargained for what surgery of the soul would entail. Ian had to get into his home before he exploded. Once he shut the door to his town house, the emotional explosion could take place. For God had shown him that somewhere deep inside Dr. Ian Lowderman—six-foot-seven, two-hundred-seventy pounds, former athlete, respected surgeon—was still a ten-year-old boy who had never recovered from his mother's desertion.

Hands trembling, Ian unlocked the door, closed it behind him, and collapsed on the sectional sofa. The sobs which racked his soul had been pounding at the door of his heart, begging for release for more years than Ian ever wanted to admit. He had smothered those sobs with his accomplishments. He had pretended he was tough. He had learned to put on a convincing front.

And in all that, Ian had never lived. Not really. He had merely existed in a world where he shut out everyone except his closest relatives. And those boys. Those hurting boys at the home. He had connected with them in a way he hadn't connected with another soul. Ian now saw why.

He was one of them.

He had never grown past the sorrow of his childhood. If he was to do more than be their companion, if he was to truly minister to them, Ian knew he must embrace God's healing. He must allow his Creator to perform surgery on the soul and remove the pain that had ravaged his very existence.

"Oh Father," Ian groaned. "Help me. Heal me."

He didn't know what time his personal phone line rang or how long he had been on the sofa. But the insistent ringing seemed to echo one name off the walls of the classically decorated room.

Andrea.

Andrea.

Andrea.

Still, he couldn't talk. Not to her. Or even to his own father. Whoever the caller was, Ian hoped they left a message.

At last, he lifted himself from the sofa, removed his sweats, and stepped into a steaming shower. He stood with his back to the water and let the hot spray wash over him. For the first time in his life, he felt his spirit relaxing. Truly relaxing.

No reason to be on guard.

No reason to hide.

No reason to cover the wound.

For the wound was being knit together by the Master Physician.

When Ian's answering machine picked up, Andrea disconnected the call. She couldn't leave a message. She had no idea what to say. Andrea wasn't even sure she should have called him in the first place.

"He wasn't home?" Felicia asked.

"I guess not. He didn't answer," Andrea said, turning from the telephone. She settled in the wing-backed chair nearest the fireplace and stared into the crackling flames.

Ed was in his study, fine-tuning his Christmas sermon for the next morning, while Felicia and Andrea had the simply decorated living room to themselves.

Andrea hadn't told Felicia what happened between her and Ian. She simply informed her birth mother that Ian had left without saying "good-bye," and that she wanted to chat with him. As Andrea admired the Christmas tree, trimmed in red bows, wooden apples, and stuffed bears, she felt Felicia's curiosity rising to universal proportions.

But what could Andrea tell her? She was so unsure of Ian's motives herself. It seemed every time he approached Andrea, he soon retreated. But somehow, Andrea didn't feel that his latest retreat was bad. Otherwise, she wouldn't have called him.

"Are you and Ian by chance. . .falling in love?" Felicia's curiosity had finally given birth to words.

Andrea pulled her attention from the Christmas

tree and dared look into Felicia's eyes.

Felicia, lowering her knitting, peered at Andrea over her reading glasses.

"What makes you ask that?" Andrea hated being evasive, but honestly didn't know how to answer.

"Because Ian has been very. . .reflective since my surgery. I didn't quite understand it until the day I went home from the hospital and saw the way he reacted to you. Then he chased you out of the room. I didn't even realize the two of you had met, except on the phone." Her forehead wrinkled as she raised her brows and continued her scrutiny.

Andrea felt as if Felicia was trying to read her mind.

"I speculated then, and especially when he called and asked for your phone number last month. But tonight. . ." She trailed off meaningfully. "I was so shocked I didn't quite know how to handle the whole thing, if you want the truth."

"You could have fooled me," Andrea chided.

Felicia removed her glasses and laid them and the knitting on the polished coffee table. "I never have handled awkward situations well, so I learned a long time ago that if I revert to humor it seems to ease the tension. I honestly didn't know what to do about all that lipstick on Ian. I thought both of you would be following me into the sanctuary, and it wouldn't take a brain surgeon to see that Ian's lipstick matched yours. I'm afraid Stella noticed right off. And Ian seemed so blissfully ignorant of it."

"Thanks for that report," Andrea said ruefully, her face warming once more. However, Felicia's mentioning

Stella Jones resurrected Andrea's pending sense of anxiety. Should Andrea go through with her plans to attend church with Felicia tomorrow morning?

Felicia, seeming oblivious to Stella's judgmental spirit, appraised Andrea with eyes dancing in mirth. They sat in companionable silence until Felicia finally rose from her chair. "Let's have some hot apple cider," she said briskly. "I always like a cup before going to bed."

Glad that Felicia had dropped the subject, Andrea followed her to the kitchen. The room's cheerful colors and simple decor reflected Felicia's personality. At once, Andrea felt as if she had known Felicia her whole life. She had always carried a part of this incredible woman in her heart.

As they prepared the cider, Andrea thought of her parents. Of the resentment she had harbored these past months. Amazingly, the resentment seemed no longer in her grasp. She thought back to the altar when Ian had prayed for her. Andrea knew then that God was cleansing her heart of that resentment and giving her a pure, forgiving, unconditional love for her parents.

No. They had not been right. They had been very wrong to hide the truth from her. But, as Ian said, they had been given limited information about the best course and did what they thought was right. Andrea would accept that. She would purpose to release and re-release the resentment should she fall prey to the temptation to pick it up again.

As she and Felicia companionably sipped their cider at the kitchen table, Felicia took Andrea's hand in her own. Andrea thanked God for her heritage. He had truly brought good from what could have been disastrous. Andrea was born out of wedlock, but God had used the circumstances of her birth to provide a family for a childless couple. And later, to give a reason to live to the woman who bore her.

Nevertheless, Andrea continued to worry that her presence might cause trouble with Ed's congregation.

Chapter 9

The next morning Andrea sat in the crowded church beside Felicia. After the congregation's warm greetings, Andrea had finally relaxed about her presence harming Ed and Felicia's ministry. The vaulted, pine ceiling seemed to expand with the glorious Christmas music, the wisdom of Ed's words, and the love of God. All morning, Andrea had searched the crowd of one hundred smiling faces to see if she recognized one specific face.

Ian Lowderman.

But Andrea hadn't seen his tall frame towering over the rest. Despite Ed's encouraging words, disappointment gripped Andrea as he began closing the service. She, Felicia, and Ed planned to eat out for lunch, and Andrea would leave the restaurant to return home. Felicia and the cast of the Christmas play would be working all afternoon toward their performance that evening. Felicia had never mentioned whether or not Ian would join them at the restaurant. If Andrea didn't see him in a few short minutes, she would not see him before she left. "Let us stand for our benediction," Ed was saying, but Andrea barely took in his words. "Just a minute, Ed." Felicia stood from beside Andrea and turned to face the congregation.

Ed's surprise was evidenced by his widened eyes. Andrea shared in his surprise. What was Felicia up to?

"I have a very important praise to share."

"Go ahead, dear," Ed said, nodding his head.

He glanced toward Andrea, and she instinctively knew Felicia's next words would somehow include her. Andrea resisted the urge to scoot down in her seat and slip from sight.

Felicia continued. "Most of you have noticed the lovely young woman who is here with me today. Several of you have commented that we must be related because we look so much alike. Well, you're right. We are related. Andrea is my daughter."

Andrea darted an anxious glance across the crowd. Each person's attention was riveted to Felicia. Except one. One person, sitting near the back, was focused on Andrea. A man with sandy hair, pale eyes, and a no-nonsense demeanor. Ian was here.

Andrea's heart gently pounded as she held his gaze. He must have slipped in after the service started. The disappointment which had previously gripped Andrea now disappeared in a whirlwind of elation. But the elation was interrupted by Felicia's next words.

"I gave birth to Andrea before I was married, before I met Ed, and before I met Christ."

The crowd gasped. Andrea stared at Felicia, eyes widened in shock. She wanted to stop her birth mother, but knew it was too late. Why couldn't Felicia just leave the congregation guessing about her relationship to Andrea? Perhaps she should have told them Andrea was her niece. But that would have meant lying. Andrea hated lying.

"When I had Andrea, I desperately wanted to keep her," Felicia said. "But I knew that it was best for her if I released her to a couple who would give her a good home. So I placed her for adoption."

Another collective gasp. Murmuring. Nervous stirring.

"You may ask why I am telling you this. It would have been very easy for me to just ignore your questions about my relation to Andrea, but I couldn't do that. This is the best Christmas I have ever had, and I felt compelled to praise God for the miracle He has brought into my life." Felicia dabbed the corners of her eyes with a tissue, and Andrea was overwhelmed with love for this strong woman standing beside her. "Many of you don't know it, but Andrea is the reason I survived my car wreck. She had a recurring dream that I was calling to her and that she should visit me. I believe that dream was of God. Andrea and I had shared a brief contact five years ago and hadn't communicated since. Still, Andrea obeyed God and called me to learn that I was dying in the hospital. Without another question, she came to my side and God used my seeing her to give me the strength to survive."

The congregation burst into spontaneous applause. When the clapping subsided, Felicia continued. "I stand before you, a woman who has sinned. Thirty years ago, I had a child out of wedlock. But God took my disobedience and turned it into something beautiful." As a tearful Felicia began seating herself, Andrea dashed away her own tears and glanced toward Ed, who was crying himself.

"Thank you, Andrea, for obeying God," he whispered.

"Excuse me," a harsh voice interrupted from behind.

Andrea turned to see a well-dressed, middle-aged man standing, his hardened face set in deep lines. With his standing, a cord of tension wove through the crowd.

"I don't happen to think this is so wonderful. I think it's a disgrace to our church and to God Himself for us to have a pastor's wife who openly admits to giving birth out of wedlock and placing the baby for adoption."

"I agree!" Stella Jones stood on the other side of the sanctuary, and Andrea suppressed a groan. "This is appalling! And on Christmas morning at that! I have a visitor here! I am deeply ashamed." Andrea noticed a young lady near Stella who tugged on her arm in an attempt to drag her back onto the seat.

"But isn't this what we preach about?" Ed asked gently. "God is in the business of forgiving. And there is not one of us here who hasn't benefited from that forgiveness. Not everyone has a child out of wedlock, but we all have sinned."

A chorus of "Amens" rippled across the congregation.

"But a pastor's wife!" the first man challenged. "Please forgive me," he continued, "but I've never had a pastor's wife who has given birth to a. . .a. . ." He ended his outburst with a weighted silence which spoke more than if he had uttered the filthy word.

"Excuse me," a familiar voice boomed from the back of the church.

Andrea scooted down in her seat and resisted the

need to hide her face. Ian had apparently decided to jump in the fight with both feet. She recalled her first encounter with him. Recalled his anger. Recalled how intimidating he could be. Despite the disgruntled man's harsh words, Andrea experienced a surprising trace of pity for him. That man didn't know what he had gotten himself into.

"I cannot let you stand there and belittle my aunt and the woman I. . .the woman I. . ."

As Ian grappled for words, Andrea, her face flaming, darted a glance his way. He caught her eye.

"The woman I love," he finally said.

The silence of a tomb permeated the room. Andrea's heart churned with emotion. Not only had Ian confessed his love, he had confessed it in front of a church full of onlookers. Trying to stay the tears, she bit her lip as her own love flooded her soul like a sweet, refreshing rain.

"Andrea had no control over the circumstances of her birth," Ian continued. "And neither did you!" His commanding voice bounced off the ceiling as he pointed a finger toward the disgruntled man.

The man seemed to wither in the face of Ian's daunting demeanor. Briefly, a trace of uncertainty scurried across his features. Then, they hardened once more. Stiffly, he turned to his bewildered, mousy wife, whispered something, and silently left the sanctuary. His wife bent her head and followed.

Stella jumped back to her feet, but the young woman sitting next to her dragged her back down, and she was silenced.

"We must never forget," Ian continued, "that we

have an example to set for others—a living example of God's forgiveness and unconditional love and. . .and trust in one another as fellow believers in Christ!"

As the congregation burst into another round of applause, Ian's last words echoed off the corridors of Andrea's heart.

Trust. Trust. Trust.

Ian had asked her to pray for him last night. To pray that he could learn to trust. Was he trying to tell Andrea that their prayers had been answered?

"I have had trouble trusting others. Some of you know that my mother left my father and me when I was only ten," Ian said, his voice softening with emotion. "But God brought Andrea into my life and made me want to trust in a way I have never trusted. And last night. . ." Ian hesitated, a hint of vulnerability back in his voice. ". . . last night, I believe that God began the healing in me, that He gave me the gift of forgiveness and trust. Never underestimate His power. He is an awesome God."

As Ian seated himself, Andrea's heart almost burst with love and pride in the man she knew beyond any doubt God had chosen for her.

A sniffle at her side focused Andrea on Felicia. Hands trembling, Felicia mopped at a torrent of tears. "I've prayed for him for so long," she whispered. "I didn't know all this would happen this way, and I'm sorry. But I'm so glad it prompted Ian's testimony."

"It's probably best that it's all out in the open," Andrea whispered. She reflected on her parents' hiding the truth, and knew she was right. The truth produced freedom and healing. Now Felicia and Ed and even Ian were free of the worry of what would happen should the congregation learn of Andrea's parentage.

Ed silently observed his congregation. At last, he spoke. "There are a lot of things I enjoy about pastoring a small congregation. But there are some drawbacks, too. It seems that we are so close to one another that we often speak harshly when perhaps we should maintain silence. For any visitors here, I would like to apologize for the scene you just witnessed. We don't do this sort of thing every Sunday." He smiled a bit.

A nervous chuckle erupted across the crowd.

"And may I take the opportunity to be perfectly candid? I knew that if Felicia told the truth that some of our members would probably leave. My hope is that none of the rest of you wish to leave." He paused as if waiting for someone to stand. "But sometimes God uses these situations to work His sovereign will. I believe that our church will experience more harmony now than it ever has." Ed left the rest unsaid, and Andrea suspected this wasn't the first scene the trouble-makers had caused.

With Ed's prompting, the boisterous congregation stood to its feet and began singing "Joy to the World." Andrea knew that joy. Indeed, she felt it in every stitch of her soul.

In seconds, the congregation began filing from the sanctuary. Even before Andrea looked toward Ian, she felt him at her side. Spontaneously, Ian wrapped his arms around her for a brief hug. Andrea clung to him, looked into his sparkling eyes, and marveled at the absence of pain and anger which once marred him.

"We need to talk," Ian whispered. "Can we go back to the prayer room?"

"Of course," Andrea said. She glanced toward Felicia, surrounded by loving friends, and knew her birth mother would never miss her.

Her hand in his, Andrea followed Ian to the dimly lit room where they had prayed the evening before. As soon as the door closed, Ian took her hands in his. "I guess everything is out in the open. . .literally," he added with a rueful smile.

"Looks that way," Andrea said through a chuckle.

"I know I've already said it once, but I want you to know that I am falling in love with you. You feel the same way?" His searching gaze requested an answer.

"Yes. And if you want the truth, part of the reason I was so defensive when Aunt Felicia went home from the hospital was because I was fighting it even then."

"Believe me, I know how you feel. You blew my socks off from the start." He stroked her cheek, and Andrea relished his affection.

"If you think you can put up with me, Andrea, I want to know if we can continue to see each other. Regularly." A teasing smile. "Really regularly."

"Thought you'd never ask." As Ian took her in his arms, Andrea felt as if she had come home. God had given her more than she ever hoped for when she found Felicia. He had given her the love of an incredible man. And in God's time, they would share a life, a marriage, a family.

Debra White Smith

Debra White Smith lives in east Texas with her husband, Daniel, son Brett, and daughter Brooke. She has authored numerous articles and books and stories, including "Castaways," a part of the CBA bestselling romance anthology *Only You* (Barbour Publishing). Her novel *The Neighbor* was voted by **Heartsong Presents** readers as one of the top ten favorite contemporary romances of 1997. In the same year, she was selected as one of the top ten favorite new **Heartsong** authors. In the last year, Debra has had 129,000 copies of her books printed. Visit Debra on the World Wide Web at http://www.getset.com/debrawhitesmith